Love,

Only Better

A NOVEL

Paulette Stout

Media Goddess Inc.

FIRST EDITION

Edited by Let's Get Booked
Cover designed by Let's Get Booked with illustrations by Catherine Clarke.

ISBN 978-1-7366371-0-4 (eBook Edition)
ISBN 978-1-7366371-1-1 (Paperback Edition)

Library of Congress Cataloging-in-Publication Data has been applied for.
Library of Congress Control Number 2021907828

Published by Media Goddess Inc., 241 Arlington Street #814, Acton MA 01720
Visit paulettestout.com for author information.

Your Free eBook is Waiting

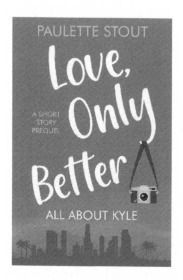

Meet the hero of Love, Only Better—before our heroine does.
Kyle's photography career is on the rise in Los Angeles, but he can't
take his mind off his ex. Her betrayal still stings, even three years and
three thousand miles away. How can he make a fresh start when so
much was left unsaid?

Get a free copy of the prequel:

Love, Only Better: All About Kyle

https://paulettestout.com/free

For my husband, whom I love more with each passing day.

Author's Note

For nearly twenty years, I was afraid to share this book with the world. Not because I was ashamed of the life experiences that compelled me to write it, but because we have so very far to go when it comes to healthy conversations around sex and women's empowerment.

What would people say? What would they think? Would telling this story limit future employment prospects? It wasn't until I didn't care about any of those things that I was free to create.

My hope is that all the mothers and sisters, cousins, aunts, and friends will be open to discussing sex and orgasms with the women in our lives. With those we know to be struggling. With those who feel broken. Sharing, without judgment. Guiding with care and tenderness.

The more women we welcome into the realm of sexual fulfillment, the more women will be empowered to achieve greatness in other areas of their lives. These aren't mere tingles. They're a catalyst for confidence. They're a catalyst for personal change and achievement.

If you're struggling, know you're not alone.

And that you'll get there.

Paulette

Chapter 1

It wasn't as if the words were unexpected. Hell, Rebecca said them to herself a thousand times over. Only, this was different. Hearing someone else say them—someone she loved. Someone who shared her life and her bed for three years—somehow made them true. And to have Ethan say them. For him to let them free that way. Now, they were alive to reverberate through the universe and rebound on her in unforgiving ways. And he'd no longer be around to save her.

Frigid. Ice queen.

Who calls someone they love an ice queen? Rebecca wondered.

That's the ticket. Ethan didn't love her. Had he ever? Or was she just a bad lay; a notch on his belt. Not even a trophy. A third-place yellow ribbon no one wanted, abandoned in the bottom of a drawer.

A wisp of spiderweb dangling from her headboard above fluttered in time with her cleansing breaths. Dust covered. Abandoned. Even the stupid spider hadn't stuck around.

Frigid. Ice queen.

She flipped up her covers to snatch a tissue from across the room, wiping her eyes and nose before tossing it into the wastebasket under her old desk. The desk in name only. Even back in high school, she did her homework on her bed. The desk chair, like now, was a glorified staging area for clothes somewhere between clean and dirty.

Did she still have it?

She yanked the center drawer open, pawing the time capsule within. Old lipstick, diaries, hair elastics, the wallet-sized card reproduction of her university diploma, tarot cards, and there it was: her third-place ribbon. She won it at summer camp for archery. She'd never held a bow before then, or since. But there it was; evidence that she was once good enough at something to warrant recognition.

The silky cord slid between her fingers until hitting the tassel knot.

So fitting. Third place. Rebecca was third place in her own life, too. She was certainly last place to Ethan. He was probably off finding himself a blue-ribbon sex machine worthy of His Majesty. Even at this hour. New York City never sleeps, after all.

Growing up in the belly of Manhattan, the buzz of life at all hours was as natural as air. The humming streetlights, the shadows, everything held a pulse. Teeming.

Except for her. Rebecca was the one spot of lifelessness in the whole city.

Frigid. Ice queen.

She dropped the ribbon in the drawer and slammed it shut, then quickly froze. Alert, she listened for sounds of stirring. Barbara, her roommate and best friend, was fast asleep in the next room. A lawyer with a big day in court ahead.

Rebecca released her breath, then strode back to bed, flopping on top of her navy down comforter and making herself a burrito with its folded edges. It was as close as she would get to an embrace for who knows how long.

Wiggling for her night table, she switched off the light. Shadows formed at familiar angles on her ceiling. The ceiling she'd pondered for twenty-eight years. Framed pictures of Salvador Dali and Kandinsky hung over her low, long dresser, once filled with frilly pink play clothes, now stuffed with T-shirts and leggings in mismatched shades of black. Her collection of discount designer shoes spilled out of the closet, distractions for the shortcomings of her noir wardrobe.

Her eyes drifted closed.

Ethan's contorted, red face jolted her awake.

Would she ever sleep again?

Would she ever love again?

Would anyone ever love her?

Was she even worthy of being loved?

She wasn't sure.

On cue, her nemesis, the mourning dove, made a fluttery landing on the air-conditioning unit blocking half of her window. The distinctive coo was maddening. Was that how Ethan felt when she was unable to climax in bed? A fury of frustration without an outlet?

Rebecca abandoned covers and leaped to battle stations. The vinyl shade creaked its objection as she bent it up to spy on the enemy. The pink towel she put out to dull the air-conditioner drips from upstairs had become a bird magnet. Twigs, leaves, tinsel? Where did they find tinsel in June?

"Shoo! Shoo!" Rebecca whisper screamed, banging on the glass with her fist.

The dusty bird settled in.

"Go on. *Go*."

"Becca! Are you fucking kidding? It's 4:00 a.m.!" Barbara shouted through the wall.

"Sorry!" Rebecca hollered back, watching the bird tuck its wings for sleep. There was a beat of silence.

"Shit," Barbara muttered. Rebecca heard her feet hit the floor and storm down the parquet hallway, a staple of 1950s' NYC apartments. The bathroom door closed.

Rebecca dropped the shade and collapsed into the cup of her papasan chair under the window, drawing a branded fleece blanket over her. It was one of the many freebies she got working in advertising; this one was from her hotel client.

After the flush and wash, Barbara exited then walked through Rebecca's perennially open bedroom door and switched the light on.

Her hand shielded her eyes from the sudden brightness.

Barbara stood in a pink satin Victoria Secret nightie, a matching sleep mask holding up her long, dark locks—a top-shelf weave and proudly not hers—flowing over ebony shoulders.

"What the hell are you doing up?"

"I'm so sorry—"

"Jesus, what happened?"

"What do you mean?"

10

"You look like a clown on acid."

Rebecca crawled out of the saucer and stood in front of the mirror.

"Yeah, not my best look."

Black mascara streaked down her face from the blotchy eyes she had been rubbing for hours.

"Where's Ethan? I thought he was staying over?"

"Gone."

"Gone home?"

"No. Just gone. We're done. Well, actually, he was done with me."

"Wow. I'm so sorry. But... not as sorry as you should be for waking me up..." Barbara said, launching herself to Rebecca's bed and sliding her sleep mask down over her eyes.

"That's it? That's all the consoling I get? I have a blowout with my boyfriend who calls me a 'frigid ice queen' and leaves, and..."

"He didn't," Barbara said, lifting up on her elbow and raising her mask.

"Oh yes he did."

"You're not an ice queen. You know that."

"Counselor, the evidence is overwhelming."

"He's a jackass. I've always thought so."

"Oh, he's not that bad..."

Barbara raised an eyebrow.

"Come on!"

"I won't lie to you and say I'm disappointed he's gone."

"But... I am," Rebecca whispered.

"All I mean is he didn't treat you right. You can absolutely do better."

Barbara patted the bed next to her. Rebecca folded her arms and looked away.

"You CAN do better. Ethan will regret losing you, and you'll look back and NOT regret losing him."

Rebecca pouted her bottom lip.

"Suit yourself. I must sleep more, though." Barbara left the bed, popped a squeaky kiss on Rebecca's forehead.

"Leave that damn bird alone, will you?" she said before leaving.

"You left the light on!" Rebecca called after her, but Barbara's bedroom door closed with a click.

Sighing, Rebecca crawled out of the chair and crossed the room to switch off the light. Dawn's blueness was already invading. She looked at her bed, but instead returned to sit under her fleece blanket, gathering it about her.

Maybe she could sleep if she was out of bed, away from his smell. She'd have to change the sheets later. She wanted to change everything; beginning with herself.

Chapter 2

"Rebecca?"

A tap on the shoulder.

"Hey, Rebecca. Wake up."

Rebecca opened her eyes to a relentless wave of jumbled consonants splashing on her computer screen. More joined every instant. She jerked her fingers back and the assault stopped.

Work. She was at work.

Rebecca looked back at the screen, the cursor blinking in mock innocence.

She swiveled her chair to face the aisle behind her.

"Lunch, do you want any lunch? Or would you like to come with us?"

Rebecca looked at Rosie and the other two girls whose names she could never remember. Their impeccably tailored Fendi outfits and Steve Madden shoes were miles apart from her bargain-basement fare. Their faces wore identical arched eyebrows of faux anticipation.

"No, I'm good, but thanks for asking."

Rosie sighed and stepped into her cube, bending to her ear.

"Rebecca, you sure? Just come. Those two look a lot bitchier than they actually are."

"It's not that. I'm just not hungry. Thanks for the pity stop, though."

The words shot Rosie upright and her eyes instantly transformed from soft to fiery. She shook her head and turned back to her companions.

"No again?" Rebecca heard Fendi #1 say as the trio walked away.

"I told you. She never comes," Fendi #2 answered.

Rosie never looked back as they made their way out of sight toward the elevator.

Rebecca spun back to her desk and hid her face in her hands. *Pity Stop. I'm an idiot. Of all the things to say.*

Rebecca squeezed her eyes shut, but the tears still came. *Christ. Not again.* If she only got paid by the tear, she'd be the wealthiest twenty-eight-year-old she knew. Too many tears and not enough laughs. At least, not lately. Ethan was all about having a good time. What was she about? Who knew anymore?

Rebecca stood up and rolled her bookshelf door up on its hinges until it rested flat on top. She popped a tissue out of the box and dabbed her eyes while staring at her favorite picture: Barbara and Rebecca mid-splash-fight at the Trevi Fountain in Rome. The photo captured a moment of pure joy, along with the pinky finger of the trio's third, Leslie, who was wisely mid-shield of the camera's lens when the photo snapped. Back then, Rebecca had no inhibitions. No fear of judgment. It was just fun and laughter and life.

Rebecca had friends. Of course she did. They just weren't in this office. She used the tear-dampened tissue to blow her nose, but needed another to clean up the mess. So much for two-ply.

With nerves subsided, hunger filled the void. She wove her way through the cubicle maze of desks to the office kitchenette. While the filth of most company kitchens was fodder for nightmares, theirs was spotless. So clean that no one dare foul it, preferring to eat at their desks or dine out instead. After all, lunches were ideal times for vendors to pump media buyers like herself with free food while prying valuable client dirt about budgets and intentions from their flapping lips. If reps were lucky, they'd also get informal commitments buyers would feel obligated to honor later. Guilt was a powerful motivator.

She opened the fridge, where the second half of her chef salad from the day before was the lone edible among the cases of Heineken and O'Doul's. Beer was always on hand for the weekly office "food fest." Each Friday, the office shut down at 4:00 p.m. for drinking and merriment. The agency's owners even catered finger food for the occasion.

A knot formed in Rebecca's chest just thinking of making small talk with all the office workers she was supposed to know. She grabbed her bag and shut the fridge.

The board room doubled as her lunch retreat. She switched on the recessed lighting, then dimmed them down. Light bounced off a warm mahogany table, and linen-papered walls contrasted with the gray cube fortress she inhabited.

Rebecca plopped into a black leather seat at the far end of the room and lingered her hands on the buttery table finish as she drew her chair in. It took major restraint not to lie down on the table for a nap using her paper bag as a pillow. The soundproofing designed so important conversations held within stayed within ensured no one would hear her snoring.

Opening her salad cover, she forked through to find lettuce that hadn't completely lost its crispness in the sea of watery-dressing accumulated in the bottom of the plastic tray. She focused on flavor over appearance, but Ethan's face invaded her weary mind.

If she were to be honest with herself, their breakup wasn't entirely unexpected. Rebecca had recently used the L-word with Ethan while they were in bed. He not only didn't reciprocate, his head dropped back in annoyance like he did when a tall person sat in front of him at the movie theater. He then stared at the ceiling for what felt like forever. Not exactly the reaction she was hoping for. The moment the words left her lips she wanted to slurp them back, but it was too late.

Ethan's behavior transformed overnight. Suddenly, he couldn't stay over as often, and canceled two dinner dates at the last minute. He kept her apart from his friends. Even going so far as to skip speaker mode on his phone and step out of the room to talk in private. Thinking on it now, they probably had already been broken up for weeks, only Rebecca had been too stupid to notice.

She was mid-chew on a perfectly salted hard-boiled egg when the conference room door swung open, and the lights turned off. It was Harry, the agency owner.

Rebecca jumped up, coughing as the egg lodged in her throat.

"Oh, excuse me," he said, flipping the lights back on and raising them to full intensity. "I thought someone left the lights on."

Still coughing, Rebecca strode to the corner sideboard and downed a warm plastic bottle of water sitting in a tray next to an empty ice bucket.

"No need to choke on my account," he chuckled.

Rebecca felt her pulse returning to normal, soothed by Harry's fatherly Arkansas lilt.

"I can leave," Rebecca croaked through egg remnants. "I just need a minute to…"

"No, no. Please, no need. But…" He glanced around, "Why are you eating in here… alone?"

Rebecca's stomach lurched. The way he said "alone" sounded particularly pathetic. She focused her gaze on the table and took a too slow sip of water.

Harry sighed and walked toward her, the room silent except for the soft swoosh of his olive suit trousers. His silver curls glowing in the overhead lights.

"Rebecca, you're not doing yourself, or us, any favors by hiding yourself away."

Her blood drained. "You're not going to mention this in the 360 evaluation, are you?"

"Yes. I think I will."

"Oh, please don't."

"Rebecca. What's the point of the evaluation if I'm not honest? It's supposed to give you the honest impressions of people you work with, junior, senior, and peers. It does you no good if we lie."

"Wonderful."

"Rebecca, you're smart and have amazing potential. Everyone seems to see it but you." Harry let his words hang in the air. Then

17

he rapped his knuckles lightly on table and headed for the door, pausing on the threshold.

"Try eating in the kitchen next time. I hear those chairs are comfortable."

"Yes, of course."

Rebecca heard him swish down the hall and returned to her salad soup. If possible, it was now less wilted than her ego. As gross as it was, she wanted to crawl in and hide.

Of all people to find her, it had to be Harry. He was the one person she admired in this hectic, type-A-infested company. Was it a career-ender? She didn't yet know. The 360 evaluation would be what it was. She had no control over that now. She'd have to redouble efforts to prove herself so he didn't think she was a pathetic loser.

But maybe it was a lost cause. She was a pathetic loser and everyone knew it but her. Ethan certainly knew, and he wasted no time cutting her loose. Rebecca couldn't afford for Harry to do the same. She'd worked too hard, and deep down, she suspected there was some promise deep within her that had yet to be tapped. At least she hoped so.

She drained the dregs of the water bottle, swishing it around in her mouth before swallowing. She trashed the remains of her lunch and turned off the lights, staring into the cool blackness before slowly closing the door.

"Don't sit down just yet. Come in here," Darcy hollered from her desk as Rebecca passed. Rebecca walked backward, pausing in her boss's doorless threshold. At *MediaNow*, all the executive offices had clear glass walls—ceiling to floor, side to side—with a tinted coating on the inside. That way, company leaders felt less on display than they knew themselves to be.

Even at eight feet, Darcy's sour odor drifted over.

"I have a project for you," she said, prim and erect as ever in her chair.

"What's all of that?" Rebecca said, noticing a sky-high pile of paper on Darcy's desk.

"Well, dear, you're not going to be happy, but we've been asked to help one of our partner ad agencies with a big billing mix-up. Their commercial was coded wrong and someone has to go through all this billing and figure out which ads were theirs and which weren't by comparing it to the submitted television buy." Darcy thumped the stack with her hand.

"Can't the stations do this?"

"They are, but Bradley & Moore want to be sure it's done right. We're getting paid for this, so it's not without revenue."

Rebecca filled her lungs and held it before walking over to retrieve the paper tower. Standing above Darcy was the worst. Her limp brown hair was pulled into a cursory ponytail at the nape of her neck, scalp generously peppered with dandruff flakes. Big ones. A winter display. Rebecca wrinkled her nose but, thankfully, Darcy misunderstood her look of disgust.

"Look, it has been assigned to you. Make the best of it." Darcy swiveled the back of her chair to Rebecca and picked up her phone.

Rebecca breathed through her mouth as she bent down to lift the stack, balanced it against her chest as she shuffled the twenty feet to her desk. She pivoted on her heels to glance back at Darcy's fishbowl, but she was no longer on the phone. Typical. A fake "we're done now" call. The receiver dropped the moment Rebecca's back turned.

The stack thumped on her desk as it landed.

Had Darcy always been such a tool? Rebecca searched the recesses, but nothing came to mind. Any pre-toolness predated Rebecca's three-year tenure at the company.

But tool as she was, Darcy left Rebecca alone to do her work, which was the asset Rebecca most prized.

Rolling in to inspect the project, Rebecca's eyes bulged. WTVV. Was Darcy playing some sadistic game with her? Rebecca leaned back to get a glimpse of Darcy talking on the phone for real this time. At least, her lips were moving and sound was coming out.

The invoice shook in her hand, so she put it down and grabbed a ruler. Client name, code, dates. Yup. This was the TV buy Darcy poached, presenting Rebecca's ideas as her own. Rows of numbers replaced by memories of Darcy basking in client praise.

They were sitting in a huge meeting when the news was announced. Darcy stood up at the head of the table and even had the nerve to act coy when compliments heaped on her for being nominated for the industry award. Rebecca glared at her across the room, but Darcy simply answered with a "sucks to be you" shrug. She then returned to revel in her unearned adulation. A shrug. Rebecca was even forced to congratulate her. What else could she do with everyone watching? To protest at that point would have made her look unbelievably petty.

Rebecca slid the ruler down the page, knee bouncing wildly.

She scrutinized each page's airing, then placed the invoices face down in a new pile when done. The steady work calmed her nerves, and when she next looked up, it was 6:27 p.m. All her desk neighbors had left. Rebecca gathered her stuff to head out, leaving the balance of paperwork behind. She could have taken it home and knocked off a large chunk, but she'd let her boss sweat it out a little. She was tired of bolstering the "Darcy" legend.

If only she knew how to build her own.

Chapter 3

The exterior frost on the pint of Coffee Heath Bar Crunch melted, a casualty of the hot takeout trays sharing the same bag.

Wasn't Styrofoam supposed to insulate both ways?

Rebecca pushed open the lobby door to her apartment, pausing to get her keys. She dipped her right shoulder to swing her handbag into grasping distance, but it slid down her arm and hit the floor.

Grumbling, she pressed the intercom with her elbow so Barbara could let her in.

At the buzz, Rebecca gave the door a sharp bump with her hip, dislodging the dinner bag which tumbled down. Out of nowhere, a guy appeared just in time to snatch it before it hit the floor.

"Got it!" he said, smiling. He handed the bag back to Rebecca.

"Thanks, you've got quick reflexes," Rebecca said. While hesitant to let strangers into the building, she figured he was too dreamy to be a threat to public safety. His wavy hair and spectacular blue eyes topped a solid build and flawless olive complexion that glowed. He was stunning but seemed unaware of his own good looks. You could tell right away if a hot guy was conceited or genuine by the way he answered your stare. If he was friendly and extended his hand, he was no Ken doll. This guy waited and let Rebecca enter first, holding the door for her.

They waited in silence for the elevator. As they stood, the unmistakable zing of sexual energy passed between them. She stole a glance, but he was already staring at her. She smiled and looked away as he chuckled.

The elevator arrived, so she entered first and pressed her floor.

"I'm going to the same floor, but I promise I'm not stalking you."

"So you say," Rebecca said. "You've probably had second thoughts and plan to steal my dinner."

"What do you have?"

"Italian."

"Good Italian?"

"Very good. I won't give it up without a fight," Rebecca said. He raised his eyebrows in mock surprise.

What was she doing? It was barely twenty-four hours since Ethan stormed out, and she was already flirting with a total stranger in an elevator! He said nothing else but continued to smile broadly.

Wonderful. He probably thought she was a desperate loser.

The elevator stopped, and they got off, each heading in opposite directions. She glanced back and once again met his gaze. Both smiling, they turned away. He rang the doorbell for one of her elderly neighbors, so Rebecca moved in half-time to listen in. Mutual hellos floated from across the hall, followed by a door slam and muffled speaking. She refocused on her task.

As usual, Barbara propped the apartment door open using the

dead bolt. She flipped it closed and let the heavy metal door slam behind her.

Rebecca kicked off her shoes and padded into the kitchen, putting the takeout bags on the counter.

"Dinner!" she yelled.

"In the bathroom," Barbara answered.

Rebecca got her handbag and walked down the hallway to her room. The Berber carpet cushioned her steps remarkably well, considering her parents installed it over fifteen years prior. She paused to lean on one of the mahogany posts at the foot of her bed, balancing on each foot in turn to pull off her black socks. Those she left in balls on the floor along with the shirt she removed next.

Rebecca was in a bra wrestling with her shirt drawer when Barbara entered.

"Hey there."

"Ugggh…" Rebecca grunted.

Barbara crossed the room to lift the far side of the long wooden drawer and together they got it open.

"Thanks."

"You know, just because you live in your childhood apartment doesn't mean you can't update your teenager furniture."

"It still feels weird to think of this apartment as my own."

"It's been six years. I don't think your folks are going to want it back any time soon."

"My mom has dropped enough hints over the years to make that an open question."

"Be that as it may. It's past time that you stood up for yourself.

I mean, buying a dresser with drawers that open and close is hardly a rebellious act. And that desk is no better."

"What's the matter with it?"

"You're kidding, right?"

Rebecca selected a black T-shirt from the mangled tees in the drawer, slipped it on, and bumped the drawer closed with her hip.

"I'll take it under advisement."

"You do that. I'll definitely give you affordable representation if your parents press charges because you replaced a few pieces of broken furniture."

"Affordable? Not free?" Rebecca asked as the duo walked down the hall to the kitchen.

"Nothing is free, baby doll. And if I'm going to be a partner and wildly successful by thirty-five, I can't be giving away my legal services."

"It's good that one of us has a plan. Perhaps by then, I'd have treated myself to a new dresser."

Barbara began the evening ritual of sorting takeout containers, sliding her meal onto a ceramic plate, and tossing it under a microwave lid to heat up.

Rebecca did the same, covering her meal with plastic wrap and popping open the microwave in progress to add her dish on top of the lid before closing and starting it again.

Rebecca rinsed the containers in the sink and added them to their recycle bucket under the sink.

After the beep, she grabbed a hot plate in each hand using a dish towel and made a hasty way to the table for two next to the window. If she timed it right, Rebecca could get the scorching plates over before her nerve endings screamed. As they began eating, Rebecca noticed Barbara staring at her plate.

"You okay?" Rebecca asked.

"Sure. Funny you should mention 'plans' before. There's something I need to tell you."

"If it's about Ethan, I'm sorry I didn't tell you when you got home last night. I was just too upse—"

"It's not about you. It's about me. Well, about Joe and me."

"Are you guys okay? You didn't break up too?"

A broad smile lit up Barbara's face, "No, of course not. In fact, it's just the opposite."

Rebecca dropped her fork with a loud clatter. "Oh my God. You're getting married."

"Whoa, now. Maybe one day. For now, I'm just moving in with him. At his place. It's a first step, but we're really excited. I wanted to tell you first."

"You're serious?"

"I know it's a shock, especially with what happened last night with Ethan, but we always talked about being totally honest with each other. I didn't want to keep this from you."

Rebecca forced her pressed lips into a smile. "It's... it's great news. Really. I'm happy for you."

She looked away, out the window. Two old ladies talked as they rolled grocery wagons. One full of groceries, one empty. Rebecca knew which hers would be.

"Becca, look at me."

"Really. I am. I'm delighted. For you both." Rebecca nodded until she had almost convinced herself. "Hell, if I knew you'd hit it off this well, I wouldn't have introduced you!"

Rebecca sniffed hard, willing her running eyes and nose to stop.

"I'm so sorry." Barbara got up and kneeled in front of Rebecca, hugging her tightly.

"No, I'm sorry. This is super-selfish of me. You're the person I care about most in the world, and I want you to be happy. You know I do."

Barbara pulled away and sat on her haunches.

"I'm just going to miss seeing you every day."

"I'll miss you too. Crap, there I go." Barbara wiped away tears with the back of her hand. She stood up to grab her napkin, dabbing her eyes with it. "Aren't we a pair?"

They both laughed.

Barbara returned to her chair and resumed eating.

"I'm not dying, you know. I'm just moving to the Upper West Side."

"We hate the Upper West Side."

"I know, but don't mention it to Joe. I didn't have the heart to tell him." Barbara winked.

Rebecca picked up her fork and commenced pushing around her linguine.

"Who knows? Maybe we'll find out we like the Upper West Side. Maybe it'll be fabulous."

Rebecca looked back outside. The woman with the empty cart was hobbling down the street, waving to friends sitting on the benches.

"I'll keep paying the rent for a few months until you can find a new roommate."

"Huh?"

"The rent. I'll keep paying for a few months. I know you can't swing it on your own."

"When were you thinking to move out?"

"On Saturday."

"What?!? That's in *two days*? How can you move in two days?"

"We figured we'd rip off the Band-Aid. My rent here will be covered, plus his cousin owns a moving service. They'll come and box up my life, move it uptown, and unpack it on the other end. The white-glove service suits me, don't you think?"

"Two days? Really?"

"You know me. Once I make a decision, I like to move quickly."

"I'll say."

"You'll be fine. I know this feels like a punch in the gut, and the timing is awful for you. But maybe it's all for the best. Even me moving out."

Their eyes locked. "What do you mean?" Rebecca asked.

"It'll give you an opportunity…"

"An opportunity to… what exactly?"

"… to think about what you want next."

Rebecca inhaled deeply. She pushed back from the table, leaving her half-finished meal.

Barbara looked up. Her hazel eyes searching for a response.

Rebecca smiled meekly and gave the seated Barbara a shoulder hug. She then went silently to her room and closed the door.

Chapter 4

Rebecca threw open the window. The floral scent of spring filled her nose. Fresh and clean, it was the antithesis of everything about her life.

She turned to face the room. Everything in it was a rotting castoff. Unwanted and left behind. The bed and night tables: abandoned by her parents. The lamps: parents. The pictures: parents. The dresser and desk: holdovers from her childhood purchased by her parents. She, too, was a castoff, unwanted by anyone.

In the span of twenty-four-hours, she'd gone from a happy gal with a boyfriend, a best friend, and a job on the rise, to dumped and alone. A pathetic loner at work whose job prospects were an open question.

She slid her phone out of her back pocket and dialed.

"Hey, it's me."

"Rebecca?" her mom answered.

She must have been as stunned to hear from her daughter as her daughter was in calling. Olivia Sloane typically launched into a rousing soliloquy when beginning phone conversations. Not this time.

"Yeah, it's me."

"It's been a while."

"There's a lot going on."

"What's going on?"

What indeed.

"A lot, Mom. Just a lot."

"Papi! Turn that down. I can't hear myself think. Rebecca's on the phone."

"Rebecca who?" She heard her father, Martin, say. But his jovial lilt shined through. The best jokes were always his own.

"Quit it, will you?"

Rebecca heard the roar of Yankee Stadium go silent.

"Ay Dios. He takes a well-deserved day off, and what does he do all day? Watch a double-header.

"Why do you have those season tickets if you're going to sit at home?" she yelled at her husband.

"Where were we? Oh. How are you?" she asked in a flat voice.

She was probably disappointed to pick up the phone and have her only daughter on the other end instead of someone more exciting. That's precisely why Rebecca never called unless everything was utterly amazing. It left no opportunity for her mother to be critical. Now, what was she supposed to say?

How was she?

She hadn't planned an answer to the most obvious of questions when she decided to call home for the first time in months?

"Everything's fine, Mom."

"You're a bad liar."

Rebecca stared at the ceiling. No way she was giving a love update—no warm shoulder forthcoming from her mom. And she wasn't unemployed just yet.

"Barbara's moving out."

"What? What happened? What did you do?"

"I didn't *do* anything. And why do you always assume I did something wrong? She's just moving in with Joe."

"Her boyfriend, Joe? Oh, that's wonderful. That man is so handsome; he's like a cross between Denzel Washington and Blair Underwood. Don't you think?"

"He is handsome, yes."

"Anyway, good for her. That's great. They're such a cute couple." She began to chuckle. "Well, that leaves you in a bind. You certainly can't afford the apartment on your own."

"I'll figure it out."

"Want us to find someone? You can't be late on that rent…"

"Please don't. Barbara's going to pay for a few months anyway, so I have a little time. Not much, but I'm grateful she's looking out for me."

"Good thing that girl is a lawyer. Well, she comes from some money anyway, doesn't she?"

It always came down to money with her mom. No matter how the conversation started, it ended in the same place. They could be talking about dolphins, or snow, or rainbows, but it always tracked back to green. You'd think she'd experienced her parents' Puerto Rican poverty herself.

"I think they're comfortable, yes."

"You know so. Don't be coy. You forget I've been to her

31

family's house. And all those trips they'd take you on. You're very lucky to have her."

Rebecca paced her bedroom while her mother chatted on.

"I always felt bad not having her over more, but I couldn't ever compete with what she was used to."

"That's silly. Barbara isn't like that. She doesn't judge people that way."

"Everybody judges. Some are just better at hiding it."

For once, her mother said something she agreed with. Broken clocks…

"So, what's going on with that guy of yours? What's his name? Andrew?"

"Ethan."

"That's right. Any big plans coming up for summer?"

"No plans. We're not together anymore."

She heard her mom's judging kick in. She never bothered hiding it, especially in person.

"Well, that's a shame." Then she whispered, "Was it the sex thing again?"

"Mom!"

"Well, you're always the one mentioning it. I'm just making conversation."

"I'm not having THAT conversation with you. Jeez. I was just thinking, maybe, I'd come up on Saturday for the day. Barbara's moving out and I don't want to get in the way."

"What time? We have shul in the morning, then we have dinner plans, but early dinner plans. What time on Saturday for dinner, Marty?"

"Five o'clock," she heard her dad pipe in.

"We could squeeze you in between 1:00 p.m. and 4:00 p.m. if you want. You can help with some yard work…"

Rebecca got off the phone. Way to make her feel welcome. Schlep out to Port Washington to play hired-hand for the parents that couldn't give her the time of day? No, thank you. Her mother expected eternal chore work because Rebecca had the gall to take residence in her belly for near ten months. Her birth rent was never repaid. Either that, or she used it as an extremely clever and effective visit repellent.

For a former Catholic, her mother took going to synagogue very seriously. Though in fairness, she'd been Jewish longer at this point, having converted before they got married.

Rebecca tried to remember the last time she sat through a whole synagogue service. Probably a random high-holidays before her parents moved. She went a few times after that. Alone she felt exposed, unwelcome. Plus, the new canter sang prayers in a different tune than she had memorized. She spoke no Hebrew, but had been able to follow along like a pro, having memorized the words and the proper tunes. With the tune swap, she was lost. And being too ashamed to ask for the phonetic prayer book, she just stopped going. Better to leave before they discovered she was a fraud.

A fraud Jew. Add that to the misfit list of places she didn't belong.

She tossed her phone on the bed and crawled in after it.

Shit. The sheets. Ethan's musky, sour, sweet smell was all over them.

She sat up, a framed picture of the two of them mocked from her night table. She picked it up. *Where to put it?* She saw the open window.

She ran over and heaved it out as hard as she could throw it.

"ARRRRRRRRRRRRRRRRRRGH!"

It tumbled three floors then exploded into infinite shards on the pavement below.

Rebecca eyed her circle of destruction, panting heavily, sweat dripping down her back. The street was empty, thank goodness. But she heard windows thrown open as hundreds of eyes looked out to see what happened.

She shrank away from the window toward the bed, tossed the comforter aside, and tugged at the sheets to force them off. The far side was stuck, but instead of walking around the bed, she wrapped them around her wrist and yanked until the tension around her hands cut off circulation.

Rip.

A slit formed from the far corner down the middle of the sheet.

Shit.

Her mother would kill her.

The sheets were hers too, just like everything else.

Fuck it.

She grabbed both sides of the tear and spit the sheet clear down, end to end. She poked new holes and split those too. She kept tearing and splitting, moving on to the top sheet next. Before long, there was nothing left but frayed mounds of white ribbons.

A glint caught her eye on the floor. She kneeled down, pawing through tangles of fabric to get at it, leaving a shredded tutu around her torso.

A condom wrapper. An empty condom wrapper. Rebecca sat, surveying her madness.

She shook her head, half grinning.

What a mess.

She looked about the room, eyes landing on her half-closed T-shirt drawer. Was she doomed to live in the trash heap of other people's lives? Nothing working, nothing new and exciting? Rebecca had become a broken-down car on the highway that everyone drove past. While they whooped it up. In convertibles. On the way to the Love Shack.

Was there any more?

Would she ever get to the Love Shack?

The man from the elevator popped to mind, but she shook him off. No chance with him, or anyone else. Not given her performance in bed. No way.

After all, how could anyone love the unlovable? The cold. The frigid.

She twirled a sheet ribbon around her finger, watching her fingertip grow white.

The condom wrapper beckoned.

Rebecca pinched the foil between her fingers. A gold wrapper with a black crest: a snake coiled around a staff. *What brand was this?* She flipped it over and saw no name or logo.

Did Ethan scam a free condom from one of his medical clients? He was in and out of doctors' offices all day as a pharmaceutical sales rep. He made good money. But was she worth a Trojan or

LifeStyles?

Nope.

A free condom for their last lay. How romantic.

But in staring at it, clouds parted in her mind. Maybe she didn't have to stay frigid forever.

Chapter 5

As it rolled past 9:00 a.m., Rebecca approached her doctor's reception desk for some face time. They were already a half hour past her appointment time, and Darcy echoed in her ears.

"Am I the next patient?" she asked.

The receptionist had her back to Rebecca, typing on a computer.

"Yes, there was only one patient before you and the doctor's with her now. I'm sure he won't be long."

She spoke the words, but her averted eyes spoke louder. They were ridiculous for being so late on the second appointment of the day. But then, her gynecologist was always late.

Always.

Her attempt to minimize the wait by scheduling an early morning appointment was already failing. At this rate, the 3:00 p.m. patients should cancel their dinner plans.

The waiting room was out of central casting. Generic Impressionist prints lined the walls at strategic intervals. Their vibrant colors blued by fluorescent lighting. Monet would be displeased. Maybe the doctors wanted patients to fall asleep so they'd lose track of time.

"Rebecca Sloane?" Nurse Molly called at 9:15 a.m. "Rebecca Sloane?"

Rebecca stood up and held her shoulder strap.

"There you are! Didn't see you hiding behind the potted tree."

Rebecca marched behind the nurse down a hallway. Open doorways came and went. Yet they kept moving until the lighting grew dimmer.

"Wait here, please," Nurse Molly said, gesturing Rebecca to sit in a secondary waiting area outside two closed doors.

Rebecca glanced up at the dark fluorescent bays overhead. "Any chance you can turn these on?"

"Sorry, no. They're on a timer. You won't be here long, though," she said while positioning a plastic indicator above one of the closed doors to red and sliding Rebecca's file into a clear plastic tray affixed to the door before leaving.

Rebecca settled into one of three connected chairs and considered the beat-up issue of *People Magazine* lying on the bench next to her.

Her cell phone saved her.

"Hey, girl! I wanted to wish you good luck. Am I too late?" Barbara asked.

"No, still waiting. He's punctual as always," Rebecca said, standing up to pace the dim alcove.

"I know Dr. Rogoff is cranky, but he's the best at the practice. See what he has to say."

"I'm more afraid he'll tell me I'm fine, and then I'll be nowhere."

"Isn't it crazy to wish for something to be physically wrong with you?"

"Nope. Then I can take a few pills or have surgery and transform into a sex queen!"

"You're insane!"

"Not insane, desperate," Rebecca said, scanning the empty hall for eavesdroppers. "Do you think Ethan was right? About me being frigid?"

"Ethan was an idiot. If anything's frigid, it's his brain."

"Oh, you're right. I'm not frigid. I'm orgasmicly challenged." Rebecca dropped into a chair.

"Take a breath. You're doing the right thing by seeing the doctor. I'm sure he can help you."

"I hope you're right. I'm so tired of feeling broken."

Rebecca bounced her knee, flipping page after page of the previously abandoned magazine. She tossed it back onto the seat, craning her neck to find signs of life. The hall was eerily quiet. Too quiet. Was that a bad omen? Was this visit doomed to fail like all her other attempts had? Rebecca closed her eyes and took a controlled cleansing breath: in through the nose, out through the mouth.

Her chest thumping subsided.

Better.

Her fight-or-flight instincts told her to go screaming through the wall cartoon style. But her soul wouldn't survive another bedroom rejection. Next time, it'd be her flying out the window instead of a picture frame.

After another ten minutes, Rebecca followed Nurse Molly into an empty examination room. It had a clean, medicinal scent that wasn't entirely awful. The tan wallpaper was covered with white hearts and topped by a decorative border featuring tulips, watering cans, and kissing hens (even wallpaper chickens were getting better action!). Exam gloves, shiny metal tools, and gauze lay neatly on a stainless tray on the counter. Nurse Molly erected the back of the examination table.

"Please get undressed behind the curtain and put on a gown with the opening to the front," she said.

Rebecca walked behind the blue curtain, tugging on the drape until it was completely closed.

"It's less than a year since your last pap smear; is there another reason for your visit today?" the nurse asked.

Rebecca's throat tightened. She didn't want the whole world to know about her problem, but she had committed to the visit. Rebecca moved the curtain slightly to spy on Nurse Molly, who was assembling the blood pressure cuff.

"Miss Sloan?" Nurse Molly asked again.

Rebecca jumped out of sight. "Oh, yes. I'm here to see the doctor about a sexual issue. I'm hoping he can help me."

The nurse's shuffling noises stopped. Rebecca grasped the edges of her gown tightly closed around her neck.

Let the judging commence.

"Hmm, okay," Nurse Molly said. "He'll likely do an internal examination anyway. Please sit on the table when you're done changing. He'll be along shortly," she added before leaving.

Rebecca tied the white strings in the front and hopped up onto the examination table, the white paper crinkling as she sat. Her watch showed it was almost 9:40 a.m. Why did they offer appointment times anyway? Maybe patients should just arrive at any time and grab an open room. Wrestle each other if needed. It made about as much sense as their current "scheduling" method.

Rebecca rolled her head around her shoulders, then stopped midway. It was Ethan's move. She pictured his Adam's apple bulging as his head tilted back, and her mouth reflexively pursed. She'd have to quit it now. He had ruined one of her favorite stretches, but she had no choice. Not if she wanted a fresh start.

Finally, her nemesis strolled in with Nurse Molly in tow. He was a tall, balding man with a ring of gray and brown hair tangled around his head like a Roman Caesar in need of a hairbrush.

Rebecca gripped the sides of the table.

"Didn't I just see you?" the doctor said. He turned away to wash his hands. The nurse handed him a clean pair of gloves, then swung the table stirrups into position.

"Not too long ago." Rebecca eyed the door, but her escape route was blocked by Nurse Molly's ample form.

Anticipating his direction, Rebecca put her feet in the stirrups and slid her butt toward the edge of the table. He negotiated a low rolling stool toward the exam table and inserted an icy metal speculum into her vagina, spreading it out for a better view.

With stiff, unforgiving edges, Rebecca had no doubt that whoever invented the speculum was a sadistic man. She heard some doctors warmed them to improve patient comfort, but Dr. Rogoff had no such concerns.

41

As much as she disliked Dr. Rogoff, having an audience was worse. In-room nurses were recent additions to her last few OB-GYN visits. Presumably, they were playing witness against accusations of inappropriate doctor behavior. Rebecca swallowed a laugh. The thought of Dr. Rogoff getting nasty was almost too much. He with the bedside manner of a decomposing fish.

Rebecca fiddled her fingers. "Does everything appear to be in the right place?"

"Yes. Does this feel tender?" Dr. Rogoff asked after removing the medieval torture device and jamming his hand up Rebecca's cervix while pressing down hard on her belly with his other hand.

Was he kidding? It hurt like hell, but Rebecca didn't think that was the answer he was looking for.

"I feel it, but there are no sharp pains," she answered.

"I'm now going to do the breast exam," he said while untying the white strings on her gown to expose her breasts. Taking each in turn, he kneaded, pressing in a circular motion until he reached the nipple which he squeezed lightly. While he did this, he fixed his gaze on the blank wall over her head. Rebecca averted hers to look at Nurse Molly, who stood in full view watching the proceedings. It did seem a strange way to earn a living.

Dr. Rogoff flipped the front of her gown closed and dropped back onto the stool.

"So, why are you here today? I hear you have a problem?"

Rebecca pushed up on her arms to sit upright, "I have a sexual problem, yes." Rebecca paused for a response. None was forthcoming.

"I've yet to experience an orgasm and was wondering if you

42

could tell me why. Whether there's something wrong with me. You know, physically."

"I see," he said, retrieving her medical file. "When you say you have not had an orgasm, does that mean with a partner, alone, or at all?"

"At all, I'm afraid. I twiddle about down there some, and it feels good, but it never amounts to anything. The same thing happens when I'm with someone. It just seems that at twenty-eight, I should have had one by now."

"Well, yes and no. Some women have difficulty in this area." He opened Rebecca's file briefly, then closed it again and resumed talking.

"The ultrasound you had back when you were having those menstrual cramps was normal. Your physical examination shows nothing physically wrong with you to prevent you from having an orgasm. Perhaps you need some additional guidance."

"Like what?" The only thing that came to Rebecca's mind was a tour guide waving a sign on a stick. If only locating her lost orgasm was that easy.

"I know of a study being conducted at Ezra University Medical Center on just this topic. The researchers are looking for study participants, and perhaps they can be of some help to you. There's no cost. Is this something that would interest you?"

"Yes, I suppose. I can at least talk to them and find out what it's all about."

"Good, here's the number. You can call Dr. Emanuel Costa, who is conducting the study. He'll be able to give you the necessary details." Dr. Rogoff handed Rebecca the number, which she checked for legibility.

"Okay, then. Take this, and you can exit to the right." He gave Rebecca the billing form with several boxes checked. Then, the duo left the room.

Rebecca used tissues to wipe off the excess jelly still clinging to her upper thighs. Again with the jelly, her friend and ally in a fruitless quest. Always lubing with nothing to show for it.

But maybe that was about to change.

Chapter 6

Rebecca quickened her pace as she headed east to York Avenue. Getting to the hospital in thirty minutes every Tuesday for the sex study was going to be a feat. Hopefully, Darcy wouldn't notice her long lunches—or ask where she was going.

"I'm going to my sexual dysfunction study, Darcy. Want to come with?" Not.

Rebecca scanned the directory for the wing Dr. Costa gave her when they spoke.

Ducky. It was at the farthest possible reaches of the hospital. She broke into a light jog, a sting shooting up her leg with each footfall of her flats. Where were sneakers when you needed them? Navigating the jumble of signage at each intersection, Rebecca spun in circles to orient toward the right arrows. She passed through airy glass rooms, functional concrete, then finally into brick, the hospital's time line laid bare.

Where is this place?

A brightly lit area lay ahead.

"You guys aren't the easiest to find." Rebecca panted, tugging her sweat-dampened shirt away from her torso.

"We've heard that before," the receptionist answered. Her name tag said Gladys, and she was a plump African-American woman with a dark-brown shoulder-length bob streaked with magenta. Pink poodles danced across her scrubs, completely at odds with their 1950s' institutional surroundings.

She handed Rebecca a clipboard with forms. "Please fill these out as quickly as you can. I'll go tell the doctor you're here."

Rebecca sat on a low wooden bench, checking boxes corresponding to the few maladies she suffered among the exhaustive list presented. When Gladys returned, Rebecca handed back the clipboard. She smiled and returned Rebecca's insurance card. It was a simple, nonjudgmental smile. She smiled in return.

Fluorescent lights buzzed and flickered overhead—*cue ax murderer.*

This is insane. There has to be a better way, she thought, eyeballing the chipped plaster walls where the seafoam green paint exposed cinder block beneath. She should have known that anyplace Dr. Rogoff sent her would be sketchy, Ivy League pedigree or no. She lifted her bag strap onto her shoulder and turned toward the exit, but Dr. Costa intercepted her.

He was a small-framed man of Hispanic descent whose dark, straight hair was cut neatly and parted on the left. He was slightly shorter than Rebecca, at about 5'5", with black trousers, a white shirt, and a red tie. His name was embroidered in blue script on his white lab coat which, she supposed, made it difficult to pilfer in the locker room.

"Ms. Sloane? I'm Dr. Costa. It's a pleasure to meet you," he said with a half bow. "Please come with me."

Rebecca's eyes darted toward her escape route, but she instead followed the doctor down the hall into a large, chilly room draped in darkness. There was one empty chair on a platform, illuminated with a spotlight. Rebecca froze.

"Please sit down, Ms. Sloane," Dr. Costa said, motioning her to the featured seat before disappearing out of sight.

"You want me to sit up there?"

"Yes, up in the light."

The beam buzzed with a dangerous energy. Rebecca strained to see something, anything, to focus on. Murmuring forms emerged from the shadows, distinguishable from the darker background behind. Why were other people here? An audience? Papers shuffled. A pen dropped, and a deep voice—a male—expelled a breathy grunt while retrieving it. Rebeca's arm tightened around her bag.

"Please, Ms. Sloane. Have a seat," Dr. Costa repeated.

"I think there must be some mistake. I thought I was here for the study consultation?"

"Yes, quite right. Please sit. We'll explain everything."

"Who is we?"

"Take a seat so we can begin."

"Begin what exactly?"

Had he said anything on the phone to indicate that there would be others there? Maybe he did. Rebecca recalled a distraction partway through the call when she became absorbed in a funny episode of *Big Bang Theory* while Dr. Costa continued speaking. It was only a minute, but he might have said something about the circumstances that she missed. It was a good lesson about the perils of multitasking, yet Rebecca knew she would re-offend. It had just been so quiet since Barbara moved out that she kept the TV on for noise. It had become her roommate, only it didn't pay rent.

A sliver of light tempted from under the door. It wasn't too late. She could probably get there without tripping over anything.

"Ms. Sloane. Please. Have a seat. I'll explain everything."

Rebecca entered the cone of light, scattering dust particles that danced above her head as she sat down in the molded plastic chair. Her arms squeezed tightly around the leather purse on her lap, knees pressed together.

"Thank you for coming today. You can't see them, but my coresearchers are in attendance: Dr. Smithy, Dr. Whitestone, Dr. Augus, Dr. Barnacle, and Dr. Roe.

"We applaud you for agreeing to speak with us today, to help us study a topic too often overlooked. We typically videotape sessions for later study and review. They are strictly confidential and will only be viewed by the doctors in the room right now who heard you speak live."

Dr. Costa cleared his throat before continuing. "Our goal is to better understand female sexuality so that we can devise strategies to help women overcome obstacles to gratification. If you agree to work with us, we will meet weekly for one hour and assign work for you to do alone at home to help you achieve an orgasm. You will then report back at subsequent sessions to let us know how things went, how you felt, what you thought, what worked, and what didn't. If you're ready, we will begin taping."

Rebecca swallowed hard. Words battered around in her brain

but refused to come out. Dr. Costa took her silence as assent and signaled a videographer who pressed record. She then silently left the room, blonde pigtail swishing as she walked briefly through the light.

A red blinking recording light penetrated the darkness.

"Are you sure no one else will see these tapes?"

"Quite so. Only this team and the videographer."

Rebecca leaned back in her chair. "Okay, then. I guess I'm as ready as I'll ever be."

"We've found that subjects speak more freely and candidly if they're not forced to look at our faces and gauge our responses. That's why the lighting is darkened this way. It seems dramatic at first, but I think that you'll likewise find it an aid."

The record light kept blinking. Rebecca closed her eyes.

Is this real?

"Let's get to know you a little first. Please tell us about your background, schooling, and sexual history," Dr. Costa started.

"M-my name is Reb-Rebecca Sloane, and I'm t-twenty-eight," she stuttered, then took a deep breath. "I'm sorry."

"No worries, no worries. Take your time. You're among friends here," Dr. Costa answered for the group.

"I'm feeling really exposed here in this chair. Are you sure it's necessary?"

"Give it a try. Your name is Rebecca Sloane, and you're twenty-eight. Go ahead…" he answered.

"Yes. I grew up here in Manhattan with my parents. I live… alone, for now. My roommate just moved out. She was my best friend, *is* my best friend."

Awkward. Truly awkward.

"My parents moved to the Island, to Port Washington, and I stayed behind—along with all the building neighbors who've hounded me since I was nine. Oh, and a few mostly dead houseplants. That's not my thing, plants. I've got a black thumb."

Not a peep from anyone. *Tough crowd.*

"Tell us a little bit about your parents," a woman, Dr. Roe, asked with a bubbly voice. Sounded blonde, whatever that means.

"Did they support you growing up? Help you form a positive self-image?" Dr. Augus asked in a silky, baritone voice.

"Well, I've had pretty low self-esteem as a rule. That's probably typical of most women my age. I look in the mirror and always notice the faults. I was a fat kid, you know. Always the last one picked at kickball, wore elastic pants, the whole nine yards. I've worked hard to be a healthy adult, go running and all that. But I always feel like there's something wrong. It's a cloud I can't shake."

"How has your self-esteem impacted your romantic relationships?" Dr. Costa asked.

"Probably hasn't done me any favors when you always feel less-than. I've read that confidence is a factor in bed, and I'm as un-confident as you can get in the bedroom."

"Why do you think that is?"

"Well, my parents were more like roommates. They were doing their thing, and the whole 'birds and bees' thing never came up. You can see how well that's gone."

Pens and keyboards went into overdrive.

"And your sexual history?" Dr. Costa asked. "When did that begin?"

"I was eighteen when I had sex for the first time. It wasn't particularly good, but I don't know that the first time is supposed to be. It was with a guy that I knew liked me, but whom I was not attracted to. I was trying to hook up with a different guy at a frat party, and when that didn't work out, I grabbed this guy. He was, of course, willing, and we left."

"Why did you want to be intimate with someone you were not attracted to?" asked Dr. Roe.

"It was almost the end of freshman year, and I thought that it was time, I guess. I thought of it as something to be over with, and I wanted it over."

"Did you have any other experiences freshman year that were more satisfying?" Dr. Barnacle, a man, asked.

Rebecca tried to reconstruct her college love life. There was one boy she liked; he was Israeli and seemed more experienced than she was. Nothing too much happened with him. Then she remembered.

"This might sound weird, but there was this boy in my dorm. He would use his hand on me, you know, down there, and it felt better than anything I'd done so far in a sexual way." Rebecca couldn't believe she was saying all of this to a room of strangers with a video camera rolling.

"And what about after college? Any longer-term relationships?" asked Dr. Costa.

"One. We dated for three years and just broke up, actually. It's because of him that I'm here."

"What do you mean?" asked Dr. Roe.

I can't believe that I have to say this out loud. "Would it be okay if I

51

stood up or walked around a little?"

"It's best you stay seated. We need to keep you in the frame," Dr. Costa said.

The red blinking light glared at her like the eye of Sauron. Watching. Always watching. Rebecca closed her eyes and laced her fingers, sliding them slowly together and apart in a rhythm to steady her breathing. *Better.* She reengaged her eyes toward the doctors.

"Ethan, that's his name. He would climax and get angry that I couldn't. Then, he'd take it personally and start bragging about his past girlfriends and how satisfied they were with him. He said there had to be something wrong with me. He called me an ice queen. Who says that to someone they care about? I just wanted to please him. I didn't even care about myself. I tried to get through it all without a fight. It became such an issue for us that finally, I tried to fake it."

"Fake an orgasm?" Dr. Augus asked.

"Yes. But I didn't know what the hell I was doing! How do you fake something when you have no idea what it is? He knew it; I knew it. It was a disaster. He called me out on the spot; called me a lying bitch. He grabbed his clothes and left."

Rebecca hid her face in her hands and wept uncontrollably. Her stomach refluxed with her every gasp for air, leaving her throat burning. She twisted toward the back of the chair; it was as much privacy as she was going to get while sitting on a stage in a spotlight. She opened her eyes and focused on the darkness. She completely understood the lighting now. If she had to watch them, she would have already left screaming.

"Thank you for sharing that. It must have been an extremely painful experience. Please know that we're here to help you. You don't have to face this challenge on your own. That's why we're all here," Dr. Costa said, walking over to hand Rebecca a paper cup of water.

Rebecca struggled to swallow in between hiccups of air. But she persisted, sipping water until she was able to breathe. She placed the empty cup on the platform next to her chair.

"Many women who come to us have had experiences like yours, so you're not alone. Please know that."

Rebecca stared into the void.

"Are you able to continue? We did have some more intimate questions to cover…" Dr. Costa asked.

"Fire away." *It can't possibly get any worse.*

"Have you ever tried to masturbate?" Dr. Whitestone asked.

Of course. Go for the jugular. "I have, but it never works. Flying solo never seemed natural. My brain refuses to play along."

"Did you ever seek advice from girlfriends or try to set the mood before you started…" Dr. Whitestone asked, before Rebecca interrupted.

"Believe me, no amount of mood lighting, candles, or quiet music can quell the critic stuck in my head, evaluating my performance in real-time," Rebecca said, pantomiming a clipboard and pencil. "I just feel silly, then give up before too long."

"How long would you say?" asked Dr. Whitestone.

"Oh, I don't know. Probably ten minutes, maybe less." At this, Rebecca heard pencils scribbling wildly.

Rebecca's gaze drifted back to the blinking red light; she

squeezed her eyes shut.

"That's likely enough for today. Do you think you'd be comfortable working with our team?" Dr. Costa asked.

"I don't know that comfortable is the word for it, but sure, I'll continue."

"We'll see you next week then. Please get your homework assignment from Gladys." He escorted Rebecca to the now open door, where Gladys awaited her.

Light blindness subsided as she staggered behind Gladys, hands shielding her eyes. She keyed on the receptionist's backside, which sashayed as she walked down the hall in a hypnotic rhythm. As Gladys reached the reception and sat down, Rebecca came around the front of the desk and sneaked a peek for other patients. Finding it empty, she let out an audible sigh.

"We try to schedule subjects over an hour apart, so you don't cross in the halls. It helps to maintain your privacy," Gladys said, reading Rebecca's mind. "Here's your homework, and good luck. We'll see you next Tuesday."

Gladys disarmed Rebecca with her smile. She was good.

Rebecca noticed the time, which snapped her back to attention. If she hurried, she could make it back to the office by 2:00 p.m.: the unofficial witching hour.

After being alone in the spotlight, Rebecca longed for the crowds and anonymity of the subway. She slid the homework in her bag, inserted earphones, and headed for the train.

Chapter 7

What have I done? Rebecca thought as she sat at her desk, face buried in her hands. She wasn't just frigid. She was a freak. Normal people don't blather on about their sexual inadequacies to faceless figures in the dark.

Wet saltiness slid down her throat. She gasped for air, a bit louder than expected.

"You okay, Sloane?" Paul, her neighbor, asked over the cube wall.

"Yeah, yeah. It's the hiccups," Rebecca said. *Please, God, if you exist, just help me get through this day.* Rebecca shifted papers on her desk, looking for a boring task to distract her.

Hours later, her ears registered the office silence. The available natural light was dimming. She arched her back to stretch, then grabbed the report she was working on and headed to Darcy's empty office. Rebecca dropped the papers on her desk beside her family picture. There she sat in a pile of brilliant fall leaves with her two sons, and her au pair, secured via an overseas exchange-like program.

Where was this one from, Sweden?

Rebecca picked up the picture to look closer. Blonde, pretty, could be Sweden, Rebecca thought. Darcy's reliance on an au pair was wholly consistent with her personality: someone to boss around on the home front and blame for parenting failures. Darcy relied too much on her au pair, Rebecca thought, but then, she wasn't a mother. That work/life thing was a delicate balance.

Barbara's face lit up her vibrating cell, so she replaced Darcy's picture and meandered into the hall before answering.

"Hey, girl, I wanted to be sure you remembered dinner. I know you get your nose buried after hours."

"I'm just finishing up. Take it easy on me tonight, will you? Today was ridiculous."

"Don't worry. It'll be fun. We won't mention work at all. We just want to hear how the study visit went."

"That's what I'm talking about," Rebecca said, ducking into the copy room for privacy. "It was awful. I felt so ashamed." She sat on a stack of unopened boxes of paper, wrapping herself in her free arm.

"Becca, don't say stuff like that."

"I want to forget everything that happened today. I hate feeling like my entry ticket for dinner is a blow-by-blow on my meeting with Dr. Costa. Promise me you guys won't make a big deal out of it? Please? I don't think I can stand another grill…"

"Becca, relax," Barbara interrupted. "Get going and let the chips fall where they may. We're your friends, right? We're on your side."

"Yeah, okay. Thanks."

"That said, you're making this all sound too juicy to ignore!"

56

"Barbara!"

"I'm just being honest."

"Are you going to behave?"

"Yes, yes. I'll behave."

"Fine then. I'll get going soon."

Rebecca returned to her desk to shut down the computer. She glanced around to see who was still there. She could hear a few buyers typing frantically and muttering to themselves. As usual, the corner lights in Harry's office were still on. He stayed late every night, as did his partner.

Neither man looked up as Rebecca left, and she was grateful for it. There was no shame in leaving a 9-to-5 job at 7:30 p.m., but they had somehow engendered guilt in many staff for doing just that.

Rebecca hopped a cab to Fourth Street between First and Second Avenue. She alighted on the corner, then stopped dead in her tracks. *Which restaurant was it?* She never could remember which restaurant her crew liked from among the thirty-odd Indian restaurants dotting both sides of this one city block. This time, Rebecca remembered she had to look for the two musicians playing the sitar in the storefront window.

The spiced perfume of curry, cardamom, and coriander greeted her as she opened the door. Her tummy grumbled. *Did I eat today?* She couldn't remember.

The décor matched the exotic flavors: red walls lined with multicolored Christmas lights and framed prints of famous Indian landmarks. Diners, at tables for two and four, crammed into the dining room. Through an arched window separating the restaurant's two interior dining areas sat Barbara and Leslie, framed like one of the landscape prints. They looked happy, chatting away, enjoying their mixed drinks. The three of them had been close friends since college, and they knew every intimate detail of the others' lives. They'd counseled each other through crises small and large, including the death of Barbara's mother, Leslie's parents' divorce, and Rebecca's overall feeling of parental abandonment and sexual inadequacy.

As she spied them, Rebecca's senses tingled. She knew her girlfriends. For sure they were plotting how aggressively to probe her for information. Exactly what she didn't want. She'd been probed enough for one day. The delicious scents from a moment before triggered mild nausea.

I can't do this.

She turned to leave, but Barbara spotted her through the arch and waved a frantic greeting.

Seeing her reluctance, Barbara mouthed a stern warning: "Don't leave."

Rebecca rolled her eyes and made her way over to the table.

"What took you long! I'm starving!" Leslie said, sliding over to make room for Rebecca, shifting her silky brown hair over her right shoulder in her signature swoop. Leslie's hair used to be long enough to sit on, and old habits die hard. Her crisp white shirt and pencil pants made her the primo fashionista in her paper's rumpled newsroom.

Rebecca squeezed into the seat, her chair barely an inch away from the patron behind her at the next table. Century-old Lower East Side tenements weren't known for roominess.

"So, how'd our liberated woman do today?" Leslie asked in her booming voice.

"Not so loud," Rebecca said, hiking her shoulders to pan the room. Luckily this was New York. People were trained from birth to tune the world out and sat eating merrily, bubbled in their own worlds.

"You don't have to answer her, Becca. It's none of our business," Barbara said.

"The hell it's not!" Leslie retorted. "We can't get every detail since the beginning of time and be denied when it gets juicy."

"I've had some juicy tidbits before now, haven't I?" Rebecca low-talked.

"None that compare to this," said Barbara.

"But I thought..."

"I tried, but Leslie made a solid case for why should you should tell all."

Impenetrable "I'm waiting" expressions breached her defenses.

"Off the record?"

"Entirely," Leslie answered.

Rebecca sighed, then relayed the odd proceedings with Dr. Costa, skipping the details they already knew from sharing her life the first time around.

"That's about as weird as I've ever heard," Leslie said when Rebecca had finished. "Did they say how many participants they have? This sounds a little fishy to me."

"I never thought to ask. It's a big teaching hospital, so I'm sure it's on the level. Besides, I don't think Dr. Rogoff would've known about it if Ezra Medical Center hadn't put the word out in the OB-GYN community."

"How often do you meet?" Barbara asked.

"Once a week. It gives me time to complete my homework assignment," Rebecca replied, sipping a glass of water.

"Homework!" Barbara exploded. "What kind of homework could they possibly require?"

"I'm not sure. Really, gals, can we talk about something else now? I'd love a distraction."

"Sure, Becca, we understand. But, just one more question: how can you do your homework if you don't know what it is?" Leslie asked.

"Oh, I have an assignment sheet. I was so glad to be out of there that I shoved the sheet in my purse. I haven't looked at it yet."

"Let's read it now. I can reach it for you," Leslie said, stretching for Rebecca's bag.

"No, no, no. Not for public consumption. Sorry," Rebecca said, shifting her bag out of reach and between her legs on the floor.

"Oh, come on."

"Look, I already told you way more than I wanted to. Besides, what happened to 'we're your friends. We're on your side.' Was that a load of crap?"

"Of course not," Barbara retorted.

"You know we are," Leslie said.

"Okay then, show-and-tell is over."

"We're just talking. There's no show," Barbara said.

"Who are we kidding? I'm a court jester singing for your amusement."

"No need to get testy."

"I think I have a right to be testy."

"Not with us, you don't."

Leslie put a hand on her shoulder, "It's okay…"

Rebecca shook her hand away, "It's not okay. None of this is okay."

"You're getting a little hot; calm down," Leslie said, lowering her voice.

"Hot? Me? Never. I've been too cold, remember? Cold. Frigid. Oh, forget it. You couldn't possibly understand…" Rebecca tried to stand but the table lifted with her, spilling Barbara's water into the Tamarind sauce and sending an appetizer plate to the floor with a loud crash.

The commotion hushed the room, drawing the eyes of every patron.

The waiter rushed over with a dish towel to dab the soaked tablecloth. He smiled meekly at Rebecca, then returned to his work, replacing the two layers of tablecloths before resetting the plates and serving dishes.

Rebecca surveyed the room. Patrons were chatting again but sneaking glances her way. Perfect. More time in the spotlight for the sexually impotent freak, she thought.

Her mind flooded with images of Dr. Costa's dark questioning room. Only this time, everyone from the restaurant was there, listening, laughing, pointing. No one understood what she was going through. Not really.

Tears welled in her eyes, blurring the colored lights into a molten kaleidoscope. Spices, staring people, laughter, clinking dishes, waiters, Indian music assaulted her senses—all crashing in waves one after the other. The room spun.

"I should never have come," Rebecca said, collecting her things.

"Wait! What are you doing?" Leslie said.

She headed for the door, bracing on the partition wall to steady herself on the way.

"Rebecca!"

"Let her go," she heard Barbara answer.

Out on the street, Rebecca paused to orient herself. She panted, but the humid air left her chest burning.

It had rained. The glistening sidewalk reflected the streetlamps waking up above in the growing darkness. Clouds of warm mist hung in stunted swirls, scattering as she hurried through.

Rebecca was alone. Utterly alone. But that was nothing new. She'd always been alone. She didn't belong anywhere. Not with her friends. Not with her parents. Not at work. And least of all, in bed. Rebecca walked, tears falling at will. She'd hidden them all day and was done. She got to the corner of Second Avenue and turned uptown.

Crowds of the East Village faded into the quiet sidewalks of Murray Hill. Her shoulders relaxed two miles later when she hit the abandoned streets of Midtown, Third Avenue storefronts dark until office workers returned in the morning. Somehow, the emptiness of it all felt like home. Rebecca first registered how far she'd gone when the sidewalk wetness seeped through her leather flats.

Then the sky opened.

She darted under the movie marquee for shelter.

The rain fell hard and steady. But instead of subsiding after a few minutes, the downpour kept coming. Perfect. A storm without a schedule.

She rubbed her bare arms to drive out the chill settling in her formerly active body. Dampness took hold, and Rebecca curled her toes away from the wet spots of her shoes.

A yellow cab pulled up to the theater with a splash. The young couple within jumped out and ran for the marquee, giggling and swiping the water off their jackets.

"Two, please," they said at the ticket window.

Seats purchased, they entered, the glass door hinging slowly before snapping closed after them.

Rebecca scanned the "now playing" posters behind her.

Why not?

She approached the ticket window.

"One, please."

"For what?"

"Whatever's starting now. You choose."

I want to be someone else right now.

Chapter 8

Rebecca stepped out of the theater into dewy coolness. The gal in the movie got the guy, along with some steamy action. Rebecca watched their lovemaking, not as a moviegoer, but as a student. But none of their interludes yielded groundbreaking insights. Only arched backs silhouetted against dark backgrounds, lit from above to suggest transcendence.

Her own sexcapades never sparked spontaneous spotlights from above. Certainly not with Ethan. More like red lights from below when she failed to climax. Ethan's body would go stiff and roll away after a moment of blissful relaxation. She'd roll her back to him, wrapped in her own arms when they should have been his. Why did he care so much about HER climax? Was he using it to measure his manhood?

Inadequacy jolted through her every pore at the thought of him. Him and her "problem." The problem that left her walking in the rain when she should have been eating with her besties.

But, she deserved her privacy—even from them. Intimate bedroom details were fine to keep to herself. She'd have to make them understand, or there would be many soggy walks ahead. But next time, they'd be the ones getting drenched.

She reached into her bag for the battered homework sheet, pressing out the wrinkles on her thigh to make it legible in the streetlight glowing overhead.

"Go to a beauty supply store and purchase a cosmetic mirror with a magnifying side. You will use this to explore your vagina and help identify the parts of your body that contribute to sexual climax."

Dr. Costa was supposed to make a lightbulb go off and send her on her merry way. But reality was never that easy. Her admission ticket to a fulfilled sex life required intimate field trips. And patience. Lots of patience.

Rebecca folded the paper and slipped it into her pocket

The illuminated red and white sign of a twenty-four-hour pharmacy across the street caught her eye. Traffic was light, so she crossed mid-block. Leaping over glistening puddles of blackness, her feet objecting as soggy soles met asphalt. She definitely needed to catch a cab home.

As she entered the store, she focused only on the overhead signs, avoiding all thoughts of why she needed the dumb mirror in the first place. Cosmetics were usually against the right or left wall, but rarely anywhere in between. The layout was likely decreed in Article 7 of the pharmaceutical constitution. This particular store had its section on the left, so she meandered over, resisting the impulse to grab a 99-cent plastic poof from a display barrel. No matter how many she owned, she always wanted another.

Lipstick, foundation, and mascara were prominently displayed in Aisle 1, most hanging in clear plastic packages. Shelf displays featured step-by-step selection guidelines replacing the personal instruction one got at a department store. She valued personal service, but just once, she'd like a cosmetics representative to admit that only two of the five hundred facial system steps were necessary. Rebecca could understand soap and lotion, maybe even toner for oily skin, but after that, it had to be a colossal waste.

Her untrained eye finally spotted the mirrors. They came in several sizes, from tabletop versions with a "backstage dressing room" vibe to small, handheld "mirror mirror" types. She opted for a modest swivel model with one magnifying lens, no lights, and a stand. Smaller was likely better given that she might be one-handed at times.

As she rode home in a cab, Rebecca forced herself to think positive. Was it folly to even try? The argument had looped through her mind for years and was hard to suppress now that she was making yet another attempt to address the issue. But if she had any chance of succeeding, she had to commit to the process 100 percent. Hopefully, the doctors would warm up a little and morph into a cheering squad. She definitely needed one.

Rebecca closed the cab door and reflexively looked up to see if Barbara was home. She began to chide herself, but noticed the light was on. She turned away to walk toward the lobby entrance. Had she left the light on? She didn't think so.

Outside her apartment door, she stood listening. However, her insomniac neighbor's too-loud TV was blaring, masking any sounds of intruders within. She slid her key in the lock and turned it as quietly as she could, pushing the door open just enough to peer in.

Nothing.

Rebecca repositioned her keys between her knuckles in case she had to jab someone and make a hasty exit, the only form of self-defense she could think of. She wished she'd listened to her mother and taken one of those women's self-defense courses. The pink advertising flyer with pull tabs taped to the bus shelter on the corner flashed to mind. Too late now.

The kitchen to her left was empty, as was the living room and hallway. She tiptoed to Barbara's old room and flipped on the light. Empty. Completely empty, at least until she found another roommate. Rebecca flipped on the light in her bedroom. The mess from her chair had spread to her entire floor, each article lying exactly where she disrobed on any given day, never making it to the now overflowing laundry basket in the corner. But no thief. Given the state of her room, she would have probably apologized that they had to wade through her dirty laundry as they robbed her apartment. Rebecca let out her breath and turned on the light to use the bathroom.

When she passed back across the apartment toward the front door, she noticed it. A note on the dining table illuminated by the pendant light overhead:

Wanted to make sure you were okay, but you weren't here. Waited, but had to get going.

Barbara says she's keeping her keys cuz she says you're a little nuts.

But that's why we love you!

Talk tomorrow,
Leslie & Barbara

Rebecca huffed a smile. Her girls *were* her girls. She never should have doubted them. She held the paper to her heart while tugging the pendant light off.

She lingered by the window. A car splashed through a puddle as it rolled past, streetlight reflecting in the ripples.

Her eyes adjusted to the darkness, aided by the ambient light streaming in through the windows. Rebecca scanned the sofa, coffee table, and the leather chair her father prized. She walked over and sat down, caressing the buttery smooth arms. She had forgotten how comfortable it was. There was leather, and there was LEATHER. This was the latter. It almost felt wrong sitting in it, dominated for so long by her dad. But he was gone, and it was all hers, at least for now.

Out of the corner of her eye, the white plastic pharmacy bag sat in a trapezoid of streetlight. Aggressively motionless. She checked her watch.

"It's too late," she yelled at the bag.

It sat in silent defiance.

She stared back.

"Ugh. All right," Rebecca hollered, getting up, snatching the bag before marching back to her room.

She closed her bedroom door and drew both window shades closed before pulling off her shirt.

Her head whipped around as one of the shades retracted a few inches. Rebecca returned and pulled it back down until it touched the windowsill, weighing it down with a green marble elephant figurine her parents bought abroad.

"That'll stop you."

She slipped off her bra and panties and sat on the bed, thinking. Her skin goose-pimpled.

"There's no reason to be nervous," she said, walking over to the bag, then locking her bedroom door.

She opened the box and withdrew the mirror. Staring at her face, she flipped it around to the 3x magnifying side.

"Ugh, bad idea," she said, flipping it back.

She retrieved her homework sheet from her pocket. The reverse side featured a line drawing of female genitalia. Every nook and cranny had a name. The clitoris Rebecca had obviously heard of, but the covering, the prepuce, she had not. The labia minora and labia majora sounded familiar, but it was nice to have the arrows just the same. The vagina and anus were closer together than she thought they'd be, and she honestly had never considered the urethral orifice in the mix at all. Properly informed, she shifted the covers and sat down.

Rebecca spread her legs to explore her anatomy. Wet and sticky. Browner than she had seen in pictures, but then it matched her complexion. She positioned the sheet closer so she could refer back and forth from the mirror to the instructions.

Gently, she moved the prepuce out of the way to expose the clitoris. A pink, glistening pearl. She tapped it lightly.

"Ahh, there you are!"

It was like putting a face to someone you had only known over email. Rebecca repeated the tapping on different parts of the labia, but nothing she touched had the powerfully familiar sensation of her clitoris.

This was a good first assignment. The entire region of her body was completely demystified. And somehow, less frightening. They were only a few flaps of skin, after all. Rebecca wondered why she had never checked it out before.

She put the mirror away, washed for bed, and settled in for what would be the best night's sleep she could remember.

Chapter 9

Darcy sat talking with her back to the door, the only way to get privacy in MediaNow's fortress of glass. Rebecca hurried down the aisle and around the bend toward the elevator. To avoid arriving at Dr. Costa drenched in sweat like she did the previous week, leaving earlier was a must. And she hadn't budgeted time for a Darcy inquisition.

The subway careened into the station with a blast of air, riders stepping forward to angle for the best door position. Rebecca wiggled into a narrow seat in between two passengers, holding her purse on her lap. Her strategic subway car choice and seat location would leave her at the foot of her desired stairwell when the train doors opened at her destination. She'd be out and up the stairs before a mass of humanity got stuck behind slow stair climbers. It'd save her at least three minutes, maybe more—an eternity in New York time.

Rebecca described New York time to non-natives as being like dog years, but in reverse. Every second was priceless, every hindrance an indescribable affront. Smart planning helped her avoid sticky confrontations thus far, a pretty good record by any standard.

She gazed around the car, searching for a safe spot to look. Eye contact was a distinct no-no on the subway, so Rebecca launched a round of her usual game. She searched for an interesting pair of shoes and landed on a worn-out pair of women's loafers covering navy socks bunched around the ankles. The soiled gray stitching held, despite threads escaping in spots. The seam pulls left gaps like tiny leather mouths. The soles were worn through, and the rubber heels had long since pounded through to the wood beneath. Rebecca let that bake for a minute and decided that the woman was a professor at a less than prestigious college or university. She had tenure and scheduled only afternoon classes. She wasn't as well regarded among her colleagues as her intelligence would warrant, and decided to publish an impressive paper to prove them all wrong and increase her stature. She was returning from a private archive where she gained special admission, a feat itself that would turn heads.

Having constructed the story, Rebecca glanced up to find a slim, almost gaunt, gray-haired Caucasian woman in her early fifties. Her shaggy bangs overlapped the top of her gold wire glasses. She wore a green and blue herringbone tweed blazer and carried a black leather briefcase so overflowing with paper that the zipper was rendered useless. The blue turtleneck under her blazer left Rebecca wondering what planet she was from that she would dress like that in mid-June. Perhaps she had a cold classroom. Satisfied, Rebecca surveyed the train's progress and made ready for her escape.

The walk east to York Avenue seemed longer than she

remembered, so Rebecca was surprised to look at her watch upon arrival and see that she made it on time. Gladys greeted her and ushered Rebecca to the room of darkness, where she took her place of honor in the spotlight. When the videographer left, they began.

"How did your week go?" asked Dr. Costa.

"Pretty well. The homework was helpful."

"Helpful in what way?" asked Dr. Augus.

"Well, I realized that I hadn't ever explored down there. The homework was oddly empowering. It made me feel like I was on the road to turning things around."

"Good. Good. We find this exercise helpful for our new clients. Most people who come to us, like yourself, have never examined their own sexual anatomy. Undergoing this process without that exploration is like trying to fix a car without seeing the parts," Dr. Costa said, chuckling at his own joke.

"Now that we've heard some of your dating history and you have been introduced to your anatomy, we would like to talk about masturbation."

"Wow. You guys just dive right in, huh?"

"You previously said that you have had difficulty satisfying yourself while masturbating. Is this true?" Dr. Whitestone asked.

"Yes," Rebecca answered, averting her eyes to a dark corner. Even with the lights off, she still could make out the dense outline of heads, shifting, watching her every move.

"Can you recall what typically goes through your mind while you masturbate?" he continued.

That was actually a good question.

"I usually think, what am I doing? This isn't going to work."

Rebecca snorted a laugh, but pencils went scribbling away. Her every word was pure gold.

"Have you ever had more positive thoughts while masturbating, perhaps invoked a fantasy of some kind?" Dr. Roe asked.

"Yeah, no. Never tried that. I wouldn't even know where to start."

"When you're being intimate, what goes through your mind then?" Dr. Barnacle asked.

"Nothing in particular," Rebecca crossed her legs, lacing her fingers around her knee. "You're asking about things I've never really thought about."

"Do your best. There's no right or wrong answer here," Dr. Barnacle said.

Rebecca stared into the blackness where Dr. Barnacle's voice was coming from. He likely wanted a deep answer. She shifted in her chair, willing a cogent thought to magically form.

"Well, I guess I try to focus on the person I'm with and do what they like. There's definitely some trial and error. So, if you want to know what I'm thinking, I'm usually running down the list and doing an on-the-fly assessment of my partner's satisfaction."

It was an impossible question: what did she think of during sex? Who the hell could answer a question like that? Do people really think of specific things?

If Rebecca were to be completely honest, she probably thought about how she could get through it without being exposed as an incompetent fool. Not likely the answer they were looking for.

The room was utterly silent. Weren't they going to answer?

Comment? Were they awake? The excruciating silence hurt more than her now-numb finger wrapped in one of her curls. Were they testing her? She unwrapped her curl and sat up straight.

"Sex is stressful, if you can't tell. My ex kept me guessing. I never knew if he'd be happy as a clam or brutish and insulting. Sex was no carefree, splendor-in-the-grass thing for me."

"You've talked about your partner's satisfaction. What about yours?" Dr. Costa asked.

"Me? Well, there's usually something that isn't how I like it. Then my mind starts running 'Gee, I wish he'd slow down' or 'he's such a sloppy kisser' or 'why is he penetrating already, it's too fast.' I guess you could say that once something starts going wrong, my mind is off to the races."

"Do you ever try to correct your partner? Guide them toward intimacy that's how you like it?" Dr. Augus asked.

"Of course not. Ethan would get really upset if I tried to say anything. But even before him, I just assumed that direction wasn't welcomed. Anyway, it wouldn't make much of a difference. And let's face it, I don't even know what I want, right? Best to go along with the flow and have it over with that much quicker."

Rebecca's cheeks burned. Admitting this out loud sounded awful. It was true, though. Most of her encounters hadn't been the best, and she now wondered why she never had corrected her partners. She hoped the doctors didn't think her stupid for not being more assertive.

Dr. Roe resumed while others still scratched notes, "It sounds like your encounters have not been that enjoyable. Were these people that you were attracted to beforehand, and their performance turned you off?"

"Some yes, some no," Rebecca said. "Some of the guys, I really didn't much like, but they seemed interested in me, so I went along with the intimacy for as long as I could tolerate it. Mind you, not all of them got into my bed. Sometimes the bad kissing and foreplay was enough to turn me off."

Who talks like this? Whores, that's who. Who screws guys they don't even like? Rebecca's bottom leg was falling asleep, so she recrossed them, ignoring the odd tingles coming from her lower calf.

"Could you share what sorts of things are arousing to you, in general?" Dr. Roe added.

Rebecca chewed her lower lip, glancing toward where the door should be. *What arouses me? What arouses me...?*

A deep throat clear brought her back. Had to be Dr. Augus. She heard another doctor tap to collect note papers into a neat pile.

Is someone leaving? Can I go with them?

"Um, sometimes when I watch movies, the love scenes get me aroused."

Dr. Smithy joined in. "What, specifically, triggers the arousal?"

"Well, there's usually some hot guy and some gorgeous girl in a skimpy dress. They are both very fit, and she is tan, and her boobs are frequently exploding out of her dress. She is going at it in some naughty situation or in a place where she could be caught." A ripple of pleasure pulsed her body. She looked up to see if anyone noticed, but they were all masked in blackness. She got a quick image of Sharon Stone—sans panties—in front of an interrogation squad. Rebecca kept talking, no longer conscious of the words leaving her mouth.

"Did you realize that in all your arousal examples, you focused on the females rather than the males?" he said.

"Did I?" Rebecca tried to remember. Fantastic. She had a Freudian slip in front of a room full of sex doctors. Just ducky.

"Well, females are much prettier to look at than are males with their saggy balls hanging down…"

Her saggy-balled doctors scribbled wildly. If they were insulted, they let it slide. Guess the benefits of darkness worked both ways.

"Have you ever been intimate with a woman?" asked Dr. Costa.

"No. Never. Not that there's anything wrong with it."

"The focus on women could be a significant finding which can help her to develop fantasies. Ms. Sloane, when you have a fantasy in your mind, it is easier to focus on the sensations you create through masturbation," Dr. Whitestone added, sounding excited himself.

"Let's move on to the mechanics of the masturbation," Dr. Costa said. "What do you typically use?"

"I'm not really equipped for the exercise," Rebecca admitted. "I just grab some phallic-shaped object and shove it in. I've tried with my fingers, but I don't really know what to do with them. I'm rather hopeless."

"Not at all. This is a very common problem for people who have not climaxed."

"Have you ever discussed masturbation with a family member, a sister or mother, for instance, to gain some insight?" Dr. Smithy asked.

Rebecca's guffaw shattered the polite volley. "I'm sorry, but you have got to be kidding. Talk to my mother? We were rarely in the same area code. Does anyone really talk to their mother about masturbation?"

"Yes, some do," Dr. Smithy answered, sounding miffed. "It is a difficult discussion, but we find that girls who get some guidance from a family member are more successful during masturbation than those who get their information from magazines or friends."

"Christ, my mother didn't even discuss menstruation with me until I was literally bleeding into my underwear. Seriously, I had no clue what was happening to me! Changed my panties three times before I had the courage to ask. No, I had no one to help with this stuff. I was completely on my own, and you can see how well that went. So, well, I'm here sitting here in a spotlight getting videoed in front of a room full of strangers."

Rebecca sensed movement of what was likely Dr. Smithy squirming.

"Well, we're not going to give you specific instructions about how to masturbate just yet. We would like you to purchase a vibrator, some lubricant, along with a book called *Hidden Sunshine*. It's a well-known book with sexual fantasies that might help jump-start your own fantasy process. We want you to do some more exploring this week, but this time, please explore your whole body. Really try to focus on the sensations and note which areas are more erogenous than others. This is all part of discovering yourself and learning how to maneuver your body to maximize stimulation. By the way, be sure that you are in a quiet place where you're undisturbed. Silence your phone, or turn it off altogether. And lock your door so you won't be distracted by the thought of someone interrupting you. Do you think that you can do this?" Dr. Costa asked.

"Yes, I think so," Rebecca answered.

"Good. We've made some wonderful progress today. The homework details are on the sheet you will get from Gladys. It has the author's name and the book title, as well as some stores that sell sexual paraphernalia. We will see you next week."

On cue, the door opened, and Gladys's frame silhouetted the doorway. They definitely had this thing down to a science. On her way out, she glanced at Dr. Costa's seat to see if he had some sort of buzzer. It was the only way she could explain it.

Rebecca followed Gladys to her desk, retrieved the homework, then booked back to the office. She made it back by two and thus avoided nasty glances from folks that would have accompanied arriving late.

She faced the aisle to scan the office. Was she the only inorgasmic woman in this sea of cubicles? Rationally, there had to be others. Hell, there had to be enough to warrant a study in the first place. But her bones ached from a deeper truth. She had no tribe. She was broken and alone, and might always be.

She spun back to face her desk and Dr. Smithy's question popped to mind. She took out a pad of paper and drew random squiggles with her blue pen. If her mother had been more helpful at the time, when she was growing up, she wouldn't be in this pickle. Whatever her pickle was. Rebecca didn't know what she didn't know, and that's a lousy place from which to begin a conversation. Especially with the absent and impatient Olivia Sloane. Her mother never liked it when she didn't understand something. It was always Rebecca's fault for not studying hard enough or not discovering answers on her own. If they were in public, her mother would smile faintly and scan the room to see if anyone had witnessed her ultimate embarrassment of having a daughter who "didn't know."

Rebecca was left to acquire sexual knowledge in the same way she did her algebra: muddling through alone. It was a fatal mistake she was still paying for, despite her extensive studying after the fact.

"Jesus Christ, why can't they ever get it right?" a buyer across the aisle from her screamed after slamming the phone down. She stormed past Rebecca's desk, nearly colliding with Darcy.

"Excuse you," Darcy said to the woman's back, bristling from being dismissed.

"She's in rare form today," Rebecca said.

"You know, you could learn a lot from her."

"Like what? How to break phones?" The woman broke so many phones that she got a Fischer Price toddler phone from her office Secret Santa the previous holiday. It went over surprisingly well, but everyone ducked just the same when she feigned throwing it after finally getting the joke.

"Snark all you want, but she's a highly successful, tough negotiator. Her style works," Darcy finished with an uptilt of her chin.

"I'm glad it works for her, but not every vendor likes being yelled at."

"Perhaps not, but you go too far in the other direction. You're way too lenient."

"I'm surprised you think so," Rebecca said, standing up to face her. "Orangina, Acura, and Hollis Hotels have all complimented the deals I negotiated for them."

Darcy glared back, forcing her lips closed so hard a bloodless ring formed around her mouth.

"All I mean is that there's no one right negotiation style for all situations. I think we need to all find the style that works for us. Don't you think?"

"Are you done?"

"Yes."

"Good." Darcy turned heel and marched down the aisle to her office.

Wow, Rebecca thought, not used to getting the last word with her overload boss. She glanced over, but Darcy was on the phone with her back to the door. Rebecca raised an eyebrow.

Another fake call?

Rebecca rarely got a mic-drop moment with Darcy. Too bad she had no such answer in bed.

Chapter 10

"Oh my God, I hate not seeing you every day!" Barbara said, embracing her in the street.

"I know. It sucks. Mrs. Portnoy talks to me in the elevator. It's like she knows I'm wounded and is going in for the kill."

"Are you wounded?"

Freudian slip. Two days in a row.

Rebecca shook her head, "Of course not. Let's go up."

The Potter's Shed, a paint your own pottery place, was on the third floor of an industrial building on Twenty-First Street off Fifth Avenue. The freight elevator doors opened like a mouth into a psychedelic wonderland straight out of the 1960s: pink, purple, and orange daisies as tall as Rebecca were painted on the walls. Bright white enamel tables sat atop legs splattered with old glaze. The floors were puddles of color, covered in drips and dusty footprints.

Rebecca surveyed the pristine shelves of white porcelain awaiting color.

"I can never decide what to glaze," she said.

"How do the costs run?" Barbara called over to the young woman behind the counter.

"The bowls, plates, goblets, and pitchers are $20 to $35 each; figurines, salt and pepper shakers, plain tiles, napkin holders, piggy banks, and the rest are each labeled in pencil on the bottom, but run $10-18 each. The oversized vases and special items on the top shelf can go as high as $60, so let me know if you want one of those, and I'll get it down for you."

As she spoke, the woman continued wrapping fired projects in pink tissue paper and placing them in white shopping bags. "You pay for the piece you want and take as long as you need to decorate it, since we don't charge a sitting fee. When you're finished, I'll help you check out, and you'll leave your piece here for firing. It will be done in a week, and you can come to pick it up. Glazes, brushes, and sponges are over there in the corner, and you can use the sink near the window if you need water. Let me know if you need any help."

"I love this place. It feels like a bohemian café lost in time," Rebecca whispered to Barbara.

Barbara chose a small bowl suitable for cereal or her favorite morning oatmeal, Rebecca thought. Rebecca chose a large bowl eighteen inches across. After grabbing a plastic palette and filling it with a choice of glazes, they sat down at an empty table in the middle of the room. Only two others worked in the vast studio: An old woman sat alone painting a woodland scene on a pitcher while a young woman decorated a vase with irises and hummingbirds at another table. Each was completely lost to their work and paid the new arrivals no attention whatsoever.

"I love how anything is possible when I do art," Rebecca said, wiping the white ceramic bowl with a damp sea sponge to remove the dust.

"You know, anything is possible in real life too," Barbara said, working with a thin paintbrush scarcely more than a few hairs.

"Doesn't feel like it."

"Becca, it's all about your frame of mind. Do you think I'm always super confident in my job? Hell, I'm the only Black face for miles. Often the only woman too. I don't always have the biggest cheering squad, if you know what I mean. The difference is, I believe in myself and forge ahead. Give it a try."

"I know you're right, but there are raging battles going on upstairs," Rebecca said, tapping her head. She then waved the idea away. "I'll figure it out."

The conversation lulled, each artist working away. Rebecca settled into the order and precision of the Greek-style border she sketched around the rim of her bowl. Straight lines interconnected at right angles without a beginning or end. She planned to paint the shapes black on a yellow background and the outside of the bowl cobalt blue. As it stood, the glazes were pale references of the colors they would ultimately become, adding further mystery to the whole ceramic process. Time would tell if Rebecca's own transformation would be as vibrant.

Barbara toiled on an intricate landscape design. Watching her work, it was hard to imagine her harboring self-doubt about anything. She was stunning and smart. A successful lawyer with a gorgeous boyfriend, now tackling the arts like it was her calling. She was fearless, precise, and engaged in her task, three qualities Rebecca could stand to emulate, especially when it came to the study.

But was achievement really all about attitude?

Barbara looked up. "What?"

"Nothing. Just watching."

"Less watching, more doing," she commanded, turning back to her work.

Two hours later and content with their work, they each paid and left, leaving the house artisans to continue their masterpieces, their progress imperceptible from when they arrived.

After they parted, Rebecca strolled home, sipping a milkshake she purchased at an ice cream shop along the way, condensation beading on the outside of the plastic cup. The evening was comfortably warm, but the mugginess hinted at the summer scorchers yet to come. When she arrived at the apartment, the front door was propped open, and cardboard boxes littered the foyer.

"This is a strange time to be moving in," Rebecca thought.

She waited for the elevator to stop and pulled open the exterior elevator door to the utter shock of a gorgeous young man in a black T-shirt standing within—the same guy who rescued Rebecca's dinner.

"Christ! I didn't see you standing there," he gasped. "I've been up and down alone so many times I forgot—hey! It's you!"

"Yup, no dinner to rescue this time," Rebecca said, toasting him with her milkshake.

"I'm Kyle, by the way. I'm moving in with my aunt in 3G."

"Oh, you're Bessie's nephew. Are you the one who lives in California?" Rebecca asked.

"Lived. I've moved back. I'm needed here, plus there were too many cosmetically enhanced actors. All that perfection got creepy."

"Well, welcome back, and don't worry. There are no perfect specimens for fifty miles around here!" Rebecca laughed.

"Oh, I wouldn't say that," Kyle said, shooting Rebecca a glance that made her blush and shift her gaze elsewhere. "Would you mind holding the door open for me so I can load up the elevator? It will only take a minute."

"Sure. By the way, my name is Rebecca. I live in 3B." She extended her hand to shake, but his were occupied with a box labeled "books." He smiled at the gesture.

"I'm afraid you'll have to shake a finger. That's all I can spare," he said, extending the pinky finger on his right hand, which Rebecca gladly shook, taking care not to dislodge his grip. It was awkward but sweet.

"Thanks for helping. I'm sure moving boxes wasn't high on your list for tonight," Kyle said while depositing yet another box into the elevator. Rebecca did a fine job of holding the door and sipping her shake while staying out of his way.

"It looks like you plan to stay for a while. Is your aunt not well?"

"Yeah, she's not doing too great. With my family scattered around the country, we debated moving her to a facility where she could have some support. In the end, we decided against it. We'll see how it goes with me around to help her. It should be fun for her, at least for a while. She's lived alone since my uncle died fifteen years ago, and she never had any kids. I'm the closest thing she's got. Me and my sister, that is."

"Is your sister moving in with you as well?" she asked, hoping not. Girls complicated things, even if they were relatives.

"Oh no, she's engaged and lives in Texas. My parents live up near Boston. Actually, Bessie is my mom's aunt. She's my great-aunt, but we just leave the 'great' off. Sounds fussy." He paused and smiled. "Sorry for the family history. I'll just keep going if no one interrupts me. It's a bad habit."

"Not at all. I like hearing about other people's families."

Kyle continued to fill the elevator and carried his last box in when the other elevator arrived, overflowing with passengers who gave Kyle dirty looks as they walked by. He didn't seem to notice. With the last box aboard, they squeezed into the car and headed up.

"Thanks for helping. I have a doorstop upstairs, so you don't need to hold the door for me," he said.

Rebecca's shoulders dropped in disappointment.

"But, if you want to help me carry boxes, you are by all means welcome."

"Sure, I'd be happy to help you. Never let it be said that New Yorkers aren't friendly," Rebecca said with a smile.

Kyle scratched his head. "Has anyone ever said that New Yorkers *were* friendly?"

"Not that I'm aware of, but I must be scoring cosmic brownie points tonight for my brethren, don't you think?"

"Absolutely," he replied while stepping out of the elevator and propping the door open.

"I'll be right back," Rebecca said, heading to open her apartment door, then closing it quietly behind her. She typically let the heavy metal door slam, but she didn't want to be rude to her new friend.

Rebecca dropped her bag and pinched her cheeks in her foyer mirror, straightening her hair. Despite her checkered dating history, she tended to be pretty comfortable around men. Back in college, she got along better with guys than girls. She liked sports and cursed like a sailor, which they all found amusing. Apparently, she retained that "one of the guys" vibe, which served her well in the short term, but didn't lead to lasting romantic entanglements.

Rebecca returned to the hallway. Kyle had shifted the boxes out of the elevator and left them scattered around the floor in front of the now-closed elevator door. Moving in at midnight had its advantages. One could dispense with neighborly courtesy since the octogenarian tenant population was long in bed. Rebecca hoped for Bessie's sake that Kyle would be neater once unpacked. She had only been in Bessie's apartment a few times, but from what she remembered it was spotless with pinpoint placement of every knickknack. Not knowing what else to do, Rebecca lifted a box and headed into the apartment.

The foyer was dark. And as Rebecca penetrated deeper, she found few additional lights. Bessie had a two-bedroom apartment like Rebecca's and, presumably, she slept in the master bedroom at the end of the hall near the bathroom. Light from the first bedroom refracted off the hall walls. It illuminated a path, so Rebecca headed there, lugging the box, trying not to collide with any of Bessie's Victorian furniture. Despite Kyle's midnight move, the apartment remained quiet, and all parcels were confined to his bedroom. That boded well for his aunt.

Rebecca entered the room, pausing at the threshold. The only furniture was a queen-sized bed frame and mattress leaning against the wall, and a dresser with empty drawers stacked next to it, both surrounded by a sea of boxes. It would be interesting to see how he addressed the space challenges. Maybe Kyle would have some creative storage solutions she could apply in her own apartment. Though she had the master bedroom in her unit, Rebecca still had more possessions than the room could comfortably hold. She was tempted to sprawl into Barbara's old room, but she knew it wouldn't be empty for long. Rebecca would have to get on that roommate thing—and soon. But she wanted to savor the freedom of living on her own for a bit longer.

The edges of the box dug into her fingers. "Where would you like this?" Rebecca asked, juggling the weight to generate blood flow.

"Oh, I'm sorry. Let me take that," Kyle said, leaning awkwardly to take the box out of her arms. "I never should have opened this box. I wanted my pocketknife to help slice tape, but it doesn't seem to be in here. Anyway, let's shift the other boxes in here so we can close the apartment door. This is New York, after all."

"Well, yes, but it's a pretty safe neighborhood, knock wood," Rebecca said, then quickly rapped on the dresser twice to be safe.

Kyle gave her a curious look. "I've heard 'knock wood' before, but what's it all about? How does the knocking protect you?"

"Don't you know? It's to keep the little trolls from making mischief and ruining whatever you want to go well. When you knock on wood, you knock on their heads, and they get distracted and confused and cannot work their ill will," she said, pantomiming the chaos.

"Riiiight…" he answered.

Back in the hall, Kyle handed Rebecca what turned out to be a very light box. He then stacked two boxes and led Rebecca back into the apartment.

"Don't you think it's a little strange to think that little creatures are living inside the furniture?" he continued.

"Yeah," Rebecca smiled back, "But it's better than having little creatures in the furniture who are aligned with the forces of evil."

"I guess if you put it that way, it makes sense." He put the boxes down upon a few others and immediately knocked on the headboard.

"What was that for?" Rebecca asked.

"I wanted to protect you from something that I was thinking," Kyle said with an impish smile. Rebecca said nothing more and helped him move the remaining boxes out of the elevator bank and into the living room as his bedroom was at capacity.

"I'm surprised your aunt hasn't woken up. Is she a heavy sleeper?"

"That and a little hard of hearing," he said dropping the last box of books with a loud thud to illustrate his point, "I can't thank you enough for helping me. I mean, you just met me in the hall. Tell me you don't do this for everyone."

"I never have and probably never will again; you're lucky you're so cute," Rebecca said, slapping a hand over her gaping mouth.

Idiot, idiot, idiot.

Kyle smiled. "You're pretty cute yourself."

Rebecca's face flashed warm. She looked away, focusing on a

brown box next to her labelled clothes.

"I should go," she said, gesturing over her shoulder while backpedaling.

"Sorry, I didn't mean to…"

"No; no worries. I just have an early day tomorrow."

He took a step forward but stopped, scratching his head. "Thanks for helping. Will I see you around?"

"Sure, yeah."

"Maybe I can make it up to you sometime?"

"Oh, no need. But thanks."

"Good night."

"G'night."

Rebecca turned tail before his blue eyes could give her the pitying look she knew was coming.

Chapter 11

"Someone had fun last night!"

Rebecca looked up to find a buyer named Maia, her face obscured behind a whale of a mug.

"There's nothing to tell, Maia. I was just up late," Rebecca said, exposing her folly with a wide grin.

"You've got the glow; I know it when I see it. Tell me everything."

Rebecca shook her head no, but her smile said otherwise.

"I'm not leaving here until I get some details, so you might as well spill it," Maia said, plunking herself in Rebecca's guest chair and pivoting to face Rebecca squarely. Maia sat silently, warming her hands on either side of her cup. The office air-conditioning was frigid, as it was most mornings.

"Come on, out with it!" Maia demanded.

"Okay, but then you have to go. I met a hunky guy last night who moved in across the hall," Rebecca rattled off.

"There's got to be more than that…"

"Nope."

Rebecca imagined Maia casing her building trying to snatch

Kyle away. Pathetic, she knew, but everyone had their insecurities.

"Does Mr. Hunky have a name?"

"Kyle."

"Oh, Kyle! That's a hot guy name. What does he look like? Where did you meet him?"

"He's about six-two with dark hair and the bluest eyes I've ever seen. He is seriously hot," Rebecca added with more enthusiasm than intended. "Okay, that's enough gossip. Break time's over."

"What? That's it?" Maia stood up, arching to evade Rebecca's shooing gestures.

"Seriously, I need to get some work done before I hit a wall. I'm sure you can understand."

"I guess. Hey, do you want to tell me more over lunch?"

"I'm sorry I can't. I have some errands I need to do today. Maybe another time?"

"Suit yourself," Maia said. She ambled away. Rebecca exhaled when she heard Maia's animated conversation after she latched onto someone else.

The morning evaporated while Rebecca submerged into media planning work for a hotel client. A gaggle of girls headed out for lunch, sales reps in tow. Rebecca peered into Darcy's office. Finding it empty, she made a clean getaway to search for a vibrator.

Rebecca's bare arms welcomed the sun's warmth as she weaved in and out of the teeming lunch crowds blocking the sidewalks. Lines spilled outdoors with people queuing for the more popular establishments. Fast was key. Good, but slow, places were best saved for dinner. Delicious scents of grilled meat wafted over from a Souvlaki pushcart, but she kept moving. The lines would be shorter on the way back.

Her mind drifted to Kyle. He had an ease and magnetism that was irresistible; pure unbridled confidence. If she hadn't left when she did, she likely would have embarrassed herself.

The way he was staring at her...

A loud horn blared, jarring Rebecca back to attention just in time to avoid getting flattened by a box truck rattling by, canvas sides flapping in the breeze. Her heart pounded through her chest. The crowds parted around her as she recovered on the crosswalk.

Why hadn't she ordered online? She stepped to the side to scan the browser on her phone for a moment before reaffirming her need to go to the store: she needed to handle the merchandise. A pause in the traffic had Rebecca resuming her stroll to the only "sexy" store she could think of: *Pink Kitten*. When had she last been there? Probably back in high school when Rebecca and her friends would gawk at the naughty wearables until the owner kicked them out. Hopefully, the cosmos wouldn't hold a grudge now that she was a real customer.

Rebecca took a right on Stanton Street and passed a few buildings before she saw the familiar black storefront with pink neon signs. The entrance was below street level, down a few steps, and partially hidden underneath the brownstone steps of the building above. Rebecca darted down the stairs and was inside before anyone could have noticed.

However, her stealth operation was quickly aborted once inside the store. Rebecca was completely exposed—spotlight in the prison yard, forget running for the fence—exposed. She entered to the mouth of a large "U" of display cases edging three walls.

There were no nooks, no crannies, and nowhere to hide, just a big open floor from side to side, front to back, and shiny glass cases filled with unmentionables. If she averted her eyes away from the feather teddies, edible underwear, and handcuffs on the walls, she landed on a double-ended dildo, anatomically correct penis (complete with bulging veins), or some other thing that made her want to run away screaming. There was not a single place to privately ponder the choices or browse while concealed. Things had certainly changed. The owners had made a conscious choice: you either bought something or got out. There was no middle ground. Luckily for Rebecca, there were also no other shoppers.

She searched until she saw a line of what appeared to be vibrators. They were long and straight with rounded conical tips. They varied in size, color, and surface texture. Some seemed to be hardened plastic, while others were apparently rubberized. In any event, they were in a display case beyond her reach. The store was as silent as it was tawdry with no salesperson in sight. Rebecca looked for a service bell of some kind.

Were they kidding? It was hard enough to approach the door, enter, and stay inside. Now they were making patrons beg for help?

"Hello? Are you open?" Rebecca hollered.

"I'll be right with you," a cheery voice called from the back. A moment later, a young woman parted the black satin curtains that led from the stockroom, and Rebecca was completely taken aback. The girl's appearance matched her surroundings, but not her voice. The girl was stereotypical goth: black shoulder-length hair with white bangs and two pigtails on top Shih-Tzu style. Her lips, eyes, and nails were done in black and joined by multiple piercings in her eyebrows, ears, and nose. She wore a white ripped shirt under a black net shirt, purple mini skirt, black and purple striped tights, and big, clunky, black boots with silver buckles. She was straight out of Halloween, but her friendly voice betrayed her mid-Western upbringing and sunny interior. She was probably once a prom queen.

"I'm sorry to keep you waiting; it's so hard to hear people come in when I'm in the back. I keep telling them to put a bell on the door—but they think a bell would put people off; too much like an arrival announcement. 'I'm here!' I suppose it might make some people look up to see who came in, and the owners want to be sure EVERYONE feels comfortable, you know? Not everyone is comfortable buying this stuff. So, what can I get you?" she said, stopping for air.

"I need a vibrator and don't know where to start. I never knew there would be so many choices."

She circled the room behind the counter and stopped at the display case Rebecca noticed. She reached in and pulled out a display tray and a few options.

"Most folks like to start with one of these. They are easy to handle, don't get too slippery with the lubricant, and are mid-sized, so most folks find them comfortable for both vaginal and anal use."

Rebecca slowly reached out and grabbed one. Her fingers wrapped around but couldn't touch. For a mid-sized model, it felt like a tree. She put it back.

"This one is covered with a thin layer of silicone, so it's a little softer to the touch. And, it's not too loud," the girl added, handing

Rebecca a different one to try. It was surprisingly heavy for its size, but it fit easily in her hand.

"It seems fine, I suppose. What kind of batteries does it take?"

"Two C batteries," she said as she put the samples back in the case. "What color do you want?"

The assortment included every color in the rainbow plus black and white. She decided on blue, and the girl pulled out the box.

"What is that thing?" Rebecca asked, pointing to an intricate metal circle hanging on the wall.

"Oh, that's a cock ring. It constricts the flow of blood to the penis, which helps some men retain their erections longer. It also hurts some guys, and they buy it for the extra sensation it provides. Do you need one of those?"

"Oh, no, no, no," Rebecca shuttered. "The vibrator is bad enough!"

"Bad enough? Come on, now! Every woman needs a vibrator. Sometimes your partner's not handy, and you gotta get some? Right?"

Luckily, Goth-Girl didn't wait for an answer and moved over to the lubrication section.

"Which lubricant would you like? We have scented, unscented, warming, gels, lotions…"

"What's cheap?" Rebecca asked.

"Oh, we have the regular KY. You can get that anywhere when you need to refill. Truth is, we overcharge a bit here."

Rebecca figured she might as well be done with it and nodded her assent. The girl reached for a KY bottle and rang up Rebecca's purchase, handing her an unmarked pink plastic bag.

"Come again!" she yelled and started to laugh, "Get it? COME again? I never get tired of saying that." She slapped her thigh and retreated into the stockroom from whence Rebecca heard her muted giggles.

Rebecca grinned. Someone ought to tell Goth-Girl that she was entirely too happy to be dressed like that. If she kept it up, she would be forced to surrender her goth privileges. Rebecca rolled up the bag and stuffed it into her purse. All she needed was for Maia to find the purchase and broadcast it to the whole office. Thinking of Maia prompted Rebecca to check the time. She had about twenty minutes to grab lunch and get back. Peeking out the door, she made a break for it.

The return trip was quick. Rebecca hid her handbag in the bottom drawer of her desk and moved the trash can in front for good measure. She wasn't back five minutes when her phone vibrated on her desk.

"Who is Kyle?" her mother asked when she answered. "Bessie called to get your phone number. I didn't know who he was, so I said I'd call back."

Kyle wanted her number? Rebecca's heart fluttered.

"He's her nephew. Just arrived from California. He moved in with her last night."

"What does he want with you?"

What indeed.

"I helped him carry some boxes. He seemed nice."

"Interesting. Well, you're certainly available with Ethan out of the picture."

"Thanks for the reminder. Anyway, you can call back and give

Bessie my number. Let me know what she says."

"I will when I call. I've got a meeting now, then a dinner later with friends. But I'll get to it tonight; tomorrow for sure."

"Mom, can't you—"

"Oh, they're calling me. Talk soon," her mother said before hanging up.

Rebecca stared as her phone, then replaced it to her ear.

"Bye, Mom. Thanks so much for putting me first and jumping right on my opportunity to talk to an interesting new guy."

It was a classic Olivia Sloane move. Play hard to get, even with her daughter's love life.

Rebecca cleared her head. What's important was that Kyle asked for her number. Rebecca clung to her phone, savoring the thought of Kyle, his dreamy blue eyes and toned physique.

"Don't make a call now; you'll be late for the meeting," Darcy barked before strutting off. "We're in Conference Room D."

Did Darcy have a happiness detector in her office? Perpetually at-the-ready with an icy bucket of water? Rebecca opened her calendar. Who was this meeting with anyway? They all blended together. She gathered her pad and pen, but when she approached reception, the reps were still sitting there playing on their phones. Rebecca reversed course, taking the long way around to the conference room. She arrived to find Darcy with her feet up talking to her husband.

Rebecca sat at her elbow.

"Darcy, the reps are here," Rebecca whispered to no reply.

Even exaggerated wrist flips every few minutes to check the time failed to draw Darcy's attention.

"The reps are waiting."

Darcy furrowed her brows, covering the phone with her hand, "I'm not an idiot. I know."

Several minutes later, Darcy hung up, "You can show them in now."

Rebecca made light conversation with the two salespeople as they walked to the room. Meanwhile, Darcy swapped seats away from the head of the table into Rebecca's chair. Typical. Would the senior salesperson now take the head table position—a direct threat to Darcy's authority—or would he wisely sit across from Darcy, showing proper deference. The "seat game" played a critical role in Darcy's meeting outcomes; a salesperson could fail before a word was ever exchanged. Given those rules, Rebecca wished they could just sit down, stand up, and leave. It would certainly save everyone a lot of time and trouble.

After proper seating and pleasantries came the ceremonial presentation of Darcy gifts—this time tickets to the US Open Tennis at Flushing Meadows in August. Those tickets sealed Darcy's power broker position, so the meeting could begin in earnest.

The presentation started, and Rebecca listened while examining the media kit they presented and scribbling questions she had about the magazine, its circulation, and competitors. Then the three of them noticed Darcy's head nodding. Rebecca arched her eyebrows in apology and took over the meeting, learning some choice tidbits about the magazine and their potential rate packages. The info would help her make final decisions about which magazines made the cut for their client.

Darcy startled awake just as the vendors were gathering their belongings to leave. Embarrassed, she bailed on the rest of the afternoon's meetings, leaving Rebecca to blissfully run through them on her own. She then stayed late to make up for the lost desk time. Deadlines were deadlines. At 9:00 p.m., Rebecca dragged herself home, eyes half-closed. That was, until she got to her apartment door.

A white envelope was taped below the peephole. It was blank on the outside.

Rebecca held the envelope, pealing the Scotch tape off the door, then slid her finger under the flap to open the note.

"Stop by when you get in. Kyle."

Beaming, she dropped her bags in place and turned to cross the hall. She stopped midway. It was almost ten o'clock. Was it too late? Then Rebecca remembered what time she met him the night before, and rang his bell.

Kyle immediately opened the door.

"Hi, I got your note."

"I didn't have your number."

"What's up?" she said, lacing her fingers to keep from fidgeting.

"I wondered if you were available for dinner tomorrow night?"

"Dinner?"

"I know a cute place, and it'll give me a chance to say thank you."

"Tomorrow?"

"If you have plans, I understand. It is last minute."

Even if she had plans, she'd cancel them to be with him. But she didn't want him to know that. Was it lame that she was available on a Friday night? But if she accepted, she would have plans and be way less lame than she would otherwise have been.

"Yeah, I'd love to."

"Great. That's great. I'll swing by at seven?"

"Seven o'clock is awesome."

"One more thing. Hold the door a sec?" Kyle said while he ducked into the apartment. Rebecca looked in, but he was gone. He came back holding an arm behind his back, then presented her with a single red rose. They jointly held the cool, thornless stem, before he let go.

"See you tomorrow," he said with a smile as big as the sky as he closed the door.

"Wait, Ky—" Rebecca said but stopped. Blood coursing, knees wobbly.

Rebecca raised her hand to ring the doorbell, finger hovering without pressing. Was he still there? Rebecca stood listening. She dropped her hand, but replaced it again without pressing. Rebecca's entire day had evaporated, replaced by images of Kyle in his hot T-shirt. She hadn't heard him walk away, which meant he was probably still standing there watching her through the peephole. Rebecca exhaled, smirking at the glass lens. She lifted the rose to her nose to inhale its fragrance before heading back to her apartment.

'Til tomorrow.

Chapter 12

Rebecca's heart was still pounding as she closed her apartment door and kicked off her shoes. The warmth of Kyle's smile radiated within her. She flipped on the kitchen light and rummaged in the cupboard for a bud vase which she filled with water before adding the stem.

Nestling her nose in the silky petals, she breathed deeply as she walked to her bedroom and deposited the vase on her night table. She lay back across her bed and shut her eyes to absorb the bouquet. Rebecca sank into her bedspread, her body completely relaxed.

I have a pink plastic bag in my purse.

Rebecca sprang up to retrieve the new vibrator box. She unscrewed the black cap to load the batteries, then stood it, cone up, on her night table.

Blue. Why did I get blue? It has to be the least sexy color ever. It's the color of sexual frustration.

Rebecca closed the shades and took the vibrator in her hand, feeling its weight. Squeezing it. She depressed a dimple into the silicone covering. Goo within seeped back to repair itself. She filled her lungs with as much rose air as she could muster, letting her eyelashes meet as it escaped.

I can do this.

Rebecca slipped off her top, her bra, and the pants, dropping them to the floor beside her bed.

She pulled her side table drawer open to retrieve the fantasy book she picked up the day before. Crisp and new, she hadn't as much as cracked the spine of *Hidden Sunshine.*

The author collected sexual fantasies during interviews with women. She discussed how they were a healthy part of sex, but that the discussion of them had been taboo, especially in the presence of men who thought that their mere presence should make every woman cream their pants.

Ain't that the truth.

The fantasies fell along common themes, including anonymous sex, rape, domination, incest, women, young boys, and many others. Rebecca flipped open the book to a random spot and read about a woman who fantasized about having sex with an octopus.

Rebecca's left eyebrow involuntarily shot up, and she exhaled her amusement.

She abandoned the octopus and flipped ahead, landing on a fantasy from a woman who imagined being entertained by naked women masturbating for her benefit. It went on in vivid detail, describing their bodies and their motions before it evolved into a pagan dance scene around a fire.

The fire dance lost Rebecca, so she skipped ahead to one about a woman who fantasized about being "taken" in an abandoned building by three women, who were also men with penises. The woman who wrote the fantasy said she hated anal sex in real life, but in her fantasy—she loved it.

Rebecca sat up.

I've been doing it all wrong.

She pondered her own fantasies: always with some faceless guy, in her own four-poster bed, with him on top and her on the bottom. How boring was that?

She could literally imagine bedding anything, anyone, anywhere, including half-man, half-woman encounters floating on clouds. Embers of creativity stirred.

Where did she want to go—and with whom?

Rebecca closed her eyes while her mind's eye took flight. She inched her hands around her body, light ripples of sensation trailing behind. Arms. Wrists. Ears. Breasts. Face. Each stirred familiar tingling from her clit. She pinched her nipples, sparking a flush across her body and a tingly ripple up her spine.

OMG. That felt amazing.

She attempted to replicate the spine tingle, but try as she might, she was unable. Finally, she took hold of the vibrator, holding her breath as she switched on the power with her fingernail. It jumped to life with an aggressive buzz. Rebecca dove her hands under the covers to smother the sound.

She paused, unflinching, heart pounding, listening.

But no one was coming.

Rebecca was alone.

She lay back, muscles tense and senses searching.

This isn't going to work.

Rebecca reached for her phone and swiped through until she

found her favorite jazz album, then paired it with her Bluetooth speaker.

Rich saxophone tones suspended in the air, blocking out all but the scent of her rose. Rebecca slipped under the covers, settling back to rejoin her newfound stories. This time when her finger clicked the button, she didn't miss a beat. She guided the vibrations toward each wrist, breast, and thigh, growing hypnotized by the quivers penetrating her skin.

Losing herself, Rebecca inserted her toy but quickly paused to squirt KY on the vibrating surface.

Wow.

Rebecca floated down a river of anticipation, which mounted, growing more intense like a dam within her was swelling.

She was with Kyle. They were in the stairwell. He was filling her. Breathless, she joined his movements. Rebecca's heart pounded; her limbs tingled down to her fingertips. Or was that because of the vibrator?

"Oh my God, oh my God, this is it! I know it. I'm going to have one this time!"

Don't stop, keep going! Wait. Am I even doing this right?

Rebecca was frantic to quiet the relentless quarrel in her mind.

Rebecca's eyes squinted tightly, willing the internal battle to end.

Then it did.

The tension evaporated as quickly as it came, leaving her hollowed out. Frustrated. Aching. The vibrator's lonely song muffled by covers.

Rebecca tried to conjure the arousal back.

Which fantasy got her juices flowing?

Was it the girls?

What was she thinking about when she got aroused?

Rebecca searched the doors of her mind but found them all locked. The toy's mocking rumble persisted, unaware the battle was lost. She fished her hand under the quilt, clicked it off, and dropped it to the floor. Her chest rose and fell as her pulse slowed.

If jazz, a vibrator, and mental foreplay with Kyle isn't going to work, I'm a lost cause.

Warm tears escaped, their saltiness pooling in the corners of her mouth. Her nose joined in. She wiped her face dry with the back of her bare hand, then sniffled hard. Twice.

Covered in wet slime, she flipped the covers back and stomped across the room to get a tissue. As she stood at her dresser, wiping her nose, she avoided the reflection in the mirror. Not a sight she wanted burned into her mind's eye. She opened her pajama drawer to retrieve an over-sized T-shirt from a charity run she'd done a few years back. Slipping it overhead, she flopped back into bed.

Rational Rebecca returned. Her body *did* respond in ways it never had before. Good ways. There were unmistakable signs of progress. She found the vibrator on the floor and wiped its silicone surface with rubbing alcohol, per the directions. She then dropped all the paraphernalia in her bedside table drawer and slammed it shut. Weapons primed to fight another day.

Chapter 13

A curl of envelopes and catalogs crammed into her mailbox past the bursting point.

"Seriously, Milton?" she yelled at the box before planning her approach.

Their mailman had outdone himself this time. Her fingers pierced the wad seeking a hold. Wrestling it back and forth, it sprung loose, but not before shredding the edges of nearly everything.

Rebecca slammed the brass door closed, shaking the sting out of her scraped hand.

"Milton only stuffs it like that to save us the hike over to the post office. He's just doing his job," her elderly neighbor Mrs. Portnoy said.

"Thanks for the tip."

"They'll charge you if you break the door," she said while rapidly pressing the button for the elevator.

"You're right. Don't mind me. I've had a bad day."

A formula error on a client budget sheet meant Rebecca had to redo an entire advertising plan, cutting its bounty roughly in half.

No wonder the client's meager budget seemed to stretch so far. It was an innocent mistake, but Darcy's ire was well founded. This time. But a month's worth of work and negotiations was completely upended.

In her current state, there was no way Rebecca should be anywhere near Kyle. She'd blow it royally if she tried. She'd insult his family, or say something breathtakingly stupid that would make him flee the dinner table, never to return. She'd get left with the check, a check she couldn't afford to pay, then get chapped hands washing restaurant dishes to pay off her meal. Disaster was guaranteed.

"Your floor," Mrs. Portnoy said.

"Huh?"

"Isn't this your floor?"

"Yes. Sorry. Thank you." Rebecca jabbed her hand in front of the closing elevator door; it immediately retracted. "Have a good night."

"You too, dear. Hope tomorrow's better."

She turned the hallway corner and saw it. Another white envelope taped to the door.

This time, it was closed with a red seal stamped with a "K."

She ran her finger over the bumpy wax. Her fingers slipped under the flap and removed the crisp linen card within. The note had two words:

"Wear pants."

This was just too much. It was too good. She closed her eyes and sighed deeply. He was making this hard to resist.

She had to cancel, for both their sakes. She'd think of a

believable excuse. He'd understand. I mean, they'd just met anyway. She really didn't have any obligation to go.

She'd just march over and… No. She'd call. She'd call and let him know.

Rebecca opened her apartment door and let it slam shut. She was standing in her bedroom before noticing that her shoes were still on. She slipped them off and tossed them through the open closet door.

Then it registered. The scent.

Kyle's rose had worked its magic. The flower was triple the size of the night before. Its bouquet transforming her bedroom into an English garden.

How can one rose smell so amazing?

"You want me to go, don't you?" Rebecca said to the flower.

"There's no way this is going to work." She looked at the card still in her hand. "Wear pants. What kind of pants? Where are we going, and why is he telling me what to wear? Should I be mad? Should I be insulted he's dictating what I put on?"

The flower bloomed back.

"Ugh. You are so unhelpful," Rebecca yelled at the cluster of petals while making her way to the closet. She slid hanger after hanger to the left in succession, choosing none. Then the doorbell double-chimed.

Shit.

She snatched a pair of dark wash jeans, slipped them on, fastening the buttons on her way to answer the door.

"Hi. Hello!" Rebecca said with a broad smile, slinking her arm up the door.

"Ready to ride? I see you're wearing pants, very good. You got my note."

Kyle wore tight black jeans and a fitted blue T-shirt that made his eyes pop. Over the shirt, he wore a black leather jacket and held two helmets at his sides.

"Oh my God, we're going on a motorcycle?"

"Your chariot awaits!"

"I'm not ready yet."

"What you're wearing is fine, but I don't mind waiting. You'll just need something to help block the wind. It's not cold tonight, but you'll feel the air more when we're moving. Let me see what you've got." Kyle came in and inspected the foyer closet.

"These are cute but not very functional," he said while reviewing the options. "Okay, try this," he stated, handing Rebecca a leather jacket, not unlike his.

She slipped it on.

"Perfect. Let's go!" He reached for the doorknob.

"Kyle, my shirt is a little sloppy for dinner. I was going to change."

"It's not the shirt that matters; it's who's wearing it."

He took Rebecca's hand and planted a deep kiss on her lips that made her body go wobbly. The strong arm wrapped around her waist kept her vertical when her knees nearly buckled. He pulled away.

"We'd better leave or we'll be late for our reservation."

"Where are we going?"

"You'll see when we get there."

They walked hand-in-hand to the street, where a shiny black motorcycle was chained to a pole. He carefully unchained the bike and wrapped it back in place, locking it tightly until they returned.

"I've never been on a motorcycle before," she said, staring at the vehicle like it was going to bite.

"You'll love it, I promise. Here, put this on." Kyle handed her a shiny black helmet with a clear face shield.

Rebecca watched him put the helmet on, mimicking his motions.

"I must be doing something wrong. My ears keep folding down."

"You can slide your head in and unfold them afterward if that works better for you," Kyle suggested. "Here, give me your purse, and I'll toss it in the saddlebag."

While his back was turned, Rebecca stuffed her shirt bottom into her jeans and zipped the jacket.

Kyle's muscular leg swept over the frame, landing on the other side. The engine roared to life, and he walked it backward out of the parking spot.

God, he's hot.

"Hop on," he said while steadying the bike with his legs.

"How exactly?"

"That black peg is a footrest." He motioned with his helmeted head. "Step on it with your left leg, then swing your other leg over."

When Rebecca landed, the cushioned leather seat welcomed her. She tested the chrome and leather backrest, her legs wrapped firmly around Kyle's perfect rump.

Am I too close? Can he feel the pulsing in my pants?

She repositioned, mistakenly knocking helmets.

"Oops, sorry! I forgot I was wearing this thing. I feel like I've got a giant baby head!"

They both laughed. "Squeeze me tight twice with your legs if you want to stop. It's easy to get leg cramps if you're not used to riding. Hold on."

The roar of acceleration plastered Rebecca into the backrest. She readjusted her feet on the pegs, grabbing the seat frame on either side with her hands. Wind whipped bits of hair hanging out the bottom of her helmet, tickling her neck. But Rebecca let them fly. Her white-knuckled hands were busy.

The sky burned an intense shade of tangerine, swirled with wisps of white clouds tinged dusky blue. Elongated shadows from passersby were just beginning their evening fade as streetlights blinked to life. Walkers moved along, unaware of her presence. It was New York, after all. Motorcycles were commonplace.

But shouldn't everyone notice how atypical it was for Rebecca Sloane to be on a motorcycle? Wasn't it obvious? Apparently not.

When they stopped at a light, Rebecca lifted the visor for a better view. Pyramids of apples and oranges were neatly stacked under a market awning to her right. A couple browsed a restaurant window menu. A woman crouched to untangle a red dog leash from around her pet's legs. Life. Same as it had always been. But also, new. Different. The light changed, and they zipped off again.

Rebecca clung to Kyle, who powered the machine. The three organisms moving as one. When Kyle tilted left, she tilted left. When he tilted right, she tilted right. Her instinctive attempts to counterbalance were futile. The bike's momentum forced a complete submission, of not just her body, but her mind too. Her senses. Her being. The wind, the sky, sights, vibrations, and sounds all collided, sending her pulse pounding.

Kyle stopped short a few times, and they clunked helmets, the forward force being so strong. After a while, Rebecca got the hang of leaning into the turns, rising up in her seat over bumps, and tightening her grip at stops to avoid head collisions. By the time she refocused on her surroundings, they were riding up the on-ramp to the Brooklyn Bridge. Rebecca loosened her grip on the bike frame.

Impending darkness shaded imperfections on the landmark she had seen a thousand times before. Tonight, it was proud. Strong stone lines led up to bright lights spanning from tower to tower, shore to shore. Seeing its rough texture, carvings, and mortar lines up close hearkened visions of the nineteenth-century workers who braved precarious scaffolding to build it.

Halfway over the span, Rebecca looked into a car next to them. Two children in the backseat spied her from behind closed windows. Rebecca wiggled her fingers at them.

Their eyes widened, and mouths noiselessly yelled to their parents within about the motorcyclist who waved to them. They looked back at her for another acknowledgment, which she gladly granted. Why not share her joy?

Kyle drove them onto the local streets, which he seemed to know well. Being a Manhattanite, Rebecca rarely ventured into Brooklyn. In fact, she had more knowledge of Queens and the Bronx than she did of Brooklyn. More of her summer camp friends hailed from those boroughs.

Though, Rebecca did go to Coney Island as a child, as well as the Brooklyn Botanical Garden and the Subway Museum, but those trips were all by train. Her trip tonight was like riding on a magic carpet with a prince into a new realm.

The bike slowed as they wove to the waterfront, stopping next to a floating restaurant called the Waterwheel. The paddle boat was permanently fixed to the shoreline, accessible via a steel walkway. It was a two-story, red, white, and blue paddle steamer with a large wheel at the stern. The sounds of clinking glasses, laughter, and blues music made it clear dinner was already in full swing.

Rebecca hopped off the bike and removed her helmet. She tossed her hair because every lady biker she'd ever seen on TV did it. Though, it was unlikely her insuppressible curls had been flattened.

Kyle removed his and flashed a wide smile.

"So, what do you think?" he asked.

"That was awesome! I didn't want it to stop," she said. "I felt like I was flying. The lights, the views…"

"Well, since you had such a good time, we should probably leave," he said, starting to replace his helmet, but instead taking Rebecca's hand and pulling her in close for a delicate kiss.

Soft, sweet, and completely unexpected, Rebecca responded instinctively to him. Body already purring, she had no time to overthink.

She pulled back, her arms still draped around his shoulders. Eyes linked, they savored the moment.

"Okay, hop on, I'll take us back!"

"Not so fast, buddy, you owe me food, and I intend to collect!"

"Oh, all right, I guess I'll have to suffer through fantastic views and lovely company."

Rebecca hid her red face behind her hands.

"We'll have none of that, young lady. Let's go inside. I ordered a primo table, and if we're late, they'll give it away."

Primo was an understatement. The table was next to the cleanest window she'd ever seen, that provided an expansive and unobstructed view of lower Manhattan. Rebecca scanned the skyline, admiring the brightly lit buildings. It was so unmistakably New York with the bridges lit up spanning the twinkling water, and the confluence of buildings jutting up at the perfect combination of random heights. You couldn't have planned it better if it had been planned.

"Have you ever eaten here before?"

"No, I've seen it from the Manhattan side, though. Have you?"

"A few times. I lived in Brooklyn for two years after college. When my parents came to visit me, they liked to come here. Smokey sports bars were more my scene and they were trying to broaden my horizons. The food is Southern/Cajun and is off the charts good," Kyle said has he eyeballed some platters passing at eye level, on route to another diner.

"Man, I'd love to shoot this menu."

"Excuse me?" Rebecca asked.

"Oh, I'm a food photographer. That's what I do when I'm not rescuing my aunt."

"That's amazing. I've always wondered about how you guys do things. One of our food clients said that ice cream is never ice cream? Is that true?"

"Well, if you're selling ice cream, then you have to use your product. Outside of that, it's usually mashed potatoes or shortening."

"Shortening! Like Crisco?"

"Well, it's either that or a bowl of soup. Those lights get pretty hot."

"That's gross. But, I guess if that's the alternative. You do have to admit it's a little strange."

"At first, it was, but I'm used to it by now. Anyhow, I've already started putting some feelers out, so we'll see if any work shakes loose."

A waiter passed wearing frayed mid-calf jeans, a loose white shirt, and a straw hat hanging down his back on a string. Metal cattails lined the posts, bouncing as the boat swayed. Paddles on the walls were painted with childlike lettering marking mileage to various points along the Mississippi River.

"When I eat here, I feel like I'm down south somewhere on a riverboat adventure," Kyle said.

"A fan of Tom and Huck, are you?"

"Who isn't? They did all the naughty stuff that I wanted to do but couldn't."

"Looking at you now with your impish grin and black motorcycle, it's hard to believe you weren't neck-deep in trouble."

"Oh, I was, but not the kind that Tom and Huck got into. They enjoyed freedom and independence that I never had as a child. The calculator in my mind would click the punishment points for every rule I broke. It was a major killjoy. It just wasn't worth it. My parents were tough, but Bessie was tougher. She watched Libby and me when my parents were off working, especially in the summers. Her eagle eye ruined a lot of the fun I *should* have been having."

Rebecca laughed to herself. She knew better than anyone how an overactive brain can ruin a fun time. She hid her face behind the menu lest he misinterpret her knowing smile for mockery. He did likewise.

They shared two appetizers, fried green tomatoes and sautéed gulf shrimp, which were a crisp, salty, tangy flavor explosion. For the main course, Rebecca ordered the very sophisticated and dainty buttermilk fried chicken with mashed potatoes, gravy, and green beans. Kyle ordered Jambalaya with basmati rice.

Rebecca figured if this relationship was going to go anywhere, he needed to know upfront that she was a big eater. Kyle would never hear the words, "Oh, I can't. It's too rich!" cross her lips. No plate would ever be left half-full while she starved. Quite the opposite; she'd eat all of hers and half of his as well if he wasn't quick enough. It was a cold reality best learned early on.

They each tasted each other's meal with abandon. He teased her like an old friend, and she laughed with him at her own failings. He paid and she let him. Afterward, they walked on the promenade, enjoying the view of Manhattan's lights rippling in the dark river below. The pair chatted about everything and nothing. At one point, they stopped along the railing to look across the water.

Shoulder to shoulder, Rebecca nudged closer.

Kyle leaned in for a kiss.

They turned to face each other, him pulling her close with both arms.

Rebecca explored his firm back through the leather jacket.

Kyle's hands slid over the curve of Rebecca's bottom, but then he pulled back.

"How am I supposed to drive us home when you make me so crazy, I can't see straight?"

Rebecca beamed, looking up into his eyes.

"Okay, this is the deal. When we get back on the bike: no snuggling close and no grabbing my torso or arms. No light touching or fondling, and we already know that you will not be kissing my neck anytime soon unless you want to smash helmets again. We're strictly business. Good? Questions?"

"Only one: where are we going?" she asked.

"To your place. Auntie doesn't take well to naked girls running around."

Rebecca's blood went cold.

Naked means sex, and sex means frigid ice queen, then bye-bye Kyle.

"You okay?" Kyle asked, his eyebrow slightly raised.

"Sure, yes. I promise no touching." *Now or ever.*

They returned to the motorcycle, barely speaking and not touching at all. Rebecca's stomach hollowed as she climbed behind him. This was exactly why she should have canceled. She wasn't worthy of bedding Kyle right now. Hell, she wasn't worthy of bedding anyone right now. She had but a few moments to figure out how she was going to politely decline without ruining what had been the most incredible first date of her life.

Kyle drove like a man on a mission. Instead of the scenic route they took to the restaurant, he zipped back across the Brooklyn Bridge and up the FDR Drive: the fastest route home. The FDR

Drive ran the full length of Manhattan along the East River. Rebecca watched lights from the Manhattan and Williamsburg Bridges undulate in the current while driving north.

The air was crisp, just cool enough to be comfortable in the jacket. Faint stars dotted the night sky, a rarity given how hard it was to see stars through the haze of New York's ever-present lights.

The sky was perfect.

The twinkling river was perfect.

He was perfect.

She was broken.

One of these things is not like the other.

By the time they pulled up to a stop in front of the building, nausea had taken hold. Nausea and utter panic rolled up into a fat ball. Rebecca's stomach churned.

I have to get off this bike.

Acid crept up her throat.

Please no. Not now.

She stood on the pegs and stumbled off the bike ahead of Kyle, struggling to unfasten the helmet's chin strap while pressing her lips closed.

"Rebecca? What's wrong?"

She flung off the helmet just in time to throw up on the lawn outside her building. She bent at the waist, hands crossed over her belly, waiting for the waves to pass.

What a mess. Rebecca rummaged in her pocket for a tissue, dabbing her eyes and mouth before standing up.

"You okay?" Kyle said, running over.

Rebecca inhaled deeply through her nose, letting the air seep out her nostrils. Standing might not have been the smartest move. She bent back over.

"Are you okay?"

"I think so. I don't know what happened. It came on so fast," Rebecca said.

"Just breathe; I'm sure it'll pass," he said, rubbing her back.

"Where's the helmet? I hope I didn't scratch it. Was it new?"

"Forget the helmet. Are you feeling better?"

"Yeah. No. I don't know." Rebecca stared at her shoes.

"You know, if you didn't want me to come over, you could have just said so."

Rebecca shot up. "What? What made you say that? It's not that—"

"I'm joking."

"Oh. Right," she said, feigning a smile. "Of course."

Kyle bent over and picked up the helmet, then handed Rebecca her purse.

"Let's get you upstairs."

Rebecca took the elbow Kyle offered. Neither spoke until they exited the elevator on their floor.

"Kyle I…"

"Hey, I had a really great time."

"Me too, until," Rebecca couldn't bring herself to say the words.

"I'll take a rain check on the good night kiss. Okay?"

"Sure."

Kyle leaned in to kiss her on the forehead. His lips soft and warm. Passionless. It was a brotherly kiss.

"Go get some rest. I'll check on you tomorrow." He stood, waiting for her to move first.

"Sorry about the whole, thing, downstairs…" Rebecca said, holding her purse strap for moral support.

"You certainly know how to make an exit."

Rebecca smiled. "I'll try to be less explosive next time."

Kyle grinned. "You do that."

Rebecca searched for her apartment key, pausing to look back before entering. But Kyle was already gone.

Chapter 14

"How did your homework go this week?" Dr. Costa asked.

"Better than expected, but I'm still not there," Rebecca said to the dark void filling in for Dr. Costa's head.

"How so?" asked Dr. Whitestone.

Everything before her vomit episode with Kyle was hazy.

"Well, I bought the vibrator and the book. I got farther along than I had before. But then everything broke down."

"Let's start with what went well. What was different this time that made you get farther along?"

What went well? Well, what didn't was that she had messed up her best chance with Kyle. The closest she'd get to him had already passed. At least she still had a fleeting memory to cling to. That triggered it.

"I did also have what might qualify as foreplay beforehand."

"What do you mean?" Dr. Costa asked.

"I met someone, a neighbor on my floor. We've had a kind of flirtation going. But I did see him for a few minutes before my homework. He surprised me with a rose; it was the sweetest thing."

"A rose?"

"Yes, right before. I used that and fantasized about him, when I was… you know."

She heard a pen bounce hard on a pad with a thud.

Chairs slid across on the floor. Voices whispered. Rebecca uncrossed her legs and sat up straight, leaning her ear closer to listen.

There were two, three, four speakers, but she couldn't make out what they were saying. Someone was animated, then shushed. It didn't sound good.

"Is something the matter?" Rebecca asked at last.

"Just a moment, Ms. Sloane," Dr. Costa answered.

Dad voice. He answered in a dad voice.

Rebecca got up and paced in the spotlight, looking back at the group periodically, which continued to ignore her. Finally, the doctors returned to their seats, sniffing, recomposing themselves. She did likewise.

"We haven't yet delved into this issue since you joined the study, and we accept that as being our fault. But it does present an opportunity for deeper exploration."

"Come again?"

"We typically prefer participants to refrain from physical intimacy until they have climaxed on their own. But we've discussed it and have agreed to allow it in your case. A beta program of sorts. It's fascinating."

"I'm really not following your meaning."

"You can continue to see this… what was his name?"

"Kyle."

"Yes, you can see Kyle, and we'll discuss your progress each week when you come. We'll use this opportunity to provide us—you—additional inputs to propel your success."

Rebecca blinked into the darkness. *Am I hearing right?*

"I meet a great guy, and you guys want me to report back on everything we do?"

"It would add an entirely new ripple to our understanding. You've already shared intimate bedroom experiences. This would be no different," Dr. Costa said, sounding aroused himself.

"And what if my chances with him are over?"

"It sounded like it went so well. What do you mean?"

"Well, the date ended, awkwardly," she said, images of splattered dinner flashing across her mind.

"I'm sure it's not irreparable. Harken back to your self-exploration. Imagine what *that* Rebecca would do, and use it to fuel your real-world behavior."

She pondered. Fantasy Rebecca would chop down his door with an ax and drag him to her bedroom. Real-world Rebecca was afraid to ring his doorbell to sell Girl Scout cookies.

"I'm not sure I can do this."

"We understand."

"You're asking a lot. You know that."

"We do. And we hope that we are likewise offering value to you, helping you find answers for an issue I believe you were desperate to solve."

Touché. Rebecca leaned back in her chair.

"Okay. I'll do it."

"Good!"

"Dr. Costa, with that resolved, I would like to get back to Ms.

Sloane's past concerns about the running dialog. Perhaps a process discussion is in order?" Offered Dr. Smithy.

"Yes, a good idea." Dr. Costa said.

"Ms. Sloane, it's important that when you are doing your homework to focus on the sensations and not on the outcome. By that, I mean that your orgasms will come with time. You cannot will them to arrive before you are ready," Dr. Smithy said.

"It's difficult to begin to get aroused or feel sensations I have never felt without feeling more hopeful that my equipment works properly. How do I shut off my brain?"

"We do not want to shut off your brain; rather, we want to refocus your brain to be an active participant. We find that for many women the mental aspects of sex are almost more important than the physical ones. Foreplay can begin with dinner or harmless flirtation that builds as the evening proceeds. Many find this to be very arousing and can contribute to a heightened level of arousal prior to intercourse. This might explain your positive response to the rose exchange with Kyle."

Dr. Roe continued, "You can have all the stimulation in the world, but if your head is not in it, most women will not climax. You must mentally commit to the action at hand to fully experience an orgasm. You may gain some pleasurable sensations from intercourse or masturbation, but if your mind is on the project at work or whether you left the oven on, you are wasting your time."

It was interesting to hear the doctors explain things in those terms. She had never considered how involved her mind was in the orgasm equation. Rebecca had focused so much on the physical part of sex that she had never fully considered the mental part. She knew that her brain could shut things down; however, she never thought about how it could contribute to an enhanced experience.

"That's why the fantasies are so important during masturbation," Dr. Roe expanded. "If you are as completely committed to executing the fantasy as you are to imagining it, your brain will already be busy. In essence, you are giving your brain something to do to help heighten the stimulation you provide during physical exploration and vaginal penetration. Did you penetrate with the vibrator?"

"Yes, and thank God for KY."

"Lubrication is essential to ease penetration and avoid skin irritation, especially in sensitive vaginal areas that may not be conditioned to vigorous contact," Dr. Augus added. "As you become more aroused, you create your own lubrication but may need some additional gel to get things going."

"Let's go back to the brain thing," Rebecca said. "I understand what you're telling me, but what I don't get is how to shut off the criticism, that nasty part of my brain that evaluates my performance in real-time. You're telling me to focus on the fantasy during masturbation, but you're not telling me how."

Dr. Costa paused then attempted to answer. "Sexual stimulation is uniquely different for each individual. There is no one way that works for everyone. We are providing you the tools to discover what is arousing to you. In a previous session, you discussed being attracted to women. Let's explore that. Perhaps there are forbidden situations that you could explore or people you know you could incorporate into a fantasy role-play to help you heighten arousal. Many people are aroused by the prospect of having sex with someone who would be untouchable in real life. The goal is to get so focused on the fantasy and the sensations, together, they help you to climax."

"Is there another way to fantasize besides making it all up myself? *Hidden Sunshine* didn't do it."

"If the fantasy book is insufficient, visual stimulation can be very effective in these cases," Dr. Barnacle said. "Magazines or videos with graphic sexual content can help to bridge the gap between what your mind can invent and what your body needs to fully exploit the physical sensations you create."

"You mean porn?"

"Well, yes. There is a wide variety to choose from, and it can help you to heighten arousal faster than would otherwise occur on your own," he answered.

"I guess I could try that."

"When you do, explore a wide variety of situations and circumstances to see what generates arousal," Dr. Whitestone added. "Some of them can be very regimented with ordinary situations while others are more ambitious with multiple partners. Don't dismiss anything until you have explored it."

"Good, good. These are all wonderful suggestions for you to incorporate into your homework this week," Doctor Costa said. "I'd now like to explore some esteem issues with you."

Rebecca's mind wandered. Buying a vibrator and watching porno were not things she would have done on her own, but was that all they had to offer? And now they wanted her to play double agent with Kyle? This was getting way more complicated than what she thought she signed up for. Rebecca kept those thoughts to herself and made it through the rest of the session.

"Here's your homework, Ms. Sloane," Gladys said as she handed Rebecca the next assignment sheet.

"Thanks," Rebecca mumbled.

As she stood there, the videographer walked by, rolling a dolly of equipment. She was slim and pretty with pale skin and pin-straight blonde hair pulled back into a perky ponytail. She probably didn't have any trouble in bed.

Likely feeling her stare, the woman looked up and smiled at Rebecca. She seemed nice, so Rebecca broadened her return smile. Cosmic compensation for damning the poor woman's bedroom habits.

On her return to the office, tension from her shoulders and neck subsided as she succumbed to the swaying of the subway car. Sex wasn't supposed to be so much work. Each session left her feeling like human spaghetti. Far from the nurturing personalities she hoped they'd be, the doctors were cold and emotionless to a level that bordered on cruelty. Hearing her words, but not empathizing or attempting to understand the impact those experiences were having on her life. Or, on her non-relationship with Kyle.

How exactly was she supposed to meet their expectations? She had to date for herself and for them too? *No pressure.* She had zero trust in them, and why should she? She bared her soul again and again, with nothing to show for it. The faster she had an orgasm, the quicker she could be rid of them. Maybe a dalliance with porn would be her ticket to freedom.

Chapter 15

The chilly supermarket air was a relief after a sticky walk home. Avoiding all human interactions for the rest of the day meant she either had to cook for herself or brave eye contact with a takeout delivery guy. And that wasn't happening.

That day's session was looming large. Not only was she on a personal quest, now she had double pressure to keep Kyle in the picture—her own reasons and theirs. How exactly did they expect her to accomplish that one?

Green carry baskets were stacked near the entrance door, but something was different. The floor tiles were clean. Actually, the whole store had been remodeled. Those projects took months, sometimes years, to complete, and she had missed the whole thing.

Maybe I should cook more than never?

She ambled up the first aisle: meat. Raw food. What a novelty? She passed over the poultry and pork. Steak. *Even I couldn't mess up steak.* A bright red one with perfect marbling called to her from its white Styrofoam tray, tightly wrapped in plastic to show off its best features. Kyle would have loved to photograph it.

She continued across the store to the vegetables and selected a small head of green, firm broccoli. She had to search to find one that was firm and didn't have any yellow bits on it or signs the yellow bits had been sawed off. Even she was onto that "freshening" trick.

A couple of nearby apples wanted in, so in the basket they went. *What next?*

A starch. One of those yummy, but completely unhealthy, pre-seasoned noodle packets would be divine. Chicken flavored. Her mouth watered as she headed over to the "pasta, rice, and canned tomatoes" aisle.

Chicken flavor was out of stock. She shifted packages around to see if any remaining packages were mixed into the other flavors. Her mother had taught her that trick. Hide an item, come back later. Maybe she'd get lucky. She wasn't feeling Herb and Butter.

Her basket blocked the narrow aisle, and a shopping cart smashed into it while her arm was sweeping packages aside at the back of the shelf.

"Excuse me, I—" a familiar voice said.

"Holy shit, what are you doing here?" Rebecca asked.

"Shopping," Kyle replied, leaning over his cart to whisper, "You know, I never got that good-night kiss…"

"Ahem."

He retreated. "You remember my Aunt Bessie?"

"Sure. Hi, Bessie," Rebecca said, but Bessie bristled.

"Sorry I haven't popped over. Auntie's been keeping me busy. Haven't you?"

"Shoot me for enjoying some company from my fine nephew."

"No need to be dramatic, Auntie."

"Really, it's no matter. I got your text on Saturday." Rebecca dismissed with a wave.

So, that's where you've been!

"Let us make it up to you. Come for dinner tomorrow. We'd like that, wouldn't we," Kyle said, leaving no doubt.

"Yes, of course," Bessie said, rolling her eyes.

"Lovely, does seven work for you?"

"Yes, perfect. Thanks so much."

"I'm getting tired, Kyle. Help me to that bench over there." Bessie grabbed her nephew and dragged him toward the customer service area.

Tired my ass, Rebecca thought.

Kyle looked back, mouthing, "I'm sorry," as his linebacker of an aunt made her way to the bench and plopped down.

It wasn't the reunion Rebecca hoped for, but at least Kyle wasn't avoiding her. He was being held captive by his aunt. But why? Rebecca tossed the thought aside and headed to the register. Bessie was still guarding him as Rebecca left the store.

Barbara lit up her phone as she was unpacking her groceries at home.

"Why haven't you called me back?"

"I never got the messages, sorry. I've been in cell phone hell," Barbara said. "My battery wouldn't hold a charge, so I had to get a new one just to transfer the numbers to my new phone because the backup wasn't right. Anyway, want to meet up for dinner?"

"Um, I just got groceries. I was going to cook."

"Cook? Are you feeling okay?"

"Yeah, I'd rather not be around people right now."

"Bad day at the study?"

"Is there ever a good day at the study?"

"Good point."

"Why don't you come over here? Who knows when I'll have the urge to cook again?"

"Sounds good. I'll be there as soon as I get a cab."

Rebecca hung up and looked at the stove. "You better behave and not burn anything."

Rebecca opened the cupboard for the two ingredients she had: salt and pepper. She coated both sides of the meat with a liberal dusting and set it aside. She then cut the broccoli into bite-sized florets and dumped the washed bits into a double steamer, but didn't cook it yet. Her mother, God love her, always served cold, over-cooked vegetables. Whatever else Rebecca accomplished in her life, she wanted to serve hot greenery. She'd wait until Barbara arrived. Vegetables prepped, she turned her attention to the bag of noodles. Barbara would probably reject them, having a more refined palette, but Rebecca would cook them just the same. She liked them and could easily polish off the whole pot herself.

After eating the meal, Barbara pushed away from the table and crossed her toned legs.

"You have way too much juicy stuff going on, girl. You say he lives right across the hall? No wonder you wanted to connect!"

"Ya think?"

"I can't believe you actually puked. You haven't done that since senior year final exams."

"Not my proudest moment. I thought I ruined things, but I was so glad to see Kyle today at the store. It's hard having him so close and not seeing him. But it's really nice getting the notes and male attention. I don't know how long it's going to last, but I'll ride the wave and enjoy it."

"What good timing. You have a man show up, right when you're trying to get your groove on!"

"According to the doctors, I officially have a threesome: me, Kyle, and the doctors peering over my shoulder," Rebecca said.

"You *are* joking."

"Wish I was."

"So what next?"

"Right now, nothing. Aunt Bessie has him under lock and key anyway. I got the sense today that she didn't like me."

"Why wouldn't she like you? She's known you since you were a kid."

"I know."

"You trick or treated at her house."

"It doesn't make sense. But it might not be the worst thing."

"I don't follow."

"Truth be told, I don't know what I'm doing in the sex department. Might be just as well to take our time."

Rebecca stacked the dinner dishes and turned to go to the kitchen, but Barbara touched her arm.

"Becca, you've been with men before. Lots of guys, most of which you didn't even like. I include knucklehead in that. Even if you don't have an orgasm, you can still be close and enjoy each other."

Rebecca felt saltiness in her throat and tried to escape again, but Barbara held firm.

"Look at me."

Hands occupied, Rebecca was unable to wipe away the warm tears sliding down her cheeks.

"It sounds like he really likes you, and I'm sure that he'll be nurturing and slow and give you a completely different experience than you've had before. I say, if you have the opportunity to hook up with Kyle, you should take it."

"We may be talking about something that will never happen, so I guess I'll worry about it when I need to. I've gotten so caught up in the whole 'Kyle' thing, that I've forgotten that we don't really know each other. I think it's okay if we take it slow. Maybe Aunt Bessie is trying to get him to slow down on purpose. For all I know, she's trying to protect me. He could have a history of womanizing; he could be a murderer or a deviant."

Barbara let go, sitting up to retrieve her red wine, which she swirled around in the stemmed glass. "Yeah, you hear a lot about cute young guys who move in with their elderly aunts to care for them as a cover for their deviant nature."

She took a big swig to empty her glass and then refilled it from the bottle she brought. "You helped to move in some of his stuff; did you see any jars of body parts soaking in formaldehyde?"

"No, but I didn't see inside most of the boxes; they could be there," Rebecca hollered from the kitchen.

A double door ring interrupted their discussion.

"Expecting someone?" she asked.

"Nope," Rebecca said, a grin erupting on her face as she

sashayed to the door. Barbara came along, but stopped at a respectful distance to watch.

Rebecca looked through the peephole and saw Kyle on the other side. "It's him!" she whispered too loudly; when she looked back, he was smirking.

Rebecca opened the door, and Kyle pounced. A long kiss accompanied a tight embrace and a dip.

"My good-night kiss. At last. I was taking out the trash. I've got to get back fast, or she'll suspect I snuck over here."

He finally looked up from the dip and saw Barbara.

"Oh, hello."

"Hello there," Barbara said, eyebrow raised.

"I'm Kyle."

"This is my friend, Barbara," Rebecca answered, still upside down in his arms. "She's over for dinner."

"Lucky her," he said, giving Rebecca another kiss. "Gotta go. Auntie's waiting."

In a flash, Kyle rounded the corner to his side of the hall and was out of sight. A moment later, Rebecca heard him close and bolt his door. She did the same.

"Are you kidding me with this guy? He is some piece of tasty—"

"Easy girl, he's spoken for."

"Well, I can see that. He is INTO you. And you know what? I think you both like this notes-and-stealing-kisses business. It's become a game. I wonder if you'll like each other as much when you're in the same room for a few hours."

"We have been in the same room for hours, on two

occasions—thank you very much. They both went very well. I can't explain it, but I am completely at ease with him. I'm not self-conscious, I'm not nervous; it just feels right. Oh, never mind," Rebecca said, shaking her head.

"I think you explained it just fine. It's a rare thing to be so connected with someone this quickly. I hope it works out for you. You deserve it. Maybe the four of us can do a double date sometime? Now, on another matter," she said, taking Rebecca's hand and leading her over to the couch. "We got sidetracked on Kyle. How are the sexual study sessions going otherwise?"

"Oh that," Rebecca said, plopping down onto the cushion. "It's okay."

"Just okay?"

"They've helped me learn my sexual anatomy and how my body responds to touch, but that's it. I still haven't had an orgasm."

"Should you have had one by now? Are they worried?"

"Not at all. The doctors think that I'm doing well. It's their methods I don't like."

"You mean the stool in the spotlight stuff?"

"The sessions are creepy. I know that it's for me that the lighting is the way it is, but it's hard." Rebecca hugged a throw pillow to her chest. "Sitting there with six doctors picking apart every word I say?"

"Sounds like you're in the witness chair at a trial," Barbara said, heading over to the table to retrieve the wine and glasses.

"Well, it basically is. They sometimes harp on me about the smallest things, yet they give me minimal direction about my homework assignments. They are even less helpful when I have trouble and ask for assistance. I don't want to beg for clarification, but when I try, they always say everyone is different. We're talking past each other."

"Why don't you ask them about that? The communication part?"

"It's not just that. The homework they give is so superficial. We'll see how it goes, but I'm starting to question whether I want to continue."

"You can't quit now. You just started," Barbara blasted. "It's a completely weird subject to be discussing with strangers, I'll grant. But they seem to be experts. Give it a chance; maybe they can help you."

"That's just the thing. I'm starting to get the feeling that I'm helping the doctors more than they're helping me. They seem very interested in my process, but I'm not sure how effective the study will be in helping me reach a climax if their tactics don't work as expected."

"Rebecca, you have the wrong attitude about this. Listen to what they say and give it more time. Don't write your own failed ending before you finish. You might be surprised."

Rebecca swallowed her words. How could she explain that the medical circus had brought her no closer to her goal? The thrill of the project had worn off. She hated herself for needing to go but forged ahead because she had no alternative.

The pair chatted a while longer, but picking up on her cues, Barbara headed home.

Rebecca put leftovers in old takeout containers, then washed up. Once done, she strolled into the living room and surveyed the room. A stack of *Vogues* and *GQ*'s had tipped over, so she righted them. Brown leaves beaconed from her spider plant. *Maybe tomorrow?* She walked to the center of the couch and sat down cross-legged to flip through a stream of television channels before turning it off with a sigh.

Her purse was in a heap on the floor. She picked it up to straighten it, and there it was. Her homework sheet.

Was she really up for watching porn?

As weird as it sounded, she didn't want to be alone. Porn actors would have to suffice. Watching them had to be better than dead-leafing her spider plant, right?

Rebecca walked to the front door, wiggling the knob to be sure it was locked. She slid the brass chain into place. She then returned to the large picture window in the living room. The street was still. A lone dog walker passed through pools of streetlight before disappearing.

She drew the shade down, turned off all the lamps, and changed into a T-shirt, pulling it down over her bare butt as she returned to the living room. She spread an old towel on the couch and grabbed her personal laptop. No way she was watching porn on her work computer. *NSFW.*

Fingers hovering over the keyboard, she paused. Searching for porn was like seeking out malware. It wasn't something she typically wanted splashing on her computer screen. More like something you exited as quickly as possible before someone over your shoulder noticed your ill-fated search term.

Doctor Costa echoing in her ears, she typed "porn women" into the search box and held her breath while the page loaded. A surprisingly normal results page appeared, sans pictures. Smart. That probably saved many a curious kid the shock of their young lives. Clicking the first link delivered a screen of grainy thumbnails, each GIF thrusting as she cursored over. It was porn *YouTube*.

"Nope," she said, clicking away.

The fifth page of search results called her. Not someplace she typically headed, but she clicked and loaded a movie site featuring simple thumbnails of porn movie covers. *More my speed.*

On Golden Blonde and *For Your Thighs Only* were the first two titles she saw. Rebecca swallowed the laugh.

Are these for real?

After seeing *The Brady Munch* and *Sorest Rump*, laughter erupted.

"This is crazy," she said through uncontrollable laughter. She covered her mouth with her hand, but giggles persisted.

As Rebecca settled, she noticed categories she hadn't seen with all the fleshy distractions. There were boys on girls, boys on boys, girls on girls, and fetish stuff. Orgy flicks and bondage were apparently premium content.

Every image had naked girls moaning in pleasure, large penises or breasts shoved in their faces. A few wore skimpy costumes to match the corny titles. Rebecca scanned for a movie jacket where the girls looked a little more normal. Movie after movie, the boobs pictured were so enormous, Rebecca wiped her cheek to be sure silicone hadn't exploded on her face.

She gravitated to blondes with big, but not mammoth, boobs and ultimately selected a video featuring three shorter vignettes and a number forty-seven on the cover. Better to not be distracted by comparing some raunchy remake to the original.

Grabbing her wallet, she finished off an old Visa gift card with a few dollars left over and pressed play.

There was no FBI warning. No coming attractions. Just the simplest of opening credits with the title and the actors' names.

The movie opened with a bare office surrounding a large brown wooden desk. A woman strolled in wearing a painted-on miniskirt and a white blouse barely able to contain her breasts. Another woman in similar porn-office clothes followed close behind and offered the first a seat. It was a job interview, and the applicant was completely unqualified. She was, however, well endowed with other talents, which she proceeded to demonstrate for the eager interviewer.

They began to kiss and fondle each other's breasts, which were exposed in short order. The applicant suckled the interviewer's breasts before pushing her back on the desk and ripping off her skirt to reveal her nakedness. The applicant spread the interviewer's legs open and licked her clit, making her moan with pleasure. A bad jump edit later had the two women, both naked on the desk, the interviewer now on top with a strap-on penis. She penetrated the applicant who was screaming for more.

It was Rebecca's first experience watching two women screw. Her heart raced and tension was building in her body. Breathless, she inhaled deeply. Nothing existed but raw sensation and the two women in front of her going at it.

Rebecca turned her vibrator on and inserted it into herself, gently thrusting.

Sensations erupted, mild at first, but they intensified. Her face and shoulders flushed hot. She blinked to clear her mind and remain focused on the screen. Tension mounted, a well of fulfillment seeking release. *Is it too soon?*

Mind a whirl, she pulled it out. The tension immediately subsided. Rebecca noticed her chest heaving up and down. *When did that start?* She couldn't recall. When she refocused on the film, the women took turns with the strap on, and then both were naked on the carpet in a sixty-nine, performing oral sex on each other. They got worked up into a frenzy, both came, and lay quietly on the floor before they briefly resumed their character roles and exchanged closing interview remarks.

Rebecca muted the film, blue light flickering across the walls. *What happened? Are my parts actually working?*

She resumed watching. This time a cleaning lady came to take the trash out of the interviewer's office, who was there working late. A similar sex scene happened to the first, but somehow, they ended up in a shower with the maid washing the interviewer with large soapy sponges.

Rebecca's pulse quickened as she worked, and the tension returned, albeit less than the first time. The vibrator failed to work its magic. *Something feels different.* She tossed it aside and played with her boobs a little until the video ended.

The room went dark when she snapped the laptop lid closed.

The light perspiration on her skin began to chill, drawing attention to her naked lower half.

The room's silence was punctuated by random sounds of life from night-owl neighbors. Door closing. Televisions. Families. Couples. Lovers. Meanwhile, she sat naked, cold, and alone. A frigid ice queen.

Rebecca groped in the dark to gather supplies, folding them into a towel taco that she carried to her bedroom.

It was nearly 2:00 a.m., but she took a hot shower then dried off before tossing on pajamas. She crawled into bed, listening. *Everybody Loves Raymond* was playing on the television upstairs. Rebecca tried to follow along to the muted dialog and bitter family dynamics filtering down. Anything to be someone else. Somewhere else.

She lay immobile, heartbeat throbbing in her chest. A nuisance. Yet another part of her body she couldn't control. It pulsed free and uninhibited, without a care in the world.

Thump, thump. Thump, thump.

Squeezing blood, pumping, living. Her eyes drooped. Heart fading, sleep ascending. It rolled over her like a dark wave. An ending. She gave way to it.

Chapter 16

Naked girls danced in her brain at work the next day. Vivid flashes of erotica flashed like a slide show. She finally understood how so many adults became addicted to porn. It was raw, primal. It was easy to lose yourself in the images and tune out real life.

Her evening's excitement was tantamount to cruelty, given how things turned out. What prevented her from getting the juices flowing again? The stopping and starting seemed to always be part of it, but she presumed people started and stopped all the time and still "finished." Why couldn't she?

"Dreaming about your hunky boy again?" Maia snorted over her morning mug.

"Hardly."

"What? Trouble in paradise so soon? Tell me what the problem is. Maybe I can help."

Maia sounded so genuine, Rebecca opened her mouth to speak but clamped it abruptly shut.

"Come on, Rebecca. I don't bite."

Man, she is really trying today. Rebecca pivoted her chair to face Maia and spoke in hushed tones.

"Okay, this is the deal. The guy is really into me, and I'm into him. He lives across the hall with his elderly aunt. She's always been friendly to me, but I'm getting the impression that she doesn't like me. She may be even be trying to keep him away from me intentionally."

"That's so not cool."

"Right? We sneak a kiss when we can, like last night when he rang my bell and planted a dreamy kiss while he was out throwing away his trash but had to quickly get back. I'm afraid we'll never get off the ground if he feels too neglectful to go out with me."

"Wow, this is even better than I thought. Did he really ring the bell just to give you a kiss?"

"Yeah. It's awesome. He leaves me notes on my door too."

"Oh, you've got yourself a good one. We have to fix this." Maia paused momentarily to think. "I've got it. Auntie needs a date. Do you know anyone that she might like? Man or woman. We're talking about good company. In fact, if there's an old-bitty who shares her interests, it would be less suspicious. I mean, she'd probably prefer good company to a romp at her age, whatever it is," Maia said before someone called for her.

"Crap. Gotta go. But if I think of anything else, I'll let you know." Maia smiled as she walked away.

She was so much nicer when she was away from the crowd of other buyers. Rebecca questioned whether she'd been wrong about her, but then Maia's body of work came flooding back, along with the remembrance to be cautious around this new friend.

Regardless, Maia's idea had merit. Bessie kept Kyle home because she didn't want to be alone. Maybe if she had convenient company, like someone in the building, Bessie would be less possessive. It was definitely worth a shot. In fact, the best person to ask would be her mother.

"Hey, do you have a minute? I need your help," she began when her mom answered.

"Oh really, you need my help?"

Olivia Sloane spoke so loudly Rebecca had to hold the receiver away from her head.

Rebecca explained the situation with Kyle. It was the first time her mom heard the full story, so Rebecca knew her reaction would be honest.

"He sounds like a nice guy; someone who is trustworthy. Good for you, muñeca!"

Rebecca's parents had honeymooned in her family's native Puerto Rico with their prized purchase being a small doll. As it turned out, the doll held a strong resemblance to baby Rebecca, so her mother started calling her "muñeca," doll in Spanish. Her mom only dropped it when proud. Rebecca reflexively smiled.

"That's why I'm trying to sort out this whole Bessie thing. She's known me forever, but it seems like she's suspicious about me for some reason. I figured if I could find someone else she can spend time with, she wouldn't be so clingy with Kyle."

"You mean like a date?"

"No, not a date. Well, actually, maybe a date would work too. I just need someone she can hang out with for company; either one would work."

"Well, let me think. There's Mrs. Cohen on seven. She's widowed too, and I know that they go to the same synagogue.

Come to think of it, I'm not sure they like each other."

"Anyone else?" Rebecca asked, scribbling away.

"There's also Mr. Patrino on two. I've seen them talking a few times and noticed some flirtation; perhaps he might be a good choice. Oh, there's Mrs. Franklin on eleven. She's a big knitter. I know that I've seen them chatting together on the benches outside. Perhaps if you approached Mrs. Franklin for some outdoor knitting instruction and planned for Kyle to walk her by, they could connect, and who knows, maybe form a friendship?"

"Do you think that she'll buy it? I'm not really into knitting and don't want to get lassoed into something long term if it won't pan out." Rebecca envisioned herself tangled in a web of yarn.

"That's a chance you'll have to take. By the way, are you really sure Bessie isn't sick? Maybe you should check that out first."

She was right. For all Rebecca knew, Bessie was ill. That was the impetus for Kyle moving in to begin with. But Bessie looked so devious at the supermarket. She had to be faking. Either way, she could scope it out at dinner.

"You still there?" her mom asked.

"Sorry. I was off in my head. You've been a big help, thanks. I should probably get back to work."

"Okay. By the way, don't agree to anything with a replacement roommate until you talk to us. We'd like some input."

"Yeah, sure."

Rebecca hung up. Did she really want to be one of those manipulating girls guys hated? Mining her building's seniors for potential playmates had to be a moral offense of some sort.

"Let's go, Sloane," Darcy said while breezing past toward

reception. The latest reps were waiting.

Rebecca grabbed her pad and client files, quickly thumbing through the highlighted notes she prepared. She shifted those to the top. That way, she could pick up the ball when Darcy fell asleep.

On the way home, Rebecca popped into a liquor store to buy wine. Nothing too fancy. She chose a bottle with a good rating and an artistically pleasing label. There were flowers by checkout, so she picked out a bunch too. Couldn't hurt.

Dressing for a dinner across the hall was a new concept. Rebecca changed jeans and slipped on a pink cotton top that hung loose but accentuated her curves in all the right places. Silver hoop earrings matched the teardrop pendant draped around her throat. She contemplated shoes but went without, taking only keys and her peace offerings.

Bessie's door was ajar, so Rebecca stepped in.

"Hello?" Rebecca called.

"Hi, there!" Kyle's face popped out of the kitchen doorway.

"Holy crap!" Rebecca yelled, her chest pounding. "You scared me!"

"Not to death, I hope. We need you to eat dinner," he said, wiggling his eyebrows.

Kyle peered briefly over his shoulder, then leaned in to kiss Rebecca. His hands found her hips, pulling her close.

Rebecca closed her eyes, letting his musky maleness fill her senses, arms limp holding her hostess gifts.

Where was he my whole life?

148

"These for me?" Bessie said, taking the flowers from Rebecca's hand mid-kiss.

They jumped apart.

"Oh yes, this too," Rebecca said, handing her the bottle of wine.

Bessie inspected the label with interest, chirped a "not bad" sound, and shuffled into the kitchen out of sight.

Rebecca slapped Kyle's arm. "You behave!" she whispered.

"I always do."

"Rebecca, have a seat in the living room. Dinner's almost ready," Bessie hollered.

"Can I do anything to help?"

"No. We're fine."

Rebecca walked into the room. It was immaculate, not a dust bunny or glass smudge in sight. An assortment of framed drawings, prints, and landscape photographs hung across the seafoam green walls.

Mahogany furniture polished to a shine lined the room, from the tabletops to the talon-footed balls at the bottom. Even the upholstered sofa had claw feet.

Rebecca approached a table of family photos, Bessie's life in pictures from her browned wedding photo, to family events, holidays, and elder years. Several had Kyle and his sister Libby as children. The family resemblance was striking. Libby was a female Kyle, and more beautiful if that was even possible. The photos captured the kids as they played with beach balls, on boats, and at assorted New York area attractions.

Of the roughly twelve pictures, six were of Bessie with her grand-niece and nephew.

"She used to watch us in the summers," Kyle said, handing Rebecca a glass of red wine. "My mom and dad were at work, and she was free, so it was a perfect match."

"Your mom is Bessie's…?"

"Niece. But we're all much closer than the relation would suggest."

"And who's this with the blonde hair?"

"Oh, that's Vivian," Bessie chimed in.

"There's a lot of you and Vivian. Is she a cousin?"

"She's Kyle's girlfriend. Kyle, I got these out today. Don't they bring you back?"

Rebecca's blood went cold. There was something about Vivian that was strangely familiar.

"Old girlfriend, Auntie. Not anymore. Vivian works in my industry too. I'm hoping she can scare up some gigs for me. I'm working all my connections; hopefully, something will shake loose."

"Oh," Rebecca said, distracted by her own thoughts.

"We can keep one out if you want, but I'm putting the rest away. I don't need a shrine to Vivian sitting out here," he said, collecting the frames and walking them out of the room.

"She just looks so familiar."

"Maybe you've seen her around the building. She comes over periodically, unlike Kyle, who's always off someplace," Bessie said, adjusting one of the pictures a fraction of an inch.

Bessie stood with Rebecca, silently blinking. A guilty blink if Rebecca ever saw one.

"It's been over for years," Kyle said when he returned. "She's really more of a professional colleague at this point. Or, like a cousin."

"They were *engaged*," Bessie snapped

"Barely. Anyway, it was a long time ago."

"Not so long ago. Vivian still calls me to say hello, you know."

"Auntie, please drop it," Kyle said, walking away to check on a boil-over sound coming from the kitchen.

Rebecca gulped down her wine. Putting the stem on the table while staring at Bessie, who hustled to pick it up and wipe the droplet that remained on the surface with a tissue from her pocket.

Bessie stood holding the empty glass, glancing around the room. No one spoke.

"More wine?" Bessie whispered.

"Yes, I'd love some," Rebecca answered, crossing her legs and sinking back into the sofa.

Kyle returned and sat next to her.

"Rebecca, I'm so sorry. I'm not sure why—"

"Bessie, tell me a little about Vivian," Rebecca hollered.

"Rebecca, please."

"No, it's okay. I'd love to learn more about her. How long were you together?

"Eight years."

"Wow, that is a long time. When did you break up?"

"Three years ago."

"Were you engaged?"

"Briefly. But it didn't last."

"What happened?" Rebecca said, leaning over to him. Their eyes met.

"She cheated on me."

Rebecca gasped and put her hand to her mouth. She reached out to touch him, but he had already stood up and was out of reach.

"Kyle, I'm so sorry."

"Yeah, well. Me too," he said, hanging his head en route to the kitchen, passing Bessie, who reemerged with Rebecca's wine. Even she noted Kyle's gray cloud as he passed.

Rebecca's heart broke. Vivian's loss was her gain, but seeing Kyle wounded so deeply only made her want him more. But would she be capable of healing his wounded soul? She wasn't sure.

Bessie put the wineglass down on a coaster and returned to the picture table, lifting Vivian's remaining picture. She folded the stand and slipped it into a drawer.

"I'm not feeling quite well. I think I'll lie down. You two eat without me."

Bessie walked down the hall to her bedroom. Rebecca heard the door close.

Kyle was banging pots in the kitchen. Rebecca made her way over.

"Hey."

"It's almost ready," Kyle said, aggressively shaking a silver colander full of potatoes. He dumped it back in the pot, drizzled melted butter into the pot, and then swirled it with a wooden spoon.

She rubbed his back. "Should I go?"

"No. Don't give her the satisfaction. At least I have you all to myself."

Rebecca smiled, inserting her body between Kyle and the stove;

she looked up into his eyes. Tilting her head up, she reached around his body and rested her hands on his butt to pull him closer.

He met her mouth, and their tongues entwined, Kyle running his hands up and down her back. He sought her neck and nibbled farther.

"Mmmm," Rebecca said.

They were devouring each other's mouths when her tummy growled. Audibly. They looked at each other and laughed.

"Guess I'm hungry," Rebecca said.

"Me too. Let's eat."

After dinner, Kyle walked Rebecca back to her apartment door.

"Tonight didn't go at all like I had planned," he said.

"Yeah, but we recovered. Bessie even ate something."

"She's protective of me. Always has been. She didn't mean anything by it, but it was rude. I'm sorry for that."

"She's a tough cookie."

"Stubborn as an ox, but I love her for it. We all do. My family, I mean. I can't say she's likely your biggest fan right now. Hopefully, that'll change over time."

"I'd like that."

"Can I come in for a bit?" he said with arched eyebrows.

Can he come in? Hell, she'd love him to *move* in. But the red neon stop sign in her mind flashed brightly, ignoring the purring in the rest of her body.

"Let's not tonight," she answered.

His shoulders slumped for the second time that evening, "Okay. That's okay."

153

"Thanks for understanding."

"I need to do some work on set tomorrow night, but if we ride over, I can show you around. Let you see where the food magic happens. Sound good?"

"Yeah, love to."

Kyle tipped Rebecca's chin up with his finger and planted a soft kiss.

"See you tomorrow," she said, entering and closing the door.

She watched him through the peephole. It was the first time he looked strained, weary. He ran a hand through his dark locks as he started back to his apartment, then turned around and stood with his hands in his back pockets. He reached for her doorbell but stopped.

Should she open the door? What did he want to say? Rebecca's eye remained glued to the pantomime outside her door.

She had a date right now. If she opened the door, he might cancel. She watched Kyle stand in place, then silently walk away.

Chapter 17

Kyle brought the motorcycle to a stop in the parking lot of a warehouse in Hell's Kitchen, a renowned red-light district despite the neighborhood renaming to Clinton. The rebranding made it easier to market the luxury high-rise apartments that dominated the skyline.

A fiery ball was setting behind the New Jersey skyline across the river. Waves of heat radiated off the pavement. Rebecca hopped off the bike, shrugging off the light jacket clinging to her skin.

"You really feel it the second you stop moving," she said to Kyle as she removed her helmet and popped her long ringlets into a messy bun.

"Summer swelter beats riding in winter slush," Kyle replied, heaving the bike up onto its stand.

"I'd kill for some winter slush right about now."

"Let's get you inside then. We keep it frigid in there so the food doesn't melt under the lights."

They walked through a rusty iron door, down a dim hallway, and into a freight elevator with a metal accordion door. Kyle slammed it shut and shifted the lever to Up. After a lurch, they bumped up to the second floor.

"Remind me, you're not an ax murderer, are you?" Rebecca said, craning her neck to survey the abandoned elevator shaft.

"Nah, I'd take you somewhere way more private if I was going to do that."

"How reassuring."

Rebecca's stomach dropped when the elevator bounced to a stop at the second floor. Opposite the cage was a solid black door set within a pristine white wall.

"See? Signs of life!" Kyle smiled.

He punched the code into the blinking keypad, and they entered one of the largest—and whitest—rooms Rebecca had ever seen. The scale rivaled the Javits Convention Center a few blocks away. Blond wood floors stretched the length of the room, front to back with white walls sectioned into defined workstations on both sides, spaced at even intervals. Each held a mix of spotlights, tripods, and lighting umbrellas ringed around empty tables draped in white cloths.

"This is quite the place."

"Yeah, this is a no-joke shoot. There's a whole line of products to shoot for Cuisinart website, catalog, and manuals. They wanted it done in one day, so it's an all-hands-on-deck situation. I knew someone on the team, so they gave me a call. It's a great opportunity."

"I'll say. I don't cook, but even I know who Cuisinart is. It's like one of those stand-in names for food processors. You know, like Band-Aid is for plastic bandages."

"Sounds like you've given this a lot of thought."

"Some. I'm in advertising, after all!"

"Good point. My station is at the end. I need to set up my equipment, and then we can head out."

They walked the length of the football-field-sized room to a lonely table. Kyle opened black cases stacked nearby.

"They rent the big equipment for us, so we all use the exact same, but I'll bring my own cameras tomorrow. If you want, you can unzip those long duffels over there and set up the tripods. I'll show you how."

The black metal stands were surprisingly heavy. Rebecca slid the pieces together before unfolding the three support legs into their full extended position. Kyle then slid the lights on top, securing them firmly and sliding them into the desired position by turning a series of knobs and folding tension clips. Bug-like creatures sprang to life with lights for heads.

Kyle's setup began to resemble the others. Rebecca watched him, thinking, wheels turning as he ran down the series of preparations he needed to make to match the other stations.

"Is all this floor marking usual?" asked Rebecca as she adjusted a tripod to match colored tape marks on the floor.

"Not for me. I usually work on my own, so this level of meticulous symmetry is almost amusing. Makes me want to move them just to mess with their heads."

"You see! There's that naughty boy coming out again. I don't buy at all that 'Bessie kept me in line' crap."

"She tried." He smirked with a twinkle in his eyes.

Rebecca sank onto a stool.

"What's the matter?" he asked.

"Why doesn't Bessie like me? Did I do something wrong?"

"She likes you fine."

Rebecca looked up, eyebrow raised.

"You're unknown to her; she's used to playing interference."

"She's known me since I was nine!"

"Yeah, but just as a neighbor. Not as a love interest for her 'prize of a nephew,'" he said with air quotes.

Rebecca sauntered over to Kyle, who had both hands positioning a pole. "So I'm a love interest, am I?"

"Did I say that out loud?"

"Yup."

"Yes. I like you a lot, and she's always been protective of me. No one is ever good enough. It's silly, but it's something I've come to expect. Now that I'm here, her fierce instinct has kicked back in."

"Wonderful."

"Just ignore it. She'll calm down."

Kyle continued working, Rebecca helping with what she could. They strolled around the cavernous room, observing the stations. Their sameness was factory-like, making the setting a perfect venue.

Rebecca was halfway down the room looking at the ceiling architecture when headlights illuminated the parking lot below.

Kyle walked over to look out the window, then ran his hands through his hair.

"Hey, Rebecca! We'd better go," he called.

When she got back to his station, Kyle was working triple time.

"You don't look done. Don't you want to finish?"

"It's okay. I'll plan to come earlier tomorrow. Get your jacket, and we can leave."

"What's the rush?" Rebecca asked.

He stacked the empty cases against a wall, pushing the remaining equipment out of the way to clear the floor around the table. Sweat beaded on his forehead, despite the cool room temperature.

"Everything all right?"

"Let's just go. We can take the stairs."

Kyle grabbed Rebecca's hand and walked her over to an emergency exit, pressing the door's metal bar with a loud snap. The door slammed shut behind them, leaving them on a black exterior staircase heading directly to the parking lot. Kyle stopped, listening to footsteps retreat.

"Kyle, what's going on?"

"Nothing." He took a deep breath and headed down the stairs.

When they got back to the lot, a red sports car was parked in the spot immediately next to his bike. So close, there was no room to get on.

"Well, that's obnoxious. This entire parking lot is empty, and they had to park right up against your bike?"

"Who knows. Maybe it's easier to see from the upstairs window. I'll pull out a bit."

Rebecca stepped back out of the way and glanced up at the second-story window. Through the grime on the windows, she could make out a figure in a baseball cap watching them from the studio they vacated moments before. She turned with a swing of a ponytail and walked away.

Her mind buzzed all night. Who was that woman, and why was Kyle in such a rush to avoid her? It was his workplace, so she didn't push the issue, though every fiber of her being wanted to. A morning run would be the antidote. At least for now.

Rebecca stretched her tight muscles, flattening her hands on the floor and feeling the familiar tugging sensation down her calves and hamstrings. Their unyielding tightness was payback for neglect. Her runs had become less frequent than the four times per week that powered her freshman fifteen weight loss years ago.

Rebecca walked briskly east to the river. Once she crossed Avenue C, she ran at an easy pace to warm up. She turned the corner on Avenue D, ran through the housing project community bordering FDR Drive. Her route then took her over the highway on a pedestrian walkway to a park along the East River.

The last time she zipped past that spot, she was behind Kyle, ready to hurl. The pit in her stomach returned, but this time, it was a wariness. From the time Kyle saw the headlights out the window, he was on edge.

He barely spoke as they headed into the building and forgot to walk her to the door when they alighted on their floor. He only returned when Rebecca reminded him to take the helmet. They made no plans as he said he'd be working late into the night and perhaps over the weekend. Something was up, but it could be days until she found out what.

The delay removed all opportunity to test her newfound bedroom skills with Kyle. Maybe the doctors had a point. Practice makes perfect, and she had the most delightful of practice partners. But what to practice and how far to go would be a difficult balancing act. If she went too far, her secret was bound to come out. But if she didn't practice at all, she would never gain the skills she needed to rock his world. *Why is my life so complicated?*

Rebecca approached the picnic area, a popular neighborhood attraction, especially on the weekends. She hopped across scattered paper plates, napkins, cups, soda cans, tin foil, wrapping paper, debris from the previous weekend's revelry. Likely a large family event of twenty to thirty people with music, balloons, and a pig roasting on a spit. More than once, she had wished to join in rather than run by as an uninvited observer. The only downside of those gatherings was the inconceivable amount of trash left behind. If the Parks Department didn't come soon, they'd have double the mess by the time Monday rolled around.

Early fishermen had already stationed themselves by the railing at the shore's edge. Each had multiple rods leaning against the fence and tended to each with care. Though edible, fish from the East River had high enough PCBs to make eating them regularly a risky affair. Women and children were best advised to skip East River fish entirely. Not seeing any coolers or buckets, they were likely there for the sport.

The Tai Chi contingent greeted the rising sun in their usual grassy patch. This particular group was all of Asian descent, all over seventy at the young end. Like a silent ballet, they moved in unison, occasionally pausing to change direction or shift weight from one foot to another. They neither spoke nor acknowledged each other, but remained focused on the task at hand.

The air warmed as Rebecca left the shady park behind and approached the sports fields. All concrete with minimal tree coverage, the last stretch of the park had successive clay baseball diamonds behind metal fencing lined with park benches. A homeless person lay on one of them, wearing all he owned, asleep next to an overburdened shopping cart teeming with belongings. The ammonia odor hit her first. She pressed her lips together and ran a wide berth.

Growing up, she wished she could invite each homeless person she saw up for a shower and a meal, but her mom simply laughed. The thought of grimy rags being washed clean seemed like a magical transformation that would help each person immediately recover. Then, she read an article in the *New York Times* about all the able-bodied "legless" people, panhandling around the city by choice. Even then, Rebecca's money donations only stopped when a "blind" person looked into her cup to see how much had been deposited. Food donations ended only recently when a beautiful round of bread was rejected in deference for the bottle of wine in Rebecca's other hand. Her empathy had reached a limit, human tragedy notwithstanding.

The end of the park was her midpoint, so she turned around. She ran back past all the same characters as well as the next group of runners just beginning their runs south. By the time Rebecca reached the picnic area, three sanitation workers were cleaning up the party remains. Each avoiding eye contact with each other— and Rebecca. No New Yorker expects a good morning.

As she ran over the highway, a motorcycle zipped underfoot, kindling her memory of Kyle. She had to do something about

Bessie if she was going to get anywhere with Kyle. Their break for a few days might allow Rebecca to prove herself in some way. The only question was how.

Chapter 18

Bessie's doorbell chimed. She waited, but no response came. She pressed her ear to the cool metal door, listening for sounds for signs of life. Of all the scenarios that ran through her head as she planned this encounter at work, none of them had Bessie not home.

She rang the bell again, shifting her bag of dinner groceries from one arm to the other. Shuffling slipper sounds approached the door. The peephole cover slid aside, then nothing.

"It's Rebecca. I wanted to see how you were feeling."

Bessie opened the door, keeping the chain engaged.

"Yes?" she said through the crack.

"Can I come in for a minute?"

Bessie closed the door and disengaged the chain. By the time door opened fully, Bessie was already retreating. Rebecca stepped in and shut the door behind her. It wasn't exactly an invitation, but Rebecca doubted Bessie would accuse her of breaking and entering. Though, it would get Rebecca out of the way.

Bessie dropped into a wing chair and released a loud sigh, as if the trip to the door had exhausted her beyond measure. If the woman was faking, she was really good. Rebecca pulled an ottoman around to face her and sat down.

"The other night didn't exactly go as I had hoped."

"No?"

"No, I hoped to get to know you better. I've been spending a lot of time with Kyle, and I think it's important that you feel comfortable with me."

"Kyle's a grown man. He can do whatever he wants," The words hung in the air, but Bessie's intimidating glare said otherwise.

"You've known me for a long time. My family too."

"I know *of* you, but don't *know* you. And what I know is from your mother, who I understand no longer lives in the apartment."

"Yes, that's right. She sends her regards, by the way."

Bessie pursed her lips, raising one eyebrow. She exhaled her boredom, shifting in her chair. *Tough crowd.*

"Is there something I've done to make you angry or suspicious?"

"I don't know, have you?"

"Pardon?" Rebecca said, leaning back.

"Why are you after Kyle when you already have a boyfriend?"

Rebecca shook her head, "Is that what this is all about?"

"Kyle doesn't need any trouble with that blond ragamuffin you're dating. Frankly, he shouldn't even be allowed in the building."

"We broke up weeks ago. There'll be no trouble from him or anyone else.

"You broke up?"

165

"Yes."

"Who's idea?"

"His, but now that he's gone, I totally recognize what a dope he was, and I'm very happy to be free of him. There's no love triangle here, I promise."

Bessie clapped loudly and leaped to her feet, "Well, I guess I've nothing to worry about then."

She stormed toward the kitchen, pausing to look in the bag. "This dinner for me?"

"Yes. For both of us," Rebecca said, still blinking away her surprise from her perch on the ottoman. "I know Kyle is working late tonight, so I thought we could eat together."

Bessie returned to where Rebecca sat, taking Rebecca's hands in hers, patting them lightly. Her hands were supple despite eighty years of use.

"I've known you for a long time. You are a good girl. I should have remembered that. And maybe even saved you from that blond fellow. He was no good. He'd go in the hallway and talk loudly and say unflattering things about you. I should have told you what I knew about him."

"No, Bessie, it's my fault. I should have seen what was going on. I think I was both too close and not close enough, you know? Well, regardless, it's over now. I am very sorry for any concern I caused you. Shall I make us some dinner? I'm not too good, but I can boil water."

"Oh, that would be wonderful. Kyle won't be back for a few hours. I told him I'd make my own dinner tonight, but I was feeling a little tired."

"Great, can you show me where you keep things in the kitchen?"

"Yes, yes! I'll keep you company while you cook and give you some of my secrets to doctoring jarred sauce. You add a few simple ingredients, and it improves the taste dramatically."

Bessie sprang into action, retrieving two aprons from the broom closet. Rebecca removed her shoes and went to work. Rebecca left the flame too high, and the sauce splattered all over the place. Bessie said she cooked in a rush and needed to make the burners lower. Before long, they were done, and Rebecca set the table so they could eat.

"I can see that you like my nephew. He is very handsome, yes?"

"Yes." Rebecca swooned, turning red.

They both laughed.

"And I've been keeping him away from you."

"Yes!" Rebecca shouted.

"I think you now understand why. I didn't want him mixed-up in whatever was going on with your boyfriend. Now that I understand the situation, I'll stop pretending to be sick."

Rebecca choked on the bread she was swallowing and started to cough. "I knew it! I knew that you weren't sick! Well, I didn't know for sure, of course, but I suspected that was the case."

"You're a smart girl, of course you knew."

"My mother thought I might've been hasty. I called her to get her advice."

"What did she say?"

"She suggested some potential companions that I might introduce to you; to make it easier for you to relinquish Kyle."

"Whom did she come up with?"

"Well, Mrs. Cohen for starters."

"Feh, not that old crone. She's such a know-it-all. You should see her at shul, marching about like she owns the place. Who else?"

"Mr. Patrino."

"Ah, she's very observant, your mother. I used to fancy Mr. Patrino. But your mom hasn't been around so much lately, or she would have known that Mr. Patrino has taken residence with a lady friend. I was too slow."

"Oh, that's too bad."

"Well, just because you're over eighty doesn't mean that you can't still be a shy wallflower."

"You're hardly a wallflower."

"You're a sweet girl, but at my age, I have a good notion of my shortcomings."

"Bessie, you're lovely. But I think that we can modernize your hair a little to better reflect your spirit. If I could arrange it, would you give it a try?" Rebecca asked.

Bessie furrowed her brows as she worked through an inner dialog, lips quivering slightly in tune with the unspoken debate.

Rebecca sat quietly, hoping she hadn't insulted her.

"Sure, why not?" she answered at last.

They finished the dinner with more lively talk, and then Bessie went off to take a bath. Rebecca cleaned up the dishes, and by the time Bessie was in her robe, Rebecca was ready to leave.

Bessie took both of Rebecca's hands and patted them. "I'm truly sorry for doubting you. You have my blessing to date Kyle. Treat him well."

Rebecca's heart fluttered. "I will. I really will."

"You call and let me know about the salon arrangements."

"Yes, give me a few days to get some recommendations. I'll let you know as soon as I have news."

Rebecca crossed back to her apartment, smiling. Perhaps her love fortunes were about to change.

Barbara returned Rebecca's call the next morning. She gave her the name of the hairdresser her aunt Evelyn used. When she heard why Rebecca was asking, Evelyn insisted on accompanying them to the appointment she had made with her stylist for Monday evening, a day the salon was typically closed. It was that or wait months, and Evelyn wouldn't have that.

Rebecca popped back over to Bessie's.

"What is the name of the salon again?" Bessie asked.

"Salon 57," Rebecca answered for the third time.

"Are you sure Barbara's aunt doesn't mind coming? I don't want to impose. We've never even met each other."

"Don't worry. Evelyn wouldn't have offered to come if she wasn't happy to help. Believe me, she doesn't do anything that she doesn't want to."

"What is she like?" Bessie asked.

"She looks like Angela Bassett, and is just as sassy. It'll be good to have her there. The stylist won't try any nonsense while she's watching," Rebecca said, patting Bessie on the shoulder.

"About my clothes, I usually wear a loose dress when I get a haircut so I don't get anything good covered in hair. What do you think of this?"

Bessie held up a turquoise smock with yellow flowers, five sizes too big for her.

Rebecca cringed.

"No good?"

"I think we can do better. Let's wear something that contrasts against your white hair and will provide a nice neckline for your new cut. What about this blue blouse with these black slacks?"

"Yes, that works. Put them on the doorknob; I'll press them."

Rebecca closed the closet and left the garments out.

"I called to let Kyle know what a nice dinner we had. I'm sure that you will hear from him soon," Bessie said.

"Called?"

"Yes, he is still at the photo shoot."

"From yesterday? Is that typical?"

"Sometimes. Those shoots can go long and start early, so they just end up staying and napping in a chair."

"That's nuts. That place is so big, I can't imagine getting a wink."

Bessie's eyes widened. "He took you there?"

"Yes, the other night."

As Rebecca crossed the hall back to her apartment, the elevator door swiveled open, and a black trunk slid out to prop the door. Kyle's laughter jolted through her, and she swirled around to intercept.

"Of course she'll be happy to see you, Viv."

Viv?

Rebecca darted back around the corner, heart pounding as she watched Vivian and Kyle unload Kyle's gear onto the landing.

Is this his chick magnet? Help me move boxes in exchange for romance?

"Okay, but just for a minute. I'm wiped," Vivian answered.

The elevator door closed, and Rebecca got a full view. Lean and tall with a heart-shaped face and *Vogue*-worthy beauty, Vivian had grown into the adolescent face pictured on Bessie's picture table. Even sleep-deprived, the woman was stunning. Her pin-straight blonde hair was tied back in a ponytail popping out the back of her black baseball cap.

Blonde hair? Camera equipment?

She watched her roll a bag of equipment into the hall.

Oh God, no. It couldn't be.

Rebecca took another good look from her hiding place.

"Thanks for driving me back. Saved me from taking a cab," Kyle said.

"One cab? I saved you TWO cabs, at least. That bike isn't very practical, you know."

"You used to like it fine."

"Well, you might want to rethink it, just the same. I can hook you up with a guy if you want to buy a car," Vivian said.

"Anyway, let's get you in to say hi. I know it'd mean a lot to her. She had your pictures out the other day…"

Bessie's apartment door slammed.

Rebecca bolted to hers and slammed back.

Chapter 19

Rebecca paced her living room like a caged tiger. Of all the worst-case scenarios, having Kyle's ex privy to her study conversations was a catastrophe worse than death. Literally, she would rather be dead than face that kind of humiliation. She should fling her body out the window right now.

Kyle rushing her out the other night to avoid them meeting face to face was a godsend. Would Vivian have told him, or would she keep Rebecca's secret? Maybe she signed some kind of confidentiality agreement. Hospitals were known for protecting patient privacy. Perhaps she was forbidden from discussing client activity. But would she hold true to that with Kyle involved? Not likely.

The loud impact of basketballs drew her eye outside. Kyle's black motorcycle was chained to the post. Behind it, with its hazard lights blinking, was Vivian's red sports car. The same car from the photo shoot parking lot.

Everything about Vivian screamed entitled luxury. Her car, her perfectly frosted blonde hair, even her stupid black cap was probably a $900 Gucci special inlaid in diamonds.

A security scooter drove by her car but kept moving. *Do parking rules not apply to Vivian either? Or is the car's price tag indicative of the lawyer fees the city would incur from being counter-sued?*

Vivian's head jogged into view. She checked for traffic, then unlocked her car, taillights blinking. Rebecca watched her through the driver's side window as she buckled her seat belt and turned over the ignition.

Fierce sound waves blasted across the expanse, reverberating in her chest three floors up. Bystanders turned toward the noise as she revved the engine, before tearing down the street out of sight.

Rebecca swayed back and forth, hands on top of her head. *How could this possibly be happening?* Now that Rebecca knew who Vivian was, it was essential that Vivian never see Rebecca together with Kyle. That could probably be managed.

The doorbell double rang.

Shit. Of all times to pop over.

"Hi, there!" Rebecca said, opening the door wide and stepping aside.

Kyle kissed her but kept walking and flopped lengthwise on the couch.

"I'm beat," he said, talking through his yawn, "Saw a bunch of old industry friends."

"Oh, that's nice," Rebecca said. *Was Vivian one of them? Did she tell you anything interesting?*

"I got a few leads for future work, so all in all, it was a productive shoot. Did I mention Vivian was there?"

"Vivian? No, I don't think you did."

"She's a jack of all trades, that girl. Tons of connections. I

173

should still be mad at her, but somehow our talk the other night helped me break my funk. Thanks for that."

"Don't mention it," Rebecca said, keeping her distance. Dead plant leaves caught her eye, so she took the opportunity to busy her trembling hands.

"Isn't that plant dead?"

"Not yet."

"Rebecca?"

"Mmm?"

"Is something the matter?"

"No. Nothing's the matter. Why do you think something's the matter?" she said, walking handfuls of brown crinkles to the trash in the kitchen, fluttering escapees leaving a trail.

Kyle sat up on his elbow. "Because you won't look at me."

"Here," she replied, wiping her hands on her jeans. "All done."

Kyle looked skeptical.

She walked over and sat next to him. "Vivian say anything interesting during the shoot?"

"Like what?"

"Oh, other jobs she has, clients…"

"No. I barely saw her. You don't need to be jealous of her, you know. We've both moved on."

"Thanks. It's just human nature to be a little worried. You have known her a long time."

"She's protective like Bessie is. Probably why they get along so well. But I only have eyes for one girl—and I'm looking at her."

Kyle scooped her onto his lap.

"Fast moves for someone who hasn't slept in two days."

"I've got a second wind. Or a twentieth. I've lost count."

He rubbed her back in a seductive way that made her tingle in all the right places. She caressed his solid arms, and they began kissing.

What would the porn girls do right now?

She slipped off her shirt entirely, and his eyes widened. She pushed him back and swept her leg around to straddle him like a motorcycle. Their mouths met, tongues dancing. He tasted like Kyle, a unique flavor all unto his own. She craved him, and let herself go.

She ran her hands up and down his arms, feeling his taught muscles flex.

He slid her bra straps down to nibble on her bare shoulders, and she grabbed his head, tangling her fingers in his dark waves.

While he kissed her throat, Rebecca ground into his pulsing groin. He released a throaty moan.

"Oh, Rebecca."

Her heart raced. This could only lead to one place.

Holy crap. What do I do now?

Her daring girl routine had worked. Too well. How could she taxi the plane back to the hangar when it was about to take off? Spontaneous vomiting wasn't an option this time.

She pulled back and slipped her bra straps back up.

"What are you doing?"

"I'm sorry. I shouldn't be taking advantage of you when you're so tired. I'm being selfish."

"What?"

"You've been up for days and I'm pouncing on you like a tabby with catnip. It's not fair."

"Pounce away, baby! I've never been called catnip before, but I like it," he said, drawing her back in, but Rebecca wiggled out of his arms to stand. She slipped her shirt back on.

"Your eyes are half-closed."

"My eyes are always closed when I kiss."

"Yes, but you're tired. We should stop."

"I'm never too tired for this. Don't put stopping on me. Come back, I'm really fine. I promise."

Rebecca sat in her dad's chair, avoiding eye contact. Kyle boosted up on his elbows.

"I don't get it. One minute you're whipping off your shirt, the next, you're telling me I'm tired. I'm a big boy. I'll tell you when I'm too tired to get laid."

"It's my fault. You're right. I shouldn't have started. It wasn't a good time."

Kyle sat up, lips pressed together, head shaking.

"I don't know what game you're playing, but I'm too tired to figure it out."

Kyle stood up and left, letting the door slam loudly behind him.

Rebecca sat hugging her knees. She didn't know the rules either, but something told her she had already lost.

Chapter 20

The rain fell with a fury. By the time Rebecca got home, her pant legs were drenched up to her knees. She dropped her laptop bag, flicking excess water off her arms. Changing was a waste. She'd only get doused again on the way to the salon with Bessie. She swapped outerwear before locking her door and walking across the hall to ring Bessie's doorbell.

This time, she opened the door immediately.

Rebecca leaned in, "Is he here?"

"No. Not yet."

"Oh, I was hoping we could talk."

"Still no word?"

"Nothing. Not to my phone messages, texts, or notes under the door."

"He's been miserable, if it's any consolation."

"That makes two of us."

"Give him time. He'll come around. Hold the door; I'll get my coat."

Rebecca had created a gargantuan mess. The more time that passed, the more time Kyle had to walk away. And the more opportunities for another girl to catch his eye. She had played with fire and burned them both.

Outside, Rebecca and Bessie slogged through puddles, fighting horizontal rain to get to the uptown bus stop. Thankfully, it was boarding riders as they arrived.

At Fifty-Seventh Street, they maneuvered through a gridlocked intersection to transfer to the crosstown bus. Bessie got a seat right behind the driver in a handicapped chair.

Rebecca held the overhead pole, absorbing jostles and umbrella pokes as each passenger boarded. By the time they reached Salon 57, the water line on Rebecca's pants had migrated from her knees to her crotch. She paused inside the door, dripping on the mat. Bessie hung her floor-length coat on a hook.

"How are you so dry?" Rebecca asked.

"I dressed for the weather, dear," Bessie said, untucking her pant legs from her rubber galoshes and shaking out the creases.

Rebecca gathered her pants, ringing out the water she could onto the doormat instead of the white marble floor. The walls were white marble too, that is, where not lined with mirrors and shelves displaying creatively packaged hair-care products.

A solid chunk of black marble carved into a semicircle served as the reception desk, but stood empty. She could see movement behind the frosted glass wall hiding the salon from view.

Rebecca sidled up to a display shelf and lifted a blue sculpted bottle of shampoo to check the price. Sixty dollars. For shampoo. *What would a haircut cost?* Rebecca scanned a few more bottles, and her mouth went dry. She'd probably be expected to pay. It was her idea, after all. She'd have to figure it out later.

Barbara's aunt Evelyn strolled out wearing a black smock and holding a white cup and saucer. Her hair perfectly accented her lovely face and delicate features. Under the smock, she wore an ivory V-neck top and coffee-colored trousers. The tips of her brown alligator pumps peeped out from her wide pant leg. Though well into her fifties, Evelyn could be mistaken for fifteen years younger, and still moved with the grace and ease of a former dancer.

"Rebecca! So glad you could come," Evelyn said as she glided over for a kiss. "This must be Bessie. I'm Evelyn, dear. My stylist will work with you today and take wonderful care of you," she said, guiding Bessie past the wall and out of sight.

Rebecca's shoes squeaked on the floor as she followed the pair into a large circular room lined with identical stylist stations. Each had a black leather chair, chrome armrests, a black blow-dryer, a round brush, comb, and scissors.

The white marble walls from reception continued into the main salon, surrounding a lively fountain gurgling at the center. With the bright lighting and false atrium ceiling, you'd never know a storm raged outside.

"This is Antonio. He owns the salon and does wonders with all kinds of hair. He's been doing mine for years. He will listen to what you say and give you gentle direction when required." Evelyn handed the floor to Antonio and joined Rebecca on a leather bench behind Bessie at the foot of the fountain. Rebecca smiled approvingly at her bench mate and received a warm one in response.

"Thank you very much, Evelyn. Nice to meet you, Antonio,"

Bessie replied.

Antonio bowed his head in deference and began his evaluation.

"My, my, tut, tut, tut," Antonio clucked his disapproval as he released her voluminous hair that hung down to her waist, "This is much too long, much too long. Too much work, no? Who wants to brush all of this? Your arms must tire, yes?"

"Yes, very. I don't know what to do with it, so I just pull it back. I get a trim at the barbershop now and then to keep it even."

"The barbershop!?" Evelyn and Rebecca blurted out in unison.

"I know it's not the best place, but it's close, and I know the people from the neighborhood. They're cheap too," Bessie added.

"Some things are worth paying for, yes? Yes." Antonio finished, not waiting for an answer. "I want to take it up to here, just below your jawline. It is still thick, which is fabulous. I will do layers for fullness and give you a wonderful shape. The platinum color is marvelous, so I won't be doing any color today. Questions?" he snapped.

"No. No questions," Bessie said.

Rebecca leaned forward, "Bessie, are you okay with what he wants to do? If not, it's okay to tell him."

"It's okay, I'm fine. I'll let him do what he wants. I certainly don't have any ideas."

Antonio helped Bessie into a black smock and escorted her away to get her hair washed. Rebecca remained sitting with Evelyn, who had finished her coffee and placed the teacup on the small table next to the bench.

"Thanks so much," Rebecca whispered to her. "Bessie doesn't get out much, so I thought this might be fun. This is quite the place. Do you come here often?"

"Yes, fairly regularly. I do facials here, nails, massages, haircuts, color, everything. You might say that I'm a high-value customer, which is why we were able to get this appointment today when the salon is closed. Barbara said that you are dating Bessie's nephew?" Evelyn asked.

"I hope so. I was. Now, I don't know."

Rebecca exhaled deeply, staring at the water pooling around her feet. Dull splats of rain dripped from Rebecca's pants onto the floor.

"Come with me," Evelyn said.

Rebecca followed Evelyn's svelte frame across rows of empty salon chairs, through a doorway, and into a back room. Supply boxes lined the shelves; stacks of clean towels balanced high in tidy rows. Evelyn took a gown out of a drawer.

"Put this on and give me your pants."

"What?"

"You're a wet poodle. Give me your pants."

Rebecca tied the black gown around her body then peeled off the wet pants clinging to her legs, handing them to Evelyn in a messy ball.

Evelyn walked to the salon clothes dryer, tossed the pants in, and turned it on to high.

"At least they'll be a little drier by the time we leave. Antonio is fast, but damp is better than soaked, don't you think?" She smiled, handing Rebecca a towel.

"Yes. Thank you." Rebecca dabbed her face and hair. "You are a no-nonsense group of strong women in your family. That's for sure."

"My grandma used to say, 'If you sit around with your hand out, your palm will get dusty.' As women, we need to believe in ourselves and act with confidence."

"Is that how you survived all those years as a ballerina?"

"Absolutely. You think they were going to roll over for me? I worked hard to earn my way onto those stages. I did so well they couldn't say no. And when they did, I found another way."

"Martha Graham. Not too shabby a way."

"Exactly. I believed in myself and went after it. If I didn't get it, it wasn't going to be because I didn't try."

"You were so lucky to have something you cared about that deeply."

"Everyone has something, Rebecca. It's not only about one's profession. What do you care about?"

Kyle flooded to mind. Evelyn smiled, raising her chin.

"You thought of something. I can tell."

"Yes."

"Well, whatever it is, go after it. And if you think of something else you want, go after that too. There is no rule you can only have one goal in life."

Rebecca gave her a hug.

"Thanks. I needed that."

"Always, you know you're family. You're stuck with all of us, not just Barbara! I see Bessie's back in the chair; let's go see. We'll come back for your pants in a bit."

"There you are!" Bessie called.

"Antonio, dear, we're using your dryer. Rebecca was soaked to the bone," Evelyn said, sitting down.

"Of course."

Antonio removed Bessie's towel and combed her hair through. He then took a deliberate cut at the back and center of her head, handing Bessie the clump of long strands.

"Oh! That much?" Bessie said, taking hold.

"Yes, we'll do layers around your head. No more Jane Seymour hair. It's too long for you."

Evelyn whispered to Rebecca, "I think that you will be surprised by the transformation. He really has a knack for matching a cut to a face."

Rebecca nodded. Bessie's wrist was frozen in an awkward kink, memento dangling.

"Here, I'll take that," Rebecca said, relieving Bessie of her former locks.

"Thank you. I was getting tired."

Rebecca coiled up the long strand in her palm to stuff in her pants pocket, but they were still in the dryer. She held them in her hand instead.

Antonio worked using two scissors and snipped her hair with both precision and speed. It reminded Rebecca of a Japanese Hibachi chef chopping vegetables.

Within a few minutes, Antonio was done. As Evelyn predicted, the transformation was dramatic.

Bessie's blue eyes popped out of her heart-shaped face. Her straight nose widened onto an ideal tip—not too narrow, not too wide. Bessie's soft wrinkles creased in all the right places as she beamed at her reflection.

"Is that me? My goodness! What a good job you have done," Bessie said.

"I'm glad you like it." He smiled back into the mirror before getting serious. Antonio bent down so his head was next to hers, still talking into the reflection, "No more barbershop!"

"No, sir. No more barbershop. I promise," she replied.

"Put it on my account, would you?" Evelyn said to Antonio, holding up her hand to quell Rebecca's protest.

"You look amazing, Bessie!" Evelyn said, "How do you feel?"

"Like a young girl of sixty-seven," Bessie said, laughing.

Evelyn stood to clap. "Bravo!"

Rebecca joined in.

"Now, how about some dinner?" Evelyn said. "I'm famished."

"That would be lovely," Bessie replied.

"Count me in. I'll just need my pants."

After a wonderful meal at a place Rebecca could never afford, Evelyn's driver delivered her guests back home. The evening had gone exceedingly well, and Bessie was on cloud nine.

"Rebecca, can you please get me Evelyn's address so I can write her a proper thank you note?" Bessie asked, pausing at her door.

"Yes, of course. I'll slip it under your door later," Rebecca said and started to turn away, but Bessie grabbed her arm.

"Rebecca, dear, thank you so much. I can't remember the last time I felt so special, so fussed over. I usually just hideaway here in my apartment, but today reminded me that I have more life to live."

"It was my pleasure. You really look wonderful. Have a good night."

Rebecca turned away and walked across the hall, glad that Bessie was pleased with her transformation.

As Rebecca closed her door, she considered Bessie's isolation. It made her wonder how many other seniors in the building felt likewise. Looking around her own empty apartment, she felt as alone as Bessie had been before her makeover. In fact, on this given night, Bessie had the emotional edge.

Chapter 21

Evelyn was absolutely right. If Rebecca wanted something, she'd have to dive in and get it. At 8:30 a.m., she picked up her cell.

"Dr. Costa's office," the receptionist said.

"I'm trying to get ahold of Dr. Costa's videographer, Vivian. Do you have her contact information?"

It took some doing, but ultimately the hospital's communications department came through. Rebecca looked up at 1085 Second Avenue. Vivian's second-floor studio had a huge V on the plate glass window with *Vivian Kane Studios* written underneath.

Did Kyle know? Everything depended on that. If he knew, that means Rebecca didn't tell him herself and she was cooked. But if he didn't know, Rebecca might have time to figure out a next move. Maybe even finish the study? Maybe he never needed to know at all?

Rebecca coiled a curl around her finger as she paced the sidewalk.

Her stunt on Saturday morning was borderline cruel. That

much she knew. He'd gone silent ever since. And who could blame him? Rebecca made him feel as frustrated as she did after one of her failed bedroom sessions. But Bessie said he was miserable. That could indicate he missed her. If he missed her, then he might not know.

All roads led to Vivian.

She looked at the V, then tugged the bottom of her top to straighten it.

It's now or never.

Vivian's door was open, equipment stacked in the now-familiar black trunks she saw Kyle use. Tripods leaned against the wall, microphones, wires coiled in piles on metal shelving. Vinyl backdrops hung in rolls suspended horizontally at the ceiling—solid colors, leaves, and cityscapes. In a photo, you can be anywhere, and all at the same time.

Rustling and clanking came from the next room. Then Vivian appeared, rolling a gray duffel monogrammed with her company logo.

"Hey, how'd you get in here?"

"The door was open."

"Do you always go barging into people's apartments?"

"I thought it was a studio?"

"It is—"

They swapped stares.

"You shouldn't be here. I'm sorry. Did Dr. Costa send you?"

"I'm here about Kyle."

"Kyle?" she asked, staring blankly.

Silence simmered.

"You're *that* Rebecca? *Kyle's* Rebecca?" Vivian's palms met in prayer in front of her mouth.

She looked up. "Does he know? About the study?"

"That's what I came to find out. You tell me."
"What do you mean?"

"Did you tell him?" Rebecca asked.

"Of course not. That would be an outrageous violation of ethics. I would never."

All tension fled Rebecca's body, forcing her to brace herself on a nearby wall. Vivian leaked a crooked smile.

"I take it you haven't told him?"

"No. Not yet."

"Interesting…"

"That's not the word I'd use."

Sounds from the busy avenue traffic outside filtered in through Vivian's open windows. Though, the noise from traffic pinging around Rebecca's synapses was infinitely greater.

"This is *beyond* none of my business, but as someone who royally screwed up, and hurt that poor boy so badly we didn't talk for years—"

"Yes?"

"Let's just say he doesn't do well with being lied to."

"I'm not lying. I'm… omitting some details."

Vivian raised an eyebrow.

"Okay, all the details. I've told him nothing. But what am I supposed to do? This isn't exactly polite dinner conversation."

"You can sugarcoat it, but he won't. Trust me."

Should I trust Kyle's ex?

188

Vivian says she's moved on, but she could very well be steering Rebecca down the wrong path to get him back. She had already cheated on Kyle once, demonstrating a certain moral flexibility. Who's to say she wouldn't toss Rebecca under a bus at the first opportunity?

"I'd like to sit here and chat, but we're both due soon at the study," Vivian said, rising. "I have no dog in this fight. We've both moved on, Kyle and I. You can do whatever you want. But don't say I didn't warn you."

Out on the sidewalk, Rebecca checked the time. It was too late to cancel Dr. Costa, though nothing would give her greater pleasure. With Vivian watching the footage—armed with the newfound knowledge that she been watching *Kyle's Rebecca* for weeks—there was no way she'd stay silent. No way.

Kyle's Rebecca? Not for much longer.

Her storefront reflection moved across a parade of local eateries as she walked uptown. Cafes, bars, coffee shops, pizza parlors, bakeries; each came and went. Her gnarled stomach kept them all at bay.

What dumb luck. The relationship Rebecca had waited for her entire life, complete with tingle-inducing chemistry, was about to vanish into the ethos forever. It was a certainty. Sun-is-rising-tomorrow, death-and-taxes, certainty. She had two horrendous choices. Either she continued to broadcast their most intimate moments to a room full of strangers—on video Vivian would watch—or she'd fall flat on her face in the bedroom in such spectacular fashion that Kyle would run away screaming. Or worse yet, he'd leave shaking his head, wondering why he'd wasted so much time on the loser across the hall.

Rebecca's pace was slowed by a woman walking in front of her carrying a baby in a papoose sack across her chest. The baby launched a pink pacifier in the air, landing on the pavement; it rocked back and forth in an arc.

The mom took one look, shrugged, and kept walking. No way it was ever going back into her precious baby's mouth after landing on a New York City sidewalk. Best to cut it loose.

She knew the feeling. To be torn away from everything you hold dear, dizzy stars circling your head as you try to fathom what happened.

And after Kyle left her behind, what next? If she didn't forge ahead, she'd have sacrificed her budding relationship with Kyle for nothing. If she continued with the study, she'd be ready when the next Mr. Right came strolling along. Theoretically. If there ever was another Mr. Right. After the way she treated the current one, she wasn't even sure she deserved one.

She pushed through the revolving door of the hospital. It was showtime.

"I don't think I understand. Can you repeat that?" Dr. Costa asked.

"I'm not in a talking mood today," Rebecca said.

"What happened this week? Did something upset you or go wrong with the homework?"

"No, it's not about the study. It's personal."

"Can you explain?"

Rebecca turned her head sideways away from the doctors, but was met with the blinking recording light from the video camera. She wiggled her fingers to say hi to Vivian.

"Do your best. Let's start at the beginning, and we'll go slow. First, did you try the homework?"

"Yes, I went online and watched porn."

"What did you think?" Dr. Roe asked.

The thrusting GIFs popped to mind.

"Yuck, if I'm to be honest. People licking, thrusting—all free on the internet. It was primal. I was peeping into people's bedrooms. Do you feel that way with me?"

Murmurs erupted. Rebecca shielded her eyes from the beam, looking for movement, but the room was black as ever. She sat, arms crossed, defiant.

"Let's get back to the homework. Were the videos more arousing than the printed materials you used to fantasize on your own?"

"They were, but I didn't want them to be."

"What do you mean? asked Dr. Argus.

"The images were raw and made my skin crawl, but my body responded. It was like a car wreck. I couldn't look away, and I couldn't stop my body from responding to the images."

Dr. Barnacles's deep baritone chimed in, "Ms. Sloane, you were watching, hoping you wouldn't respond. Is that right?"

"Essentially. Yes."

Pens went scribbling, fingers typing.

"Responding how? What were you feeling while watching?" asked Dr. Costa.

Rebecca closed her eyes. She was back in her dark living room. Pulse racing, eyes transfixed, senses on high alert. Naked bodies writhing in front of her. Breathless, her clit begged for attention. Yearning for the closure that forever eluded her. She opened her eyes.

"You were thinking of your experience just now. Tell us," Dr. Costa said.

"No."

"Why? Why not today when it was yes other days, yes when you first called me?"

"Being here feels wrong. Baring my soul this way. Can't you see how humiliating it is? To have to come here and do this? It's such a betrayal."

"How?"

Rebecca leaned forward, "I did what you said. I used the videos as motivation. I actually experimented with Kyle. I played porn kitten. And you know what? He responded. He responded just like I responded to the videos I was watching."

"That's wonderful."

"No, it's not wonderful. Don't you see? It wasn't me."

"Living in the moment is what intimacy is all about. It's a surrender to sensation," Dr. Costa said. "It sounded like it was working for you this week."

"For my body, yes. For my mind, for my humanity, no. I was intentionally experimenting. Pushing buttons to see what happened with him, with me. He was goo in a petri dish. We both were."

For once, none of the doctors responded.

Rebecca's leg bounced a mile a minute. "You all don't get it."

"Help us."

"I wasn't free. I was a puppet. Your puppet."

"We understand this process is difficult, but remember why you came to us. You were looking for help."

"True. But the more I think about it, the more I realize the cost is too high."

"Ms. Sloane, you're only a few weeks in. You've yet to begin reaping the benefits."

"I'm a few weeks in with you. I'm twenty-eight years in with me. But I'll admit it. You've helped me. You've helped me realize that I don't like being a passenger in my own life."

"Ms. Sloane, we need you to be more cooperative," Dr. Costa said.

"Haven't I answered all your questions truthfully and without modesty? Haven't I done all your homework? Watched porn? Purchased books, masturbated more than I ever had in my life, and then crawled in here to tell you every fucking detail?"

"Yes, yes you have. But, please. Mind your lang—"

"You might not remember this as you sit in this black room, but life is moving out there. I have a job, stresses, and opportunities for love. I'm not going throw it all away for this. For you."

"It's not for us. It's vitally important work that will help women everywhere," Dr. Barnacle chimed in.

"Please, Ms. Sloane," Dr. Costa pleaded.

Rebecca stood up, "I'm sorry, but I'm done letting you in my bedroom. I'm not one of those porn videos. It's my body, and we're leaving."

"Ms. Sloane…"

Rebecca stepped off the stage. "Thanks for the good start, but I'll take it from here."

Rebecca shouldered her purse and headed for the sliver of light under the door.

Gladys jumped to attention as Rebecca marched past.

"Ms. Sloane, would you like your next homework assignment?"

"Sorry, Gladys. There won't be any more homework assignments, not for me anyway," Rebecca said without breaking stride.

She pounded the hospital's entrance door open, stopping to draw air. It filled every crevice before exiting in a firm stream through her nose. For first time in weeks, she was leaving the hospital with more clarity than when she arrived.

Chapter 22

Rebecca popped in her earbuds for her three-mile walk home.

It had to be tempting for the doctors to discretely leak video clips of ungrateful patients. With Rebecca's luck, her most intimate moments would end up on the jumbotron in Times Square. Payback for her walking out. What a laugh riot that'd be? While not physically naked in front of the doctors, with all the gritty detail she provided, she might as well have been. She was a whore in a peep show. They got their sex fix then pumped in quarters for more.

Breathe.

It's over. No more Dr. Costa.

As she headed south, the sign for Thirty-Ninth Street loomed above. Only a few blocks away from Dr. Rogoff's office. Rebecca should've known that anything he recommended would lack empathy, humanity, and any tangible help. Would it have been so hard for one of the nine hundred doctors in that room to help the patient they had sitting right in front of them? They were doctors, after all. Sex doctors. Paper shufflers and mumblers was more like it. Mumblers with no common sense.

Music left her too alone in her head. She tapped onto one of her radio apps to catch a live stream. The top of the hour news, weather, and traffic was finishing. The opening music for the next show started, a program called *Radio Witch*. It wasn't in Rebecca's usual repertoire, but it was preferable to New York City street noise. And the noise in her head.

The Witch's earthy voice oozed sex. Were she listening at work, she'd definitely find it hard to concentrate. Probably why the woman was partnered with two goofy, male sidekicks:

"Hey, ladies, I know New York is a tough town to meet a good man, and we girls have to sometimes 'take care of our own needs,' if you get my drift?"

"Hey, Witchy, don't get us kicked off air!"

"Nah, nah, it's all good, fellas. Anyway, everyone has their own 'technique,' shall we say, about how to best do the deed, so next hour we will have a head-to-head comparison of vibrators. Live in studio, we'll have three lovely ladies trialing three different models of vibrator to see who comes out on top."

"Hey, I know who will come on top, me!"

"Cool it, Jerry. You're not going anywhere near these girls. Each girl will have their own private space and report back once they have climaxed. We will time each girl with each vibrator to see which one works quickest and which one gives the most satisfying orgasm."

"Hey, Bruce, guess that's why the brown paper is covering the studio windows today!"

"Keep it up, guys, and you'll scare the girls away. Anyway, that will be next..."

Her earbuds fell silent. Rebecca had signal bars, but it was no use. Heart pounding, she checked her watch. Fifteen minutes. She could make it home in fifteen minutes, well enough time to hear the show. She tugged out her earphones and walked like her life depended on it.

Rebecca's keys landed with a clatter on the floor as she ran to her bedroom. Her bedside alarm clock was the only radio left in the apartment, a fact she deduced on her frenzied walk home.

Shit.

Rebecca turned around and ran back to her bag for her phone.

Dial position. What was the dial position? Ninety-eight point seven.

She slid down the parquet floors in her socks, kneeled by her bed, blinking as her eyes adjusted to the interior lighting. Rebecca scanned her way to the station. A Dunkin Donuts ad was playing.

Awesome. Donuts are standing between me and my orgasm.

Then, the show resumed.

"Hey, you're back with the Witch. I was completely slammed by emails and texts wanting an advance scoop of the test results, and I kept telling people that this is, truly, a live demonstration. I have not the slightest clue about which vibrator will come out on top."

"This has to be the first day my wife was looking forward to hearing the show."

"What's the matter, Bruce, can't please your old lady?"

"Not in the slightest! I'm not sure what I'm doing wrong. I'm okay with how stuff goes, but let's just say that she's not exactly lighting a cigarette after we're done, if you know what I mean..."

"What a great segue into our main event today, your timing is impeccable,

Bruce."

"I aims to please, Witchy."

"Okay, we've set up our gals in isolation. Each has three vibrators: a Magic Wand, a Heart Throb 2000, and a Venus 3. All three are electric models that do not require lubrication. Jerry, what are you doing?"

"I'm taking notes for Bruce's wife!"

"Cute, fat boy, very cute. Please continue, Witchy."

"Thank you. We did some informal polling and landed on these three. Don't call up here saying that we picked the wrong ones. If you like another one, more power to you. Anyway, each girl will start with a different toy, that way, each can have an equal shot at the quickie orgasm. We'll then rotate until each girl has climaxed with each device, and then we will have an informed discussion about the results. We have an intercom that the girls can contact us to let us know when they're done with each model as we will be timing them."

"No pressure there. Can all these girls, you know, have that many in a row?"

"Yes, Jerry. They can. We checked their references, and they come very highly recommended. Okay, ladies, can you hear me?"

"Yes."

"Start your engines."

Rebecca paced the room through a few minutes of idle banter. Then jolted to attention.

"I hear we have our first winner. It's the Magic Wand. Okay, I'm hearing the Heart Throb 2000 has climaxed, too," Radio Witch reported.

"It's a regular Kentucky Derby, Witchy!"

"Jerry, keep taking notes for my wife. I'm too nervous to write."

"Who you kiddin'? When'd you learn to write?"

After the next break, the Venus 3 girl finished. They switched around, and again, the girl with the Magic Wand came first.

Rebecca's heart pounded as she rocked back and forth, hands clasped.

Finally, all three women finished and joined the hosts in the studio. Rebecca opened and closed desk drawers, looking for pen and paper. Finding both, she took a seat on her bed next to her pillow, hands primed for dictation.

"Frank, help the girls with those headsets, will ya? Okay, we have Brandi, Samantha, and Julia here with us. First of all, thank you so much for your assistance today, ladies. Let's start with you, Brandi, how did things go?"

"Really well. I got myself really hot before I started so I would be in the mood. That's what I usually do at home."

"Good tip. What did you think of the vibrators? Which did you like best?"

"Oh, there's no doubt. The Magic Wand is awesome. It was comfortable to hold, the cord was really long so it didn't get in the way. It did the job really quickly. I have three vibrators at home, and I'm going to go out and buy one of these."

"Okay, one vote for the Magic Wand. Samantha, what did you think?"

"Witchy, I had the Venus first, and it is really loud, so loud that it interfered with my fantasy. I mean, if I did this while at home, my mom would probably bust in wondering what was going on."

"Wouldn't that be a surprise? Say, maybe you should get your wife that one, Bruce. That way, you'd know to stay clear until she was finished!"

"Jerry, can you lay off for a few? We're doing some serious investigative

journalism here on the Radio Witch Show.*"*

"Sorry, Witchy."

"Anyway, which did you like best?"

"I'd have to say the Magic Wand. I'm been a fan of the pen——. Can I say penis on air?"

"You just did, sweetheart."

"Sorry, Witchy. Anyway, I have a penis-shaped vibrator, so I thought this looked a little weird at first. But this thing is amazing. I'm going to throw my others away."

"That's two votes for the Magic Wand. Dare I ask, Julie, are you a Magic Wand gal as well?"

"Witchy, I am so a Magic Wand girl. I own a Venus 3, so I thought that I would do best with that one, but man! That Magic Wand is incredible. I've never flipped that quickly on a third one before. I was a little thrown off by the look of it with the ball on the end and all, and it is a little big, but who cares, right? If it can work like that, I'd strap on an elephant!"

"Well, I have to admit, ladies, I'm a Magic Wand girl myself. I have never used a 'personal massager' that could work like this thing does. Thanks so much for coming in today, and as a token of our appreciation, you can each keep the three vibrators you used today. You may not want the other two, but maybe you can re-gift them for the holidays! You're listening to the Radio Witch.*"*

Rebecca switched off the show and walked to the window, holding her notes.

"How could they climax on command like that?" Rebecca barked at the radio. "Is that even possible?"

She paced back into the center of the room, fingers tightening around the pad still in her hands. "Magic Wand" was scribbled in block letters and circled three times.

There was only one way to find out.

Googling "Magic Wand" brought up a slew of articles about Hitachi discontinuing production of the device. Rebecca grimaced as her eyes scanned the details.

"This can't be right," she whispered. "Where did they get theirs for the radio show?"

She navigated to the Hitachi website and clicked on all the options for consumer products, from refrigerators, microwaves, and rice cookers. No supersonic personal massagers. She checked Bed Bath and Beyond, Sharper Image, Amazon, Macy's: no luck.

Rebecca revised her search terms to include the word "masturbation." Up popped a flurry of new options. She clicked on the first, a website for someone named Heidi Quinn, masturbation counselor.

Masturbation counselor?

Rebecca leaned into her computer. The page was her sales portal for the Magic Wand, but Rebecca immediately clicked back to the homepage.

Heidi Quinn, sex therapist.

Words exploded in her mind as she skimmed the page: "Inorgasmic, struggle, shame, help, self-fulfillment."

Heidi got it. An orgasm was about so much more than having sex. It was everything. It was self-worth. It was confidence. It was companionship. It was a happy future, and yes, it was also about sex, all rolled up into one package. One event that had eluded her, and was destined to always elude her—until now. She finally found someone who understood. But even more than that, someone could actually help.

Rebecca rolled her shoulders and took a breath before clicking the "Videos" link. The page loaded with three videos, one with step-by-step instructions in the art of masturbation. Christ, who knew there was anyone like this out there? Why had she not ever looked? She could have skipped the invasive medical probing by the dear doctors had she known someone like Heidi Quinn existed.

The video description shared how Ms. Quinn helped several women overcome common masturbation issues. Women from different backgrounds who agreed to have their sessions recorded for the betterment of others.

Wow. That took the on-camera intimacy to a whole new level.

There was a discount on the Magic Wand when purchased with the video. Rebecca jogged to the dining room and palmed her wallet, unzipping it to find her credit card. She'd not only found her Magic Wand, but a treasure map as well.

She typed in her information and clicked "Order Now," then leaned back on her headboard. Heart beating wildly, fingers tingling with anticipation.

Cleansing breaths were of no use, not at a time like this. Barely a few hours after imploding her clinical assistance, she was back in business. But now she'd have to wait. Too bad patience wasn't one of her strong suits.

Rebecca strolled down the hall to the kitchen and opened the fridge, letting its coolness wash over her. Sighing at her paltry options, she grabbed an individually wrapped slice of cheddar cheese out of the package in the appropriately named "Cheese Drawer" and closed the door. Tearing the wrapper, she nibbled on a corner while walking to the sofa and flipping on the television.

Talk show, talk show, early news, infomercial. She certainly wasn't missing anything good while at work. Not that early evening television was ever high on her priority list.

Track and field was on ESPN, qualifying heats for the US Team going to Worlds. Runners sprinted around the track with breathtaking speed. Just as one rounded the last turn, she came up lame and stumbled to the ground in a heap. The crowd gasped, her coaches—with worried expressions—dashed out in the opposite direction than the lead athletes nearing the finish line. Undeterred, the injured runner rose to her feet, waving off her coaches as she began her hobble to the finish. She was out of contention, but she won the hearts of the crowd.

Rebecca toasted her with her last morsel of cheese before popping it in her mouth. Hopefully when her package arrived, she'd hobble to her own finish.

Was that a sound?

Rebecca muted the television to a double doorbell chime.

That's how he rings.

Rebecca stood, cheese wrapper in hand. She stuffed it in her pocket and primped her hair. Holding her breath as she looked through the keyhole.

It was Kyle.

She opened the door enough to squeeze her face through.

"Hey," she said.

"Hey. I heard the TV. Surprised to find you home this early."

203

"Me too."

"What do you mean?"

"It's not important. Did you get my messages?"

"Yeah. Do you have a minute?"

Rebecca wrapped her hair behind her ears.

"Yeah, sure."

Rebecca closed the door silently behind him but remained facing the door, light-headed.

I have to tell him.

"You want something to drink?" she asked.

"Yeah, some water would be great."

Rebecca poured cold water from the fridge into a glass which immediately began sweating. She grabbed a paper towel before walking to the living room. She placed it under the glass on the coffee table in front of Kyle, who was sitting on the couch.

Kyle downed the entire glass of water.

"Thirsty?"

"Yeah. Look, Rebecca…"

She sat next to him. "Let me go first, please."

"Okay."

"I am so sorry. About Saturday. About everything. About acting… so hot and cold all the time."

"Go on."

"I'm not trying to play games. I've got a problem I haven't been comfortable talking about with you."

"A problem?"

"A sex problem."

Kyle's eyebrows shot up, "Really. You didn't seem to have a sex problem on Saturday."

He's not making this easy.

"I've never..."

She looked up; he was waiting, arms folded.

Don't look at him.

She closed her eyes, losing herself in the blackness. *Just like the study.*

"I'm just going to say it. I've never been able to have an orgasm. With someone or alone. It doesn't matter. It's caused relationship problems in the past, so I try to avoid sex for as long as humanly possible."

"That's not where I thought you were going to go, but okay."

She released a breath. "There's more. I've been getting medical help to try to fix the issue."

"A doctor?"

"A group of doctors. I've been... in a study."

"What kind of study?"

"For people in my situation. I go and talk to them about it."

"Like therapy? That's not so bad. Lots of people go to therapy," Kyle said, warmth returning to his voice.

His warm hand caressed her back. She squeezed her eyes shut tighter to hold back the tears escaping. *Is this the last time he'll touch me?*

"They give me homework. Things for me to try, then I tell them how it went. How it felt. What I was thinking. Anything sexually related. I have to... share with them."

She opened her eyes. Kyle slumped on the sofa, wrapped in his own arms, looking through her as he processed the information.

"Everything."

"Everything."

"So, when we…"

"Yes."

"You told them?"

"Yes."

"About us? What we do together. Rebecca, that's for us. That's private between us. How could you?"

"I'm sorry. I wanted so badly to fix myself. So we could be together. So you would like me."

"We are together. I do like you. Did. Do." He shook his head violently side to side. "Why didn't you tell me, ask me? You've been lying all this time."

"No. Not lying. I haven't been lying."

"Was it real? Was any of it real? Or, were you just using me to get your juices flowing for your experiment?"

"No, of course it was real."

"Was Saturday real? Is that what you were up to?"

Kyle stood up, pacing back and forth in front of the where she sat on the sofa. She raised her eyes, searching, but his pools of blue had frozen over.

"I open myself. Freely, I get that. But, I expect to be treated as a human being. Not a plaything. I expect honesty. I deserve honesty."

"I have been honest, about everything else."

"Yeah, that's what Vivian said too. 'It didn't mean anything,'" He gestured in air quotes. "Well, it means something to me. You meant something to me. A lot."

Kyle headed toward the door.

"Where are you going?"

Rebecca intercepted him, hands on his chest, walking backward to stem his advance.

"I thought you were different."

"Kyle, don't go. Please don't go. I'm sorry. I'm so sorry, but I was afraid. Afraid of losing you if you found out."

"Yeah, well, you were right."

"Don't say that. Please. We can work through this."

"We could have. *If* you had been honest with me," he said as Rebecca's back hit the door.

"I didn't know how to talk to you about this. It was so personal. It's not something I could talk about."

"You couldn't talk to me, but you could talk to a room full of *strangers*?"

Their eyes met.

"Please let me out."

Rebecca stood aside. He slammed the door with such force it echoed in the emptiness where her heart had been.

Chapter 23

The Great Lawn in Central Park was packed with picnickers and dog enthusiasts. Leslie, Barbara, and Rebecca made their way through the sunbathing hordes enjoying the late-afternoon sun.

"This is great. I've wanted to use my picnic basket for ages," Leslie said. "It's not exactly practical, but it's adorable."

"Adorable is what counts," Barbara teased, looking for Rebecca who had fallen behind. "Look lively back there. There's only one patch of open grass, and it's mine."

Rebecca rolled her eyes. Barbara and Leslie meant well. She knew that. But a summer picnic the day after her life imploded wasn't her first choice of activities. Not unless they were digging a hole she could crawl in.

"Perfect! There's no one for at least ten feet."

"Go ahead. Lift the lid," Leslie said, bursting with delight.

"Cute! Very cute. Gingham is quintessential picnic décor." Barbara said.

"Right!?" Leslie said, unfolding the red and white checked sheet. "I love how everything has a compartment. Look how darling the wine glasses are!"

"Very nice. My Zinfandel will taste amazing, I'm sure."

Rebecca flopped down on the sheet. "Why did you bring me out in public? I should not be out in public right now."

"It's the perfect place for you to be. Look around. Life. Life is here. Trees, grass, fuzzy creatures…" Barbara said, eyeing a black lab that ran dangerously close to their bread and cheese.

"They're called dogs, you know," Leslie said.

"Whatever. Okay, dogs. See? If you were home, you would have missed that charming dog run by."

"And I would have missed you navigating grass in stilettos?" Rebecca said.

"Exactly. Though, it's very doable. It's all about how you carry your weight," she said, sitting down with her legs curled under herself and setting her red-soled Christian Louboutin stilettos to the side.

"Cheese?" Leslie asked, offering Rebecca a plate with a cloth gingham napkin.

She shook her head.

"Hand it over, I'm starved," Barbara said. "And add a few of those cornichon and salami slices, too."

"Mmmm, so good," Leslie cozied into her raised shoulders as she chewed.

"I needed this. Court was a bear today. Why do people run for judge if they're going to be complete assholes to everyone who comes before them?"

"Because they can be complete assholes to everyone who comes before them," Leslie said, taking a sip of wine. "Politicians. They're all politicians at heart."

"True," Barbara answered.

The conversation lulled. Barbara and Leslie exchanged wary glances. Leslie flicked her head, egging Barbara to speak first.

"Hey, Becca?"

She looked up from finger tracing circles on the checked cloth.

"You are more than what you do in the bedroom."

Rebecca pursed her mouth.

"For as long as we've known you, you've beaten yourself up for not having a tingle at the end of sex. It's eating you away. You are so much more than that. Don't let it define who you are."

Rebecca sighed and sat up. "I appreciate that, but how would you feel if there was a joke. The best, most satisfying joke in the world. People's bellies rolled, their eyes teared; they laughed so hard they couldn't breathe. They'd look at each other after, wink and nod, 'wasn't that joke just the best" and they'd answer, 'oh, yeah. Sooooo funny. Loved it!' And you're just standing there, 'I don't get it.' That's how this sex thing feels. It's the best joke in the world, and I'm on the outside looking in. It's lonely."

"I hear you. But what if the person who didn't get the joke, thought that one small failing was the essence of who they are. They were the 'girl who didn't get the joke.' Like Harry Potter, 'the boy who lived.' Would you shake that person and tell them how wrong they were? They didn't get *one* joke. There are *so* many jokes in life. They got *all* the other jokes. Plus, they had other talents. They could dance and sing and climb mountains. Big deal, they didn't get one fucking joke."

"Did you mean that pun?" Rebecca asked.

"No. I got lucky. Let's go with it," Barbara winked.

"Never argue with a lawyer, at least THIS lawyer," Leslie said, smearing ripe brie on a slice of baguette.

Barbara swirled her wine in her plastic stemware and took a sip.

"You know I'm right. I can tell," she said.

Rebecca had been bested. She tilted her head to look at the sky; clear blue with the faintest hint of sunset tinging whisps of clouds. She closed her eyes and let the sun's warmth nourish her.

"It hurts. I just want to be like everyone else," she said, a tear streaking down her face. Rebecca wiped it away.

When she opened her eyes, Leslie was there. As she always was. "Come here," she said. Her hug was tight. Leslie's energy filled Rebecca, forcing out her breath and a small measure of shame.

"You'll get there. You can do it on your own," Leslie said.

"That's right. Take what you learned there and apply it yourself. You don't need those doctors," Barbara said.

"You think so?" Rebecca said over Leslie's shoulder.

"I know so."

"I know so too," Leslie said, loosening her hug while keeping hold of Rebecca's arms. Their eyes met. "Deep down, I think you know so too."

Rebecca shrugged, "Maybe, yeah. I do think so. I was so close the other day. That porn really got me going."

"See, you've got internet porn. Who needs a group of doctors?" Barbara said.

Maybe the girls were right? She could do it on her own. Truly, all the progress she made was on her own anyway. The Magic Wand and videos would arrive any day, and she'd soon be back in business. Rebecca would figure it out. Then she and Kyle could…

Kyle. Her stomach dropped out.

"What about Kyle? I don't think he'll ever talk to me again."

"Of course he will. He just had a shock," Barbara said.

"You had weeks to get used to the study idea. It freaked you out too, if you remember? Yesterday was his first time hearing of it. Just make him understand the truth."

"And what is the truth? That I totally betrayed him?"

"You were insensitive, at best," Barbara said.

"That's the lawyer talking."

"True, but it's a negotiation. You like him; he likes you. You had a difference of opinion—different expectations. Just clear the air and be honest. He'll come around."

"And what if he doesn't?"

"Then find another way," Leslie said.

"Find another way? You sound like Evelyn."

"You could do a lot worse than sounding like my powerhouse of an aunt," Barbara said.

"Ahhhhh, ahhhhh-men," Leslie sang in a tune Rebecca recognized from synagogue. "Not bad for a shiksa, huh?"

"Totally. You're the ultimate shiksa, yes. Any man would be lucky to have your blonde, gentile ass," Rebecca said, smiling despite herself.

"Thanks!"

"And Kyle is lucky to have your sultry, Jewish-Latina-ass. Don't forget that," Barbara said.

"You think I'm sultry?"

"Way sultry."

"Totally. You talk yourself down and act like he's the only

212

prize," Leslie said. "He's a big winner too. He gets you."

Rebecca never envisioned herself as a prize worth winning; more like the consolation prize guys settled for when she was the only viable option left. But maybe her pals had a point? She was underselling herself. After all, both Kyle and Ethan fell for her, at least for a time. Both were prime catches by any measure, and they chose her. But she allowed them to choose her. It was her choice as well. She had agency. Just like with the study, it was time for her to seize control and fight for what she wanted.

"I feel it. I can do this," Rebecca said, sitting a little taller.

"Of course you can," Barbara said.

Rebecca had two tasks: slay the sexual demons and battle for Kyle. He was too important to let walk out of her life. Not that way. He had to know the truth about how she felt. Not half-truths shrouded in mystery and evasion games. The full truth. She was in this mess because she kept her secrets hidden. From her mother as a teen, from herself, and from Kyle. It was time to forge a new path.

Kyle valued honesty, so she'd give him honesty. If she came clean and he stayed, then she'd know it was because he cared for her too. It'd mean he was willing to accept her as she was. Broken, but, hopefully, lovable too.

The scent of fresh bread penetrated Rebecca's senses. Her stomach growled. Leslie was about to eat a stack with bread, salami, and cheese, but Rebecca snatched it away and popped it into her own mouth.

"Hey!" Leslie said.

"I'm ready for a plate," Rebecca said. "I'm starving."

Chapter 24

Armed with a fresh outlook, Rebecca entered her building and bounded up the stairs. Kyle's door loomed like a porthole. To what she wasn't sure. But she marched right up and rang the bell.

Bessie's slippers approached, the peephole cover slid open and closed before she opened the door.

"He's not here. He went for a walk."

"Any idea when he'll be back?"

"No. Why don't you go back home. I'm sure he'll call you at some point."

At some point. That didn't sound promising

"I was about to lie down."

"Go ahead. Thanks. Tell him I stopped by?"

Bessie smiled and closed the door.

It wasn't the reunion she had envisioned. Her standing in the hallway with a locked door in her face. When she was a teenager, she would occasionally get locked out of the apartment while her parents were at work. To get in, Rebecca would have to call the apartment complex's security officer. He would eventually come to open the door, but she'd have to wait. An hour, sometimes longer. The guy would produce a signature card to sign, and it was a miracle they ever let Rebecca in at all. At her age, the signature never looked the same twice. But that moment of unbridled relief when the door swung open on its hinges made the tense hallway wait worth it.

If anyone was worth the wait, Kyle was. Rebecca eyed the linoleum floor.

"Hello, friend," she said, sliding down the wall until her butt made contact.

Civil disobedience, for one. Muted sounds of evening activities filtered into the hallway from the other apartments. There were the original old timers on the floor, like her family, Bessie, the Nussbaums, and the O'Reileys. The other apartments had turned over multiple times, and many of those tenants kept to themselves. No chatting by the elevator, in the laundry room, or around the neighborhood. They'd pass like they didn't know each other.

Her chest tightened. Would that be her fate with Kyle? Strangers who could have had something special, but let it get away.

Never. They did have something special. Rebecca felt it. It was exciting and fresh and real. She fit in her skin when she was with Kyle. No wishing she was someone else, or with anyone else but him. Even the worrier in her brain found moments of peace when they were together. She could just be. It was scary, but scary good. She needed more of it.

Rebecca shifted her legs out straight, massaging a leg cramp out. It'd already been forty minutes. How long would she stay? Should she text him? No. He'd probably wait her out and avoid returning.

She opened her bag to check her phone when the elevator door opened.

Keys jingled.

Footsteps.

Kyle came around the corner, stopping in his tracks.

"Rebecca? What are you doing here?"

"Waiting for you," she said, scrambling to her feet.

Kyle's hands slid to his hips, faded Levi's clinging to every muscle and curve. A jersey gray T-shirt, lightly damp from his walk. She inhaled his earthiness and felt a familiar thrill.

Easy girl. Don't get ahead of yourself.

"I was hoping we could talk."

Her heart raced as he looked away, not answering.

"Please?"

"Rebecca, I…"

"Please, Kyle. Give me a few minutes. It won't take long."

She gestured toward her apartment and followed along behind him. She ushered him in and flipped on a few lights.

He stood unmoving in the foyer.

"Have a seat," she said.

He walked into the living room, but instead of sitting in his usual spot on the sofa, he sat alone in her dad's leather chair.

Things change fast.

Carrying the fridge pitcher and two glasses, Rebecca set them down on the coffee table, then poured them each a tall glass. She downed hers, but his remained untouched next to where she sat on the table to face him.

"You wanted to talk. Let's talk."

"There's no good way to say this, so I'm just going to say it. I told you about my… problem, but I didn't give you the full extent of it. It's been an issue for years. Past boyfriends have been pretty abusive about it."

"Abusive?" Kyle said, sitting up.

"Not hitting me, but calling me names. Insulting me. Calling me worthless. A punch would have almost been better. Easier to heal—"

"Hey, don't ever say that," Kyle said, reaching out for her hand. "No one has the right to treat you that way."

"Yeah, I know. But they do. Treat me badly, that is. So I have a lot of fear when it comes to sex. Shame. Emotions most other people don't have. It makes it… complicated… when I meet someone new. I don't know what to expect, and I'm always expecting the worst."

They sat silently as her words baked.

"Rebecca, I'm so sorry for how I…"

"I should have told you, or asked rather. I was already seeing the doctors when we met. We were so new. I was afraid if I'd just mentioned it, you'd be out the door."

Kyle cracked a smile.

"What?" she asked.

"Truthfully, I might have bolted. It is weird, you have to admit."

"See? I didn't know how to bring you into my world without 'us' falling apart. It felt like a choice. I chose wrong. I know that now, and I'm so sorry. I left the study. So it's all over. At least for me."

"Wow. So did you…?"

"Not yet, no."

Kyle nodded his understanding.

"I'm sorry. I didn't mean to mess up your therapy."

"It's okay. It *was* weird. Even for me. I'll figure it out."

Kyle reached for his glass and took a long drink.

"Maybe I can be of some assistance?" he said, wiping his mouth with the back of his hand.

Their eyes met. Breathless, they dove at each other, urgent mouths seeking a home in the other.

"I'm so sorry."

"No, *I'm* sorry."

Kisses smacked frantically, then Rebecca wrapped her arms around Kyle's neck, burying her face in his chest. His head found a home on top of hers.

"I thought I'd lost you."

"Me too."

"I was so afraid. Let's never fight again."

"I'll try. I'm a big lug, I know it. But you make me all squishy on the inside. I can't explain it."

She laughed. "You make me squishy too."

He slid her from the table onto his lap in the chair, holding her tight. Stroking her hair.

I could stay here forever. Even better, it seemed like he could too.

His breath on her neck tickled, and she reflexively squirmed. It was brief, but he picked up on it.

"Ticklish, are we?"

"No," she said, grinning so wide he likely felt it through his shirt.

"Only one way to tell," Kyle said, blasting a strawberry on her neck. She launched into a writhing belly laugh.

"Kyle!" Rebecca tried to wiggle out of his lap, but he held firm and blasted her neck again. Her laughter rolled, a thrilling release of all the tension and doubt she'd been harboring for days.

"Oh my God, I can't breathe," she said as their tickle session tumbled onto the floor.

"Not ticklish, huh?" he said, pulsing his fingers into every funny place she had, including ones she didn't know existed.

"I can't, stop, I can't," she breathlessly panted. A power abs class couldn't give her tummy this much of a workout. Then he abruptly stopped.

She lay panting on the floor, recovering.

"Rebecca?"

A few residual giggles escaped, along with a happy tear.

"Rebecca, the door."

"Mmmm?"

"The door?"

"What?"

"There's someone at the door."

"The door?"

A loud knock reverberated, followed by three urgent doorbell rings.

"What the hell?" Rebecca climbed out from under Kyle. "Talk about bad timing."

"Oh. I have a feeling the timing is perfect," he said, stretching so he could see the visitor.

"What?" Rebecca yelled as she opened the door.

"Well, no need to be rude," Bessie answered.

"Oh, sorry."

Bessie pursed her lips, "I wanted to get Evelyn's address to send a thank-you note. You did say you'd get it for me."

"You're right, I did. Hold on, I have it in my purse."

Rebecca walked away, making way for a Bessie inspection.

"Kyle, what are you doing on the floor?"

He grumbled and stood up. "Auntie."

Bessie stood in the doorway, holding the apartment door open.

"Here you go. Sorry for the delay," Rebecca said, handing her a slip of paper, which Bessie promptly checked for legibility.

"I didn't want Evelyn to think I wasn't grateful. It was so very generous of her. I wanted to thank her properly."

"I'm sure she wouldn't think that." Rebecca took hold of the door as Bessie retreated into the hall, stopping to look back.

"Kyle, you coming?

"No, Rebecca and I—"

"If you weren't going to eat home, you should have told me. I've been keeping it warm for you. I'm sure Rebecca understands, don't you, dear?"

"Yes, of course."

Kyle made his way to the door, mouthing "I'll call you later" as he passed the entryway.

Rebecca closed the door but couldn't help smiling. Everything was back as it should be.

Chapter 25

With all the craziness of the week, Rebecca completely lost track of her meeting with Darcy and Harry about her 360 evaluation. She was flying so high after her reunion with Kyle that even a clunker of a review wouldn't bring her down.

She pulled into her desk and opened the computer file for her self-evaluation. Skimming through, she examined the grades she gave herself across the exhaustive questionnaire. The questions weren't numbered, but there had to be at least sixty of them. How would her scores compare to the other evaluators? Would they find hers overinflated? She'd know in a few hours.

Rebecca bit her pen as her eyes tracked the columns down, doubting everything.

"Ready?" a voice behind her asked.

"Excuse me?" Rebecca swiveled her chair around to face Whitney, one of the junior media planners.

"You said to stop by today, so you could help me with the training. It's ten o'clock. Do you need to reschedule?"

"No, it's good. I just... never mind. Now is fine."

Rebecca shifted her loose papers into a pile, put it aside, and pulled her guest seat over for Whitney to sit down.

"So, remind me, what are we reviewing today?"

"I have a new client, and I'm supposed to run the syndicated research. But, I'm not sure where to start," Whitney said.

"When I get a new account, it's important to gain a baseline understanding of their business category. Who are their customers? What's their typical age, gender, lifestyle? Where do they live in the country?"

"Slow down a sec; I want to be sure to get all this down," Whitney said, scribbling madly on a notepad.

"The reports you run will give you all these answers," Rebecca said, typing on the keyboard to enter the SRDS media planning platform. "I usually compare the product and its category against the demographic information file. I also add the media usage quintiles to get a sense of the type of media they use most frequently: TV, radio, magazines, Internet, etc."

"Okay, first we figure out who they are, then we figure out what media they use?"

"Exactly. By the end, we'll know users of high-fiber cold breakfast cereal are adults twenty-five to fifty-four, with incomes of $70,000 plus who have two-plus years of college, two kids, and watch a lot of cable news."

"Then when we know what they watch or listen to, that's what we recommend in our plan?"

"Well, there's a bit more to it than that. Advertising isn't typically effective until you reach a certain percentage of your audience several times."

"What percentage is that?"

"As planners, we typically do the best we can with the budget we have and the geography we need to cover. That's why rate negotiation is so important. The less you spend on one outlet, the more money you can put toward another. Managing your budget well is how you get there. The goal is to reach as many people in your client's audience as many times as possible."

Whitney stopped writing and cocked her head. "So, what do you mean about managing the budget? I know this is off topic with the SRDS stuff, but what you're saying is way better than what I learned in orientation."

Rebecca smiled. "Managing the budget well is everything. We're always asked to do more with less, so the more you can do with what you have, the more successful you'll be.

"Part of that is getting the best bang for the buck. Is the client a national brand that needs to cover the whole country, or are they a local advertiser that only sells products in Georgia and Alabama? When do they advertise? Is there any seasonality? Are they trying to reach new customers or increase usage by their current customer base? All these will factor into which media make the most sense to use. And will dictate where and when you spend your budget."

"Sorry to be thick, the 'when?' Don't you plan for the whole year?"

"Ideally, yes, but if your client can't afford to run all year, you need to schedule the advertising when it can be most effective. If you're working for a client selling allergy medication, they may only want to be on air in the spring and fall in the north, but on more regularly in warmer areas of the country where plants are blooming year-round. Make sense?"

"Sure. It's just a lot to remember," she replied.

"You'll get there. Now, let's run through what you need for your client."

They worked for the next ninety minutes, going through Whitney's work. When the young planner seemed in command, Whitney returned to her desk.

Darcy strutted over moments later. "Harry has a conflict later, so he'd like to meet with us now."

"Now? Wow." Rebecca grabbed her laptop and notepad and followed behind Darcy as they walked the length of the floor to Harry's corner office.

Light streamed in. He waved them in as he finished his call.

"Sorry to shift the schedule, but it can't be helped sometimes," he said. "As you know, this is an important part of our development process. Gathering assessments from people junior to you, peers, and those senior to you gives a well-rounded view of what you do well and where you can improve. It's anonymous, as you know. Our goal is complete honesty."

Honesty; there's that word again.

Darcy smirked as she looked sideways at Rebecca.

Did she know what was coming? It was supposed to be secret.

"Looking at the results in your case, the biggest discrepancy was between the ratings others gave you and those you gave yourself."

"Oh," Rebecca said, accepting a copy of the printed report he passed her and Darcy.

"Overall, you did extremely well and should be proud."

"I did?"

"Yes, you got consistently high marks across the board."
"She did?" Darcy said, flipping the pages ahead to scan the results. She looked more shocked than Rebecca did.

"The biggest delta was between their marks and your self-assessment."

Rebecca's stomach dropped. *Here it comes.*

"You gave yourself much lower marks than everyone else did." He paused and looked over his glasses. "Here it is in black and white. The person with the least confidence in you is you."

Rebecca ran her finger down the rows. A quick calculation showed her own marks were about 30 percent lower than the ones her colleagues gave her. The ones she worried were self-inflated.

"There must be some mistake," Darcy said.

"Why?" Harry asked.

"Well, she—"

"Yes?"

"She demonstrates poor negotiation skills and a bad attitude."

Harry flipped one of the pages and tapped it with his finger, leaning back in his chair. "She scored high on negotiation skills, and I disagree with you about the bad attitude."

With Harry championing her, Rebecca sat back and let them battle it out. Her money was on the agency owner.

"One of the reviewers touched on this, let me find it," he said, linking his finger to page through the report.

A deflated Darcy looked across at Rebecca. Rebecca cocked her head and stared back. Two could play the death-stare game.

"Here it is. It's a quote from someone senior to you," Harry said, reading the quote aloud:

"Rebecca is a bundle of optimism with an infectious can-do spirit, but needs to improve her self-confidence. Left unchecked, it could undermine her effectiveness with others. Clients specifically could doubt her ability to effectively execute her work if she signals she doubts herself. She's better than she gives herself credit for."

"It's not an attitude problem, Darcy, it's a confidence problem. This is what I was trying to say the other day in the board room, Rebecca. What are your thoughts?"

"Maybe."

Harry raised an eyebrow.

"Yes. I agree. I need to speak with more conviction and confidence."

"Good. Darcy, would this address the concern you had?"

Rebecca slow-blinked her boss. *Let her squirm for once.*

"Perhaps."

"Good. Now, one way to build confidence is to lead others. It'll allow you to demonstrate mastery and bring others along with you."

"Did you have something in mind?" Rebecca asked.

"I overheard you training Whitney earlier."

"Oh boy," she moaned.

Harry shot her a cautionary glance.

Rebecca sighed. Acting confident was going to be hard.

"You should absolutely be running our orientation program."

Darcy huffed a pained laugh. "Do you really think this is a good idea? I mean, onboarding is a critically important function for the planning organization."

"I couldn't," Rebecca added.

"Pish posh to you both. I think it's a splendid idea. I was working nearby and heard how you ran through things with Whitney. She was right. You did a much better job than our orientation manual."

"Wow, thanks. It's overwhelming at the beginning. I find it helps to keep the 'why' behind the 'what' in mind at all times. At least, it helped me."

"Since you have a lot of junior people working with you, I'd love for you to put together a presentation sharing where you think we could be doing a better job of training. If junior planners can't take work off your plates, we need to be doing a better job."

"Really?"

"Where's your confidence?" he said, smiling.

Rebecca laughed. "Sure, I'd be happy to. I appreciate the opportunity."

"Isn't this something better handled by someone more senior?" Darcy said, leaning into Harry's desk to box out Rebecca with her body. "I could take a look at the problem myself."

"Why don't we circle back after I look at Rebecca's proposal."

Darcy sat back. "Of course."

"A week enough time?" Harry asked.

"Can I have until the next Monday?"

"A week from Monday it is," Harry said, slapping both palms on the desk and standing up.

"Let me or Darcy know if you have any questions about the 360 report after you read it. We'll schedule a follow-up in three months to check in. Keep up the good work!"

Rebecca beamed as she and Darcy exited.

They hit a safe distance, and her boss pounced, "Don't let your work suffer for this side project."

"I won't."

Darcy flushed and went back to her fishbowl.

Rebecca returned to her desk, the quote echoing in her ears, "*Rebecca is better than she gives herself credit for.*"

For the first time, she was beginning to believe it.

Chapter 26

Rebecca slid her black mascara brush back into the tube, then dashed to answer the door. Mid-opening, Kyle wrapped her in an embrace, dipping her backward in a dramatic pose.

"Good eve-va-ning?" he said, wiggling his eyebrows.

"Back at cha," Rebecca said, her neck stiffening from the long dip.

He set her upright.

"I'm almost done putting on my face."

She returned to the bathroom, where her makeup was spread out on a towel covering the closed toilet seat lid. She reassumed her mascara position.

Kyle followed, leaning in the doorway to watch.

"You're beautiful, you know. Even without the makeup."

A lump formed in her throat. "That is the sweetest thing to say. Thank you. You're beautiful too."

She air-kissed him, a squeaky smack.

"How about the real thing?" he said with a pucker.

"Not right now; we'll be late."

"You can skip the lipstick. That way, you can have your way

with me, and not leave any evidence."

"Maybe I want to leave evidence," she said, twisting up the plum tube of Berry Blast.

Kyle stood next to her in the mirror, holding a tube of Rebecca's firehouse-red lipstick he snuck out of her makeup bag.

"Maybe I want to leave evidence too." He puckered and put a soppy smear of lipstick across his own lips.

"Holy shit!" Rebecca giggled, covering her gaping mouth with her hand.

He put his head on her shoulder, blinking innocently.

"You're nuts! I can't believe you just did that!"

"Yeah, but how do I look?"

"How do you look? You look like Ronald McDonald on acid."

"Kiss?"

"No way!"

"Then no kisses for you either," he said, strutting out of the bathroom.

She looked at the tube. Old Rebeca would have caved. New Rebecca sported confidence, even with Kyle.

"I'm a strong, modern woman, and if I want to wear Berry Blast, then I'm wearing Berry Blast!" she yelled.

Kyle answered with a loud smooching noise that sent her giggling.

She finished and surveyed the results. Eyes smokey, cheeks rosy, lips—yes, they were sultry. She Vogued at her reflection, laughed, then grabbed a clean tissue and the remover, and went to find Kyle, who had switched on ESPN.

He looked up as she entered the room. "Berry Blast is almost as lovely as you."

"Thanks, but Firehouse Red isn't!"

"Oh. Forgot."

"I should have let you go out that way!"

Rebecca wet the tissue and carefully wiped his face. He was astonishingly handsome, lipstick notwithstanding. Blue eyes, midnight hair, and that amazing stubble that was always the right length to send her heart pounding.

"Lovely cleavage," he mumbled into the tissue.

"Shhh," she replied. "There. I got most of it off, but the rest will have to wear off. Make sure you eat a lot tonight and wipe your mouth well, and it should be gone by tomorrow."

"Can't you kiss it off?" he said, sneaking a hand up under her dress to pull down her underwear. She moved his hand away.

"We agreed to take it slow, remember?"

"Did we? Is it too late to change my mind?"

"Yes. Besides, we don't want to be late for Barbara, Joe, and Leslie. They'll be waiting."

"What's a few more minutes. Life is too short, don't you think?" he said, nibbling her ear.

Rebecca stepped back to exit the danger zone.

"Dinner was your idea. 'I can meet your friends and stay out of your pants all at the same time.' Ring any bells?"

"Vaguely…"

"Good. Let's go."

Rebecca held the sides of her minidress down as they rode the motorcycle downtown. New Yorkers didn't need a front-row view of her underwear. The dress briefly blew up despite her best efforts, causing heads to snap around as they passed. It was hard to care about it too much, though. She would never see those people again. She could make an ass of herself any day of the week pretty much without consequence. That is, as long as her overactive brain kept quiet.

They were meeting the gang in Chinatown at another nameless restaurant the girls frequented. They knew it by sight. It was on the east side of Mott Street just south of Canal Street, in between an import/export place that sold the usual mix of vases, tea sets, and bowls, and a grocery market with a large street display of fruit and vegetables.

Kyle usually pulled right up to where they were going, but Mott Street was jammed. They circled around the block and parked on Elizabeth Street, then walked back. Rebecca rubbed her arms, chilled from the breezy ride.

"Come here," Kyle said, pulling her close with his right arm and holding her tight to his furnace of a body as they navigated the crowds.

"You'll love Barbara, and Joe is amazing. He used to be my rep from *Sports Illustrated*, but once they started dating, I switched to be safe."

"Couldn't you have gotten a family discount?"

"Or an earful when I cut his budget."

"True."

"Best to remove any entanglements. Anyway, I wanted to warn you that Barbara and Leslie say exactly what pops into their heads, without much filtering."

"That's interesting."

"Things might come out sounding like an insult, but I promise you, they won't mean it that way."

"I'll be fine," Kyle said, squeezing her shoulders as they maneuvered around wooden crates of shellfish blocking the sidewalk. Crowds intensified as they turned onto Mott Street, so they abandoned walking side by side. Rebecca grasped Kyle's hand and tried to lead him around shoppers and sidewalk displays until they reached the restaurant.

The place had a large window where pedestrians could watch the chef cooking inside. Glazed ducks and unfamiliar herbs hung from strings in the window, presumably just for decoration as Rebecca had never seen the cook use any of them. That same duck had been there for years, easily identified by the gimpy left wing.

Inside, the restaurant had no decorations save a colorful calendar on the wall over the cashier and the fragrant scent of garlic, sesame, and ginger. The remaining walls were white with mirrors on the top half. The black-and-white octagonal floor tiles had seen better days. Many were penetrated by yellow cracks, though they remained intact underfoot.

The dining area was one room, and the waitstaff accessed the kitchen through a pair of white Formica swinging doors with tempered glass portholes. Rebecca wondered how they decided which dishes the guy in the window prepared, but guessed it didn't really matter. The food had been consistently good every time they came, décor notwithstanding.

"Hey, you're here!" Barbara said, springing up to greet them. "Kyle, how are you? We met briefly on a trash run, not sure if you remember?"

"Sure, good to see you."

"Joe will be along soon, and Leslie is running a little late."

"No worries," Rebecca said, giving Barbara a kiss.

"While we wait, Mr. Kyle, let me get a good look at you," Barbara said, rounding the table and grasping Kyle firmly by both shoulders to spin him entirely around.

"Girl, he is one fine specimen. My birthday is coming up, you know? You can get me one of these."

"Liar. Your birthday is in November," Rebecca said as they all sat down. "And you forget that I was the one who got you the current 'tasty specimen.' Remember? The one on the way here?"

"Oh yeah!" she said, bursting into laughter.

"Almost done, Kyle. The lawyer in me just has to dig deep and ask the pressing questions everyone else is afraid to ask," Barbara said, unfurling an imaginary notepad and licking her imaginary pencil. "Question one: boxers or briefs?"

"Both."

"At the same time?"

"No, each for their own purpose. I also sometimes wear boxer-briefs." Kyle answered.

"Is this necessary?" Rebecca said, but was waved off.

"Question two: electric or manual razor."

"Electric," Kyle answered.

"Really? That's very interesting," Barbara answered, ticking off the answers on her invisible list.

"Deodorant or antiperspirant?" Barbara asked.

"Deodorant, of course," Kyle answered.

"Me too!" Rebecca blurted out. Kyle smiled in her direction but refocused on the inquiry.

"Final question: General Tso's or chicken with broccoli," she asked in a slow, deliberate voice.

"That's tricky," Kyle said, playing along. "General Tso's, definitely."

"You have chosen wisely, young Kyle. You have passed the test."

"What the hell was that?" Rebecca asked Barbara. "General Tso's or chicken with broccoli? Boxers or briefs? You certainly didn't give this a lot of thought, did you?"

"I was in court all day, okay? I'll have a better list next time."

Rebecca turned around in time to see Leslie exhale a puff of smoke and toss a cigarette down to the ground before entering the restaurant.

"Since when is Leslie smoking?" Rebecca whispered across the table to Barbara.

"Just act normal; I'll tell you about it later," Barbara answered.

Leslie approached the table with a slightly forced smile. "Hey, everyone. Sorry I'm late. My car hit traffic." She stooped to give kisses around and then noticed Kyle. "Hey, you're Kyle! My goodness, Becca, he is WAY cute," she added before sitting.

"No wonder she's been hiding him. I'd hide him too." Leslie slid across the remaining empty seat to Barbara before remembering that Kyle was within earshot. Leslie glanced up and offered him a smile. Which Kyle returned, shaking his head.

"What's so funny?" Rebecca asked.

"New Yorkers are awesome. It just takes getting used to the

directness again. Out west, folks will think things all day long, but only speak honestly after slinking away to whisper in the corner. Here, everything is right out in the open."

"I think we're unusually direct, even for New Yorkers," Barbara said.

"I have to agree, I work with professional hustlers all day long," Leslie added.

"Me too, sorry," Rebecca said.

"Well, that's okay. It's entertaining if nothing else," Kyle answered.

"What happened to Joe?" Leslie asked.

"I don't know. I was a little fuzzy on the directions. Maybe I'll go look outside to see if I see him wandering around," Rebecca said, sliding out of her chair. "Barbara, can you come with?"

"Okay," Barbara said, rising. "Kyle, Leslie is a journalist. I'm sure she'll have more fun questions for you."

Rebecca could hear the two chatting as they walked toward the restaurant door and stepped out.

"What's up?" Barbara asked.

"We decided to take the intimacy thing slow."

"Okay?"

"At the end of tonight, he'll likely want to, you know. And the trouble is, I will too."

"And that's a… problem?"

"Yes."

"Why?"

"He knows about my problem, but experiencing it live and in-person is something different. I'm still nervous he'll change his mind and dump me."

"Becca, that's ridiculous. He really likes you."

"Exactly. That's why I need you to keep us apart at the end of the night."

"How am I supposed to do that?"

"You're the brains in this operation. I hadn't gotten that far," Rebecca said, twirling a curl and tucking it behind her ear.

"You could have given me some notice."

"Well, I know you do your best work thinking on your feet."

"True. Okay, I'll think of something. But you'll have to go along, even if you want to get into HIS pants. Right?"

"Yes, exactly."

"You're lucky I love you, you know."

"Yes, I know."

"I'm going back in to think. You wait for Joe," Barbara said, returning to the table.

Rebecca dialed Joe's phone. It rang only once before he answered.

"Where in the hell is this place? I've been up and down Mott Street a thousand times," Joe said above blaring traffic.

"Where are you now?" Rebecca asked.

"I'm near the corner of Mott and Pell. Where are you?"

Rebecca looked up and saw the address number of the restaurant. "We're at 77 Mott Street, just south of Canal. I'd pronounce the name for you, but I can't read Chinese. The restaurant has a yellow sign with red letters, and there's a window in front where you can see the chef cooking."

"Is there a sassy gal with a black dress out front?" Joe asked.

"Huh?" Rebecca said before realizing that he was standing next to her, still on the phone, "I don't know about sassy, but definitely hungry!" she said into the phone. They both hung up.

"Sorry about the directions," Rebecca said.

"That's okay. I got an intimate tour of Mott Street that I will not soon forget. I was almost attacked by an angry old man who started yelling at me after I passed his store for the eightieth time."

"Before we go inside, I've asked Barbara to help me with something tonight. Just play along, yes? Not sure yet what Barbara is planning, but I presume we'll know when it happens."

"You ladies certainly keep things interesting," Joe said as he held the door open for her.

"Hey there," Barbara said, craning her neck for the kiss she knew was coming.

Joe obliged, then turned to Kyle.

"I'm Joe," he said, reaching across the table to shake hands. "Glad to have some testosterone along for the ride tonight."

Joe sat down between Leslie and Barbara and slid his briefcase under his seat.

"That was one long week!" he said, clapping his hands together and rubbing them eagerly. "Drinks? Drinks? Nothing yet? Oh, we can't have that." Joe hailed the waiter and orchestrated the table's drink order.

"Joe, you're such a charmer. In a matter of seconds, you've whipped us all into shape," Rebecca said.

"That's why they pay me the big bucks, you know." Joe smiled. "But despite your flattery, I will not be expensing dinner tonight."

"This is bullshit. I'm leaving," Leslie joked, jumping to her feet and tossing down her napkin.

"I got a load of crap the last time; so you fine folks can pay for your own damn Wonton soup."

"Tre harsh." Rebecca smiled and have ger hair a toss.

"Are we going to get a bunch of stuff and share?" Kyle asked, scanning the large menu.

"I don't much like sharing, but don't let me stop you guys from doing it," Barbara answered without averting her eyes from her menu.

"Why doesn't everyone get what they want, and whoever wants to share, can share," Joe suggested.

Folks nodded in assent, and they were off to the races.

Drinks were served, dinner ordered, and the waiter immediately returned to pass around cups of tea and those wide, puffed, greasy noodles that Rebecca loved. She reached for one, dipped it in the orange Duck Sauce, and popped it in her mouth.

Bowls of Wonton soup swimming in golden broth arrived next. Rebecca inhaled the flavorful steam before dipping her spoon in. She usually got Hot and Sour, but switched allegiances when she ate there. The Wonton was just that good. Rebecca took great pride in ordering Hot and Sour when everyone else was getting Wonton. Hot and Sour oozed sophistication. She could not fathom why anyone would eat Egg Drop soup. It was just plain nasty. The broth was the color of yolks and those thin shreds of egg looked pre-eaten. Just the thought of it made her queasy. The only person she had ever met who liked Egg Drop was Darcy.

Leslie sat staring at the door, twirling her napkin.

"So, what's up with the smoking thing?" Rebecca asked after

draining her bowl.

"Cravings come when I'm stressed, and it's been super stressful at work. It's hard not to bring the job home."

She leaned in to Rebecca. "Mind if we talk outside."

Rebecca rose. Kyle glanced up briefly but returned to his conversation with Barbara and Joe. Once outside, Leslie stuck a cigarette stick loosely between her lips and rummaged through her bag for some matches. The matchbook she found was from a bar called Arrow. It wasn't far from Kyle's warehouse in Hell's Kitchen.

"Why do you have matches from Arrow?"

She took a drag and head flicked Rebecca to come closer while blowing the smoke sideways away from her face.

"I've been investigating a sex trafficking ring; very dark stuff. It's taken me to some seedy places. If I'm just sitting there doing nothing, I stick out like a sore thumb. I started smoking again to kill time. Unfortunately, my undercover work has been a bit too convincing," she said, a smokey exhale escaping her nostrils and mouth.

"Is it safe?" Rebecca asked.

"Not exactly, but it's hard to get the information for the story without hobnobbing with some shady characters. Some of my informants look out for me and steer me away from the worst of the worst. I'm trying to minimize my field work, but it's unavoidable."

"How much longer?"

"I found most of what I need with database searches and visits to archives. Fascinating stuff. I enjoy that far more than slogging around taping interviews. But, I need a few witnesses to pull it all together."

"Be careful."

"My editor knows when I'm out in the field, and we even notify the police sometimes. But, that's not always safe depending on the story, as you never know who's on the take."

"Try not to go too far down the rabbit hole."

"Always," Leslie said, but her mind was already elsewhere.

"You up for something fun after dinner?"

"We'll see. I don't want to bring everyone else down…"

"Absolutely not, you're staying, and you WILL have a good time. Look, our food just arrived. Let's go eat," Rebecca said.

Leslie ground her butt out under foot, and they returned to the table. Barbara and Joe had switched seats, and Kyle and Joe were deeply involved in some conversation. Barbara looked up from her phone.

"We're all good here," she said to Rebecca, with a wink.

"Really?"

"Yes."

"Okay, then let's eat!" Rebecca said.

The group bantered as they passed around various dishes, fumbled through fortune cookies, and divided up the check. Karaoke was the unanimous choice for a next stop, so they began the short walk over.

Kyle had become fast friends with Joe, and the two were way ahead of the rest of them, laughing loudly. Rebecca, Leslie, and Barbara walked behind, periodically stopping to inspect shop windows.

At the bar, they took a large horseshoe-shaped booth in full view of the stage where the tallest, most masculine Chinese woman Rebecca had ever seen was singing with a sweet voice completely at odds with her appearance. There was a large projection screen behind her, flashing fuzzy video images and lyrics for the Chinese tune she sang. Knowing the lyrics well, she sang with her eyes closed, thoroughly owning the performance.

"I wish I could understand what she was saying. It sounds really good," she whispered to Kyle, though with the loudspeaker system, she could have yelled, and no one would have heard.

Cheers erupted when the song finished. Joe jumped to his feet and let out a loud whistle with his pinkies, clapping like a maniac.

"Yeah!" he yelled.

Rebecca shot Barbara a glance. She looked away, trying not to laugh. Joe was the most reserved, polished guy she knew, so this outburst was totally out of character. Things were afoot.

"So, what do you think of this place?" Rebecca asked Kyle, reaching across his shoulder to play with his hair.

"It's very red."

"Red?"

"Red walls, red upholstery, ceiling, tables lamps, carpeting. Very red."

She hadn't even noticed, but now she couldn't unsee it. Beyond the redness, there was a long black lacquer bar that ran the length of the room along the left wall ending at the man-lady's booth. It was the only non-red item in the place. The stage at the rear was a plain section of parquet floor, lit by overhead lights. The red paper lanterns over the tables illuminated the thick, white smoke emanating from every patron save those alongside Rebecca. The ashy-smelling fog swirling around them made Rebecca question the effectiveness of whatever fire alarm system the bar used.

The next few singers were drunk and off-key, which even their Chinese couldn't disguise. They laughed as they scanned the Karaoke selection list in indecipherable Chinese characters and asked the server to bring a list in English, to which he both nodded and rolled his eyes. Kyle and Joe were still at it, but it didn't stop Kyle from inching his hand up her thigh under the table.

This was the exact scenario she predicted. Moving his hand would draw attention to the fact that it was there in the first place. If she didn't move it, she was liable to drag him under the table herself. She plastered a smile on her face, doing her best to ignore her mounting arousal as his fingers lapped the edges of her panties.

Meanwhile, Leslie seemed to be loosening up. She was the first of the group to attempt a song, selecting *A Kiss From a Rose* by Seal. It played alongside random photographic vistas of mountains, valleys, fields of flowers, and crashing waves.

Barbara smiled and shook her head. "She's awful!" she said.

"Yeah, but it's good to see her up there blowing off some steam."

"She tell you about her undercover work?"

"Yeah, I'm glad she agreed to come. She needed this."

Next, the man-lady retook the stage for another Chinese selection. Rebecca was lost in her voice, and her mounting sensations in her body. Her arm instinctively draped across the booth behind Kyle, her fingers playfully tangling in his hair.

243

Barbara's eyes nearly popped out of her head.

"What are you doing?" she mouthed across the table.

Kyle leaned into her for a quick kiss.

"Your turn for a song!" Barbara yelled, yanking Rebecca out of the booth.

"Wait, what?" Rebecca said to Barbara as she pushed her onto the stage.

"I had to get you away from him. You asked for this, remember?"

"Yeah, but—"

"No, yeah but. You sing, or at least pretend to."

Rebecca hit the stage just as the song Barbara picked began: *It's Raining Men* by The Weather Girls. She took the mic handed to her by the hostess and faced the crowd.

Colored spotlights backlit the smoke, rendering the room impenetrable.

Spotlight. People watching. Just like the study.

Rebecca froze.

The music played on, the screens hanging from the ceiling scrolled lyrics.

People whistled and clapped, cheering her on.

"…half-past ten…." Rebecca whispered into the mic.

Before she knew it, Kyle was next to her, holding a second mic singing the anthem to her while pantomiming the lyrics.

"tall, blonde…strong… mean," Kyle sang the lyrics to her with abandon.

She hid her face, but the crowd loved Kyle's antics. He sang, circling her, then grabbed her hand to twirl her while he sang. The craziness of it all made her lift the mic and join in.

Claps thundered in time with the music until they sang the last refrain as a duo. Cheers erupted. Kyle bowed, and she curtsied, before leaving the floor to make way for the next singer.

"Thanks for saving me," she said.

"Anytime," he answered, planting a kiss on her waiting lips.

"Bathroom run," Barbara and Leslie said, linking her elbows and pulling her along with them.

"Hey!" Rebecca protested.

Inside the single-stalled room, the music muted enough to speak.

"You, my dear, are making this very difficult," Barbara said. "We have a plan. I'm keeping my end of the bargain."

"Becca, you need to try, at least a little, not to jump his bones. We are in public."

"You're right. Sorry. But you see what I'm up against. It's not easy."

"When we get back to the table, we're going into execution mode. Please. Go along with it and we'll get everyone home safe and you lovers away from each other. Deal?"

"Yes. Sorry. I totally owe you."

The trio returned to the table, and Rebecca slid back next to Kyle, keeping her hands to herself.

"All good?" he asked.

"Yup."

"Yes, this is nuts, this place. Joe is totally entertaining, and he knows like every single athlete on the planet having been at SI for so long. He's full of stories."

"Yes, Joe is certainly entertaining."

On cue, Joe picked up his empty scotch glass and wiggled it at the waiter. Barbara lowered his arm and canceled the order with a stern stare.

"Think you've had enough for tonight."

"What? No, it's Friday! I'm just starting to loosen up!"

"You're so loose you're slipping out of your pants," Barbara said.

"What about my pants?" Joe said, looking down, confused.

"Sweetie, I think we'd better go."

"What do you mean?"

"It's time we headed home."

"No, no, no. Kyle and I are talking. Aren't we, Kyle?"

"We were, but we can pick it up another time."

"But I wanted to show you my signed memo-ra-bilia?" Joe slurred.

"Maybe next time," Kyle said, putting his arm around Rebecca's shoulders.

"No, let's go. Let's go now. I can show you." Joe was looking around, trying to slide out but was blocked on both sides by his table mates. Meanwhile, Barbara had grabbed the check and was signing for it.

"Kyle, dear. I know we just met, but I'd be forever grateful if you could help us get home. Looks like Joe drank a little too much, and we live on the third floor of a brownstone. I'm not sure I can get him home alone."

"Um." Kyle looked at Rebecca.

Rebecca looked at Joe, whose head was resting on Barbara's shoulder. He winked imperceptibly. It was enough.

"Hey, Barbara. Why don't I come with you instead? Kyle has his motorcycle here, and it's not in a terribly secure spot. Would that work? I think the two of us can manage."

"No, he's too heavy. I can do it. The bike will be okay until tomorrow."

"Rebecca's right. If you don't want that bike stripped for parts overnight, best you get it home," Leslie said.

"We can manage," Barbara added. "Kyle, this is so unlike Joe. It's embarrassing."

"No worries. Who hasn't gotten a bit wrecked from time to time? It happens," Kyle said.

"Let's talk tomorrow, yes?"

"Sure."

Kyle drew Rebecca in with one arm for a long, deep kiss. Parts of her soul melted. Rebecca opened her right eye to the stern glances of Joe and Barbara. She pulled away.

The group headed outside, and Rebecca hailed a cab while Kyle and Barbara held up Joe, who was doing a bang-up acting job.

"Kyle, wait till you see my collllleeeection of sports memorabilia."

"Not tonight, sweetheart. You're not going anywhere but to bed," Barbara interrupted.

"NO!"

"Joe, Kyle has to drive his motorcycle home tonight. Maybe next time," Rebecca said, opening the taxi door.

"Hey, I have a great idea! I'll drive Kyle's bike back for him,"

Joe offered.

"Great idea. Let's get in the cab, and we can talk all about it. Rebecca, you get in first, and we can get him in the middle," Barbara said.

"Sure," Rebecca said, climbing in and mouthing "sorry" to Kyle from over the prone body of Joe.

"Thanks, Kyle. It was great meeting you." Barbara gave Kyle a brief kiss on the cheek, kissed Leslie goodbye, climbed in the cab, and they were off.

Rebecca watched the sad forms of Kyle and Leslie standing together, before the two shook hands and went their separate ways. She turned around to face forward.

"Thanks, guys," Rebecca said.

"Don't mention it," Joe said, sitting up and adjusting his shirtsleeves, "Was I good or was I good?"

"Both." Barbara smiled, and the two kissed. "Very convincing."

"What now?" Rebecca asked.

"Well, we'll drop you off at your apartment, and you'll keep your lights off. That way, when he arrives, he won't know you're home."

"Can't I just sleep over at your apartment?"

Joe and Barbara exchanged a knowing look.

"Not tonight. Just because you're not getting busy doesn't mean no one else is."

Chapter 27

The sputtering engine of the mailman's truck whirring away drifted in through the open window. After a visual confirmation, Rebecca slipped on a pair of laceless sneakers and raced down the stairs. The Magic Wand package was already a day past the expedited shipping date. If there was no package notice in her box, she'd have some choice words for their shipping department on Monday. Amazon had spoiled her with their instant delivery.

She turned her key and smiled as she grasped the few envelopes surrounding the canary yellow slip. The box was checked for her to pick up the package at the Twenty-Third Street post office. There used to be a closer one, but it closed. Sure it was small, forlorn, and had inconvenient hours, but "consolidating" post offices still seemed like an odd concept. The same thing was happening to hospitals in Manhattan. Former pillars of the neighborhood boarded up or converted to luxury condos. She exhaled the negative energy. Today required positive thinking.

Heading out, a pit formed in her stomach. She couldn't avoid Kyle forever. Her hasty escape with Barbara and Joe the night before only bought her two days, tops. She palmed her phone to check for text messages. Nothing; no emails either. It was 1:25 p.m.

She furrowed her brow. Maybe her plan hadn't been as covert as she thought. But it was for their own good. Taking it slow with him across the hall was a tall order. A little help and distance were best. But not too distant. With a smile, sunshine, and magnetism oozing from every pore, she'd have no chance of keeping him if hotties started snooping around. Hopefully, her package would make cloak-and-dagger games a thing of the past.

At Third Avenue, she turned uptown, passing a pharmacy that had once been a toy store. The stationary store where she bought Hello Kitty stickers in fifth grade was now a chic café, the bakery had become a dry cleaner, the restaurant was still a restaurant, but had changed over six times since she was ten. It was hard to pass the thresholds of these "new" businesses without pangs of regret. Neighborhood loyalty runs deep.

Saturday window service at the post office was reduced to two agents. Patrons ahead of her in the line juggled stacks of packages, waiting for the woman at the counter to quit fussing over stamps and make her choice: flowers or flags. Despite the inconvenience, Rebecca could relate. She did the same thing herself back in December.

Christmas, with all its sparkle, bows, and trimmings, was her favorite holiday, and she dove into it in a way she wasn't able to growing up. Her mother took her adopted Jewishness very seriously and gave her hell if her holiday cards looked too "Christian." Olivia Sloane had rejected rural tree trimming and snow scenes, *Shoebox* joke cards about elves, *Peanuts* cards, Santas, and elves. Apparently, Rebecca hit pay dirt the year she'd sent a silver and blue card with snowflakes. In the end, she bought holiday stamps for most, and a separate Jewishy book for her family and immediate relatives. That way, Rebecca would be safe if her mom was out visiting and saw her card among someone else's holiday mail.

"Next!" the agent called.

Rebecca approached and handed the agent her slip, who then disappeared into the back to retrieve the box.

Then, Rebecca had a panicked thought. *The packaging.* Would it be a plain brown wrapper, or would it have MASTURBATION VIDEO AND VIBRATOR plastered across the label? Or worse yet, be the photographed carton with a shipping label slapped on. How could she walk through the streets with that? Why hadn't she thought to bring a bag?

Drumming her fingers on the counter, she half-smiled at the woman next in line. She leaned over the counter to see if she could see the agent approach.

The "naughty" magazines she'd ordered with friends in college came in opaque black plastic wrappers showing nothing. But everyone knew what was inside just the same. The privacy wrapper almost defeated the purpose of hiding the recipient's privacy. Almost. She'd kill for a black wrapper right about now.

As the agent sashayed back, she gave the bouncing Rebecca an odd look. She slid the package across the counter: plain white plastic shipping bag wrapped loosely around a box within. Disaster averted.

"The bathroom is behind the PO Boxes."

"Huh?" Rebecca answered.

"The bathroom," she said, tilting her head with raised eyebrows.

"Oh, I don't… Thanks," Rebecca said, taking her package.

I'm an absolute freak. Calm down.

The box was heavy, considering. She gathered the bag into a makeshift handle, swinging it as she walked. It's just a package. It could be anything on the planet; it could be new shoes.

Keep moving.

Each time Rebecca hit a red light, she crossed the street in the other direction. She sailed through her open lobby door. Neighbors waited for the elevator carrying bags of their own, including Mrs. Portnoy. There was no way Rebecca was going to ride up in an elevator with her wandering eyes. She could probably scan the bar code on the shipping label and tell what was inside the box. Rebecca smiled to all as she passed the elevator bank en route to the stairs. Mrs. Portnoy's mouth silently opened and closed a few times like a fish before snapping shut.

Rebecca hoofed it up the stairs and was inside her apartment before she heard the elevator pass. She closed the door, bracing it with her back, her shirt sticking to the light sweat trickling down her back.

Grabbing scissors, Rebecca sliced open the end of the bag, careful not to penetrate the cardboard box within. Once opened, she slid out the box to find it sealed within a second opaque plastic wrapper. At this point, she almost wished for less packaging.

"Holy shit, you're giant," Rebecca said to the device as she slid it out of the box.

Nearly a foot long, the device was entirely white. She held the hard plastic shaft in her right hand, assessing the weight. Its bulbous head, covered in a leathery-plastic, was filled with some kind of gel. Rebecca depressed her finger, but it yielded reluctantly. Firm. Halfway down the shaft was a black cradle switch with high and low settings. The cord was neatly coiled and bound with a twist tie.

"A lot less threatening than the crap at the Pink Kitten."

Rebecca set it down and the tossed the loose packaging materials around until she found the DVD at the bottom of the bag. The jacket pictured black silhouetted profiles of three women against a hot pink background, backs arched, mouths open.

She smirked as she read the title: *Fulfilled, with Heidi Quinn.*

"This better not be more BS," she said, using her fingernails to rip off the tight plastic wrapper. Leaving her packing mess on the floor, she walked to the living room and popped the disk into the DVD player, checking the television volume to be sure it was as low as humanly possible.

The screen filled with a woman who identified herself as Heidi Quinn. She was the epitome of Irish, with fair, freckled skin and wavy red hair streaked with gray. Closeups revealed deep-set wrinkles around her eyes and mouth, creased in all the "happy" places. She was likely in her mid- to late-fifties. Rebecca sat back, shoulders relaxing. At least this gal looked experienced. Rebecca's past forays into self-help materials were penned by those so young their success could as easily have been luck as skill.

Heidi stood in her studio, a mostly bare room with plush carpet and pillows on the floor; two small sofas faced each other in the background. The unadorned walls were a pale peach color, which harmonized with the pale woods of the coffee tables and trim. Heidi wore a black unitard, black flats, and spoke in a calm, confident voice. It was only a first impression, but those count too.

"Orgasms are not a Holy Grail reserved for a lucky few, leaving the rest to either pine away hopelessly, or worse, not pine at all. Sex is as important to life as food or air. And it can be enjoyable for all women given the right techniques, practice, and commitment. Today we will visit with three of my clients who each came to me suffering with difficulty achieving orgasms. They left feeling whole and empowered to take on the challenge of their sexual gratification."

"You've got my attention."

Bright sun was streaming in, so Rebecca drew the shade to make the TV screen more visible.

Woman number one was called Stephanie, she was a forty-five-year-old mother of three whose marriage had suffered because of her lack of interest in sex. She was attractive, tall, and slender with the supple limbs of someone naturally thin who probably never exercised a day in her life. She had blonde hair, and her pale skin was covered with a visible layer of perspiration.

Who wouldn't be nervous under those circumstances?

"Why don't you want to have sex with your husband?" Heidi asked.

"Why should I? What's in it for me? He thrusts away and is done, and I'm left feeling frustrated and used. For me, it's better to avoid the whole mess entirely."

"Do you ever masturbate?"

"Goodness, no. I don't even know how," Stephanie chortled.

"What brought you to me? Why are you here?"

"I love my husband, but I think our marriage won't last if we can't get

past this sex situation. I owe it to both of us to try."

"It's good you came to me. I'll walk you through a series of masturbation exercises that should help you to feel the wonderful sensations that your husband experiences. Then you can go home and share what you have learned and start a new sexual chapter in your marriage. Let's begin."

Stephanie changed into a black satin robe with red lining and returned to Heidi in the studio, her naked form clearly visible through the open front. Heidi positioned her on the floor with her head propped up on pillows. She talked Stephanie through a series of warm-up exercises where she explored her body and concentrated on the sensations—the same exercises Dr. Costa gave her. Rebecca folded her arms and kept watching.

The woman next explored her labia gently and periodically inserted her finger in her vagina to increase her vaginal lubrication. Heidi then instructed her to bend her knees, let her legs drop to the sides, and take some deep breaths. Heidi then handed her a Magic Wand to move around her body and feel the sensations while avoiding her vagina.

"Popular culture has taught us that the vagina is ground zero for organisms, but for most women, that's just not the case. The clitoris is the engine that makes this train run, and you have to nurture her gently until she is ready. For some, this takes quite a long time, an hour or more, for others, it is faster, but everyone is different, and there is no one right way."

That description made a lot more sense than anything the doctors ever said. The video had already paid off, she thought.

Stephanie resumed her exploration, using some situational fantasy scenarios that, from the sounds of it, were based upon preselected choices. Heidi gave her some lubrication, and she resumed her work, sliding her fingers around her labia and then closer to her clitoris until she was rubbing in a fast side to side motion with her fingers. Stephanie's breathing intensified. She moaned. Heidi encouraged her on. Finally, Stephanie moaned loudly, arched her back, and held herself taut for a moment frozen in space before collapsing, motionless, into her pillows.

Through the sobs, Stephanie spoke about the decades of lost life, for wasted time with her husband, and for her pre-orgasmic self who would never again walk the earth. Heidi congratulated her and spoke soothingly to explain all that had happened and help her to understand the process, so she could duplicate the results at home.

Heidi then walked Stephanie through the process again using the Magic Wand for clitoral stimulation, and she very easily repeated her orgasm from her already heightened state of arousal. This time Stephanie was jubilant, drunk on sensations, and desirous of more.

Rebecca paused the video as a tear escaped. Stephanie achieved her dream—a dream they shared and that many women shared. She stood to pace the living room, breathing, her mind a whirl. *Why this reaction from a video? She was acting like Stephanie was an old friend rather than an anonymous woman flickering on a screen.*

"How could it be so easy?" Rebecca said to the television.

"What had they done off-camera to get her ready beforehand?"

She resumed the video for the second woman called Margot. She was twenty-two and had never had sex because she was afraid of getting pregnant. She tried to masturbate on her own, but to no avail. Margot came from a very religious family and had no woman in her life to confide in about sexual issues.

"I see people having affairs and getting divorced because the husband and wife are not on the same page when it comes to the bedroom. I don't want it to be that way with me when I get married someday."

"You are smart for such a young woman. If more couples addressed their issues of sexual intimacy, far fewer would separate and divorce. Sex is a powerful bonding tool, and sexless couples often see a quick deterioration in their marriages. Many blame child rearing for their reduced sex drive, but more likely, it's a lack of effort or unequal priorities. Sex and the rituals surrounding foreplay take effort and occasionally planning, many don't make the effort because they have never experienced those sensations and don't know what they are missing."

"Can you help me?"

"No, but you can help yourself."

Heidi walked Margot through the same process as Stephanie. Heidi did the same things in the same order: light body exploration, focus on sensitive spots, bent knees, spread legs, vaginal penetration, incorporate fantasy, increased intensity, deep breathing, heightened fantasy, bingo!

Margot was so surprised by the intensity that she shrieked loudly and was embarrassed afterward. Heidi was pleased that Margot had abandoned her inhibitions and embraced the moment. Heidi demonstrated the work with the Magic Wand, but Margo's second orgasm wasn't as strong.

"I can tell your mind wandered; what were you thinking about?"

"I couldn't get my mind around that fact that I had finally had one. I was trying to think of all the girlfriends I would tell."

"How did that distraction affect your sexual sensations?"

"They were less strong. I didn't realize that my mind was so important to the whole affair."

"Your mind is almost more important than your clitoris. You must always focus on what you are feeling to get the maximum benefit. Think of something extremely arousing, some sexual scenario that turns you on. You can picture whoever you wish or whatever you wish. If you want to fuck a guy you saw once at Starbucks, have at it. Some women visualize the sensations as colors or heat radiating out and spreading throughout their bodies. Whatever works for you is great, but you must stay focused."

"I will. Thank you!"

This procedure seemed infallible. Rebecca wasn't necessarily learning anything books, doctors, and videos hadn't already taught her. But this woman put it all together and—most importantly— she removed the shame. Heidi made it okay to want an orgasm. More than okay, essential. Tears were streaming down Rebecca's face as the stories rolled on.

The third woman was Josie, aged thirty-four.

"I've had orgasms before, not the greatest, but I can only have them with a partner. I haven't dated anyone in forever, and I'd like to have an orgasm again."

"That problem is more common than you might think, Josie. What enables you to reach climax with a partner?"

"Well, there's usually some foreplay, sometimes lots of flirting for hours throughout the night, so I really get going. I can feel her twitching down there when I'm fully clothed sitting in a restaurant. Anyway, I've been fortunate to date guys that love oral sex, so I get to sit back and let them munch away. Sometimes I get really aroused by giving him oral sex. Anyway, by the time he penetrates, I've probably already had an orgasm from the oral and foreplay

alone. Now that I'm not dating anyone, I've been unable to duplicate that intensity on my own."

"This sounds like something that we can easily fix. It should begin with prolonged self-foreplay. You should feel free to use erotic videos, magazines, or books to help you get into the mood and set the stage for a role-play. Pick a character and a scenario you can focus on while you physically heighten the sensations with your hands and with a vibrator. Let's begin."

Heidi went through the same steps as with Stephanie and Margot, but helped Josie along in the fantasy department by having her speak her fantasy aloud, then asking probing questions to move the plot forward. She was in Josie's brain sharing her most intimate personal fantasies and witnessing their culmination in an intense orgasm that made Josie stiffen and scream aloud. This time, Heidi did not go for number two with the Magic Wand. Maybe they did that off-camera afterward, but Josie looked spent.

Rebecca shut off the DVD.

Should she try for one right now?

In a strange sense, she had already shared five orgasms with her sisters-in-arms. How could she possibly top that?

Chapter 28

The doorbell double rang.

Shit!

Rebecca stood naked from a shower with no exit plan. After the afternoon she'd had, she wanted sex more than anything. She threw on a robe to answer the door, opening it just wide enough to peep her head around.

"Hi," she said.

"I see you got home."

"Yeah, getting drunk was very unlike Joe. Sorry about that," Rebecca said, shifting a mass of curls behind her right ear.

"Can I come in?"

"Um. I'm not dressed."

"That's fine by me," Kyle said.

"Um."

"Are we okay?"

"What do you mean?"

"Hiding behind the door, escaping with Barbara. Something feels different."

"Northing's different."

"Can I come in, then?"

"Yes, of course." Rebecca stood back so Kyle could enter.

Kyle spun around to face her. "Did I do something wrong?"

"Oh no, really. It's me. I just…"

"Just what?"

"It's nothing."

"Well, it could be a lot of things, but it's not nothing."

"It's stupid."

"I'm all ears," Kyle said, sitting down on the sofa.

"I've been worried about being alone."

"With me?"

"Yes."

"You think I'm going to hurt you?"

"No, nothing like that."

"Then, what? Help me out here, Rebecca, because I'm lost."

Rebecca sat down next to him, legs folder under. "It's because of me."

He raised his eyebrows with an "and" look.

"I'm just going to blurt it out."

"Okay…" Kyle said with a smile.

"I think you're super-hot, and I can't really control myself around you."

Kyle's face erupted into a broad smile. "Is that so?"

"Yes."

"So, this coy thing is…?"

"For your protection."

"Well, that's a first." Kyle sat back, arms folded behind his head. "A girl trying to protect my honor."

Rebecca slouched. "I'm so glad you understand."

"But what if I don't want to be protected? My honor, that is. What then?"

"Um."

"Um, what?"

"You're really making me come clean, huh?"

"No more secrets."

"No more secrets. Got it."

Something about him made her melt into a puddle. She couldn't explain it. Telling him was suicide for their bedroom life, but not telling him would likely mean no bedroom life at all. She'd already used eight of their nine relationship lives in short order. She couldn't blow the last one. His blue eyes bore holes in her defenses.

Rebecca squinted. "I've also been told that I'm not very good. You know. In bed."

"I don't believe it."

"It's true. My last boyfriend said so."

"Really?"

"Yes.

"Well, I've never met him, but I can tell he was a putz."

Rebecca laughed. "Yes, he is. Was. A putz. He's the royal king of putzes."

"I don't take dating advice from the putzes."

Kyle had lifted her onto his lap. Cupping Rebecca's head, he drew her in for a deep kiss.

His scent filled her senses. She sat back, staring into his celestial eyes.

"Are you sure?" she asked.

"Are you?"

"I'm not sure about anything anymore."

They kissed again. Kyle slid his hands inside her robe. He caressed her shoulders and passed his lips ever-so-lightly over her breasts. Rebecca arched into his embrace, and he drew closer. She wrapped one leg around him and could feel him growing hard in his pants. Rebecca reached down to unfasten his zipper, but he moved her hand away and continued to nibble her neck.

Rebecca closed her eyes to focus on the sensations of his soft lips on her body. No one had ever spent this much time just kissing her neck, ears, and face. Her clit pulsed, begging for attention.

Kyle gradually moved south, kissing Rebecca's collar bones until getting thwarted by the bathrobe which constrained her arms. He rectified that by removing the robe, and she sat up slightly to assist in the maneuver. Rebecca reached to his waist, grabbing for the bottom edges of his T-shirt. Kyle intervened, removing it with one graceful motion.

Rebecca gasped. It was the most magnificent torso she had seen outside of *GQ*. She devoured his chest with her eyes. It was the first time she caught him relishing his hotness. He knew that his smooth olive skin, toned chest, and tight abs were impressive. Rebecca ran her hands across his body from his abs up to his shoulders before grabbing him and pulling him down on top of her.

She wrapped him with her legs, and he cupped Rebecca's bottom, gently squeezing it and pulling her in closer to him. She was lost in her senses when Kyle suddenly stood up with Rebecca clamped on.

"It's time for me to see your bedroom," he said, carrying her down the hall and depositing her onto the bed with a bounce. He scrambled out of his clothes and shoes, crawled on top of her.

Rebecca rolled over on top of him and smiled down. He smiled back and gently slid her forward, so she was sitting on his face with her elbows resting on the headboard.

This is new…

She never liked guys to do oral sex, and Ethan had never tried. Rebecca closed her eyes and mind, focusing only on sensations. His tongue was flicking, exploring her. Warm and wet, just the thought that the warm wetness was coming from Kyle was…

Mmmm!

Should I be doing something for him?

Am I being selfish?

She reached her arms back for his head, but it was useless; out of reach.

She returned her arms to the headboard, letting him probe and tickle away. He caressed her thighs, then moved his arms up her belly to her breasts, squeezing lightly, pinching her nipples, again, and again and again…

Quick as lightning, tingles radiated outward from her core, up her face and down her arms to her fingertips.

"Oh my God!" Rebecca yelled. Jerking backward, she windmilled her arms before reverse-somersaulting over Kyle, falling off the bed completely.

"Ouch!" she said.

"What was that?" Kyle asked, sitting up, laughing. He wiped his glistening mouth with the back of his hand.

"I'm not sure. I've never felt anything like that before." Rebecca struggled out of her tangled landing position. "I'm so sorry."

"Don't be sorry. I didn't hurt you, did I?"

"No. Quite the opposite," Rebecca said, standing to rub her rump where a bruise was mobilizing. "I told you I was bad at this."

Kyle rested his hands on Rebecca's hips and flopped her back down on the bed.

"Well, I don't want to brag, but I usually have that effect on the ladies."

"Lucky me," she said with a smile.

Rebecca wasn't keen on kissing him after oral, but he had no reservations. She could taste her own saltiness, but having just emerged from the bath before he arrived, that was the extent of it. She would have to remember this bathing before sex thing. It made post-oral kissing much better.

They kissed some more, and this time he let her hand wander and stay on his hardness. Hot and firm, with a smooth tip. A few drops of semen escaped from the tip. Rebecca slid her finger through the wetness and around his helmet before firmly grasping his shaft and working her hand a bit. He let out a deep growl then gently removed her hand, lifted her by the waist, and was about to fit her on him when she slid sideways.

"Shouldn't we put?"

"Sorry, got carried away. Do you have any?"

"Condoms? I don't."

Close call. Condoms were the only thing she could depend on Ethan for.

"I can go get some."

"No. We should stop."

"For real?"

"It's best," Rebecca replied.

"That's not the word I'd use. We're right in the middle here…"

"It's a sign. By the time you get back, the mood will be gone."

"That can be rectified," he said, motor purring.

"Kyle."

"I may have some in my apartment?"

Rebecca made a pained face.

Kyle raised an eyebrow.

"Let's not."

Kyle exhaled loudly and rolled on his side, flashing a crooked smile of futility. "You do realize you're giving me a serious case of blue balls?"

"Not having balls, I wouldn't risk making a diagnosis."

"It's not good. Trust me."

"Thanks for understanding."

"I don't understand. But I'll respect your decision."

"Thanks."

Kyle smothered his face in a pillow. Rebecca lifted it off and kissed him tenderly, no tongues.

"Mind if I have a shower?"

"Help yourself."

Kyle scampered out of bed, scratching his head with both hands. He paused at the doorway, "You definitely keep things interesting."

He entered the bathroom and closed the door. Rebecca heard the water turn on and the shower curtain slide closed.

"I hope I'm worth it."

Chapter 29

It was there, and then it was gone. The blood coursing through Rebecca's ears began to subside. Her pounding heartbeat slowed. She swallowed hard. The Magic Wand wasn't so magic after all. It was just an odd-looking and useless piece of plastic and wire. She released it through her fingers, its cord slipping until it hit her bedroom floor with a dull thud.

She rolled on her side, gathering the sheets over her naked form in a messy pile.

"What a waste. What an awful, awful waste," she whispered into the darkness.

She was a dysfunctional, sexual mess. No guy wants that. And as much as Kyle was worlds apart from her ex, he was still a guy. A sexual being who wants a partner of equal caliber. She played a good game, but she was an impostor. A fraud. He'd learn it soon enough and be gone. Like all the others.

A sob escaped, but she curled the pillow around her head and squeezed tight with both palms. Her chest heaved, then bitter acid burped up her throat.

"Arrhhgh!" Rebecca said, tossing the pillow aside.

Her feet stomped across the carpet to the bathroom. She turned on the cold water, cupping her hand under the stream of water to drink.

She gulped, water dripping in sheets down her chin and neck, before dribbling between her breasts and splattering on the tile floor.

Rebecca dabbed her body dry with a towel and stuffed it back into place. The puddle would dry.

She dropped on the edge of her bed, pulling the quilt around her. The room was dark, but the windowpanes cast parallel bars on the ceiling.

"I'm in a fucking prison. A prison that I can't escape no matter what I do."

A taxi passed, bleaching the shadows with halogen blueness, before retreating down the street. She shuffled to the window, quilt dragging like a robe. Kyle's parking spot was still empty.

Her bed was empty.

Her life was empty.

She walked to the living room and lifted the remote. But put it down.

Rebecca sat on the sofa, pulling the quilt tight.

What now?

Everything around her represented the carcass of the life her parents built together. A married life. A happy life. But it was theirs.

She deserved a life too. Her own. With a mate. To build something lasting. To have adventures; maybe one day have children.

I deserve to be happy.

I deserve to be whole.

Rebecca reached for her laptop on the coffee table. Lifting the lid, the machine woke out of sleep mode. Her eyes blinked to adjust.

In the browser she typed "Heidi Quinn," then clicked on the recently visited web page that populated first.

"So, Heidi, do you have a section for losers?"

Her eyes scanned the navigation menu.

"Holy shit."

A header said: Private Lessons.

How could she have missed it?

She clicked it and the page loaded.

"I have created a series of books and videos to help each client independently reach her own sexual fulfillment. However, should you decide you require individualized attention, I offer a very limited number of personal one-on-one coaching sessions for individuals and couples. Please call the reservation number for more information."

She looked up, then back. Blinking, clearing her eyes. Putting the open computer on the coffee table, Rebecca tossed off her quilt and strode to the kitchen. Opening the junk drawer, she shifted napkins, menus, and takeout soy sauce packets around until she found a pen. She returned and wrote Heidi's number on a notepad retrieved from her briefcase and underlined it twice. No way she was going to forget the number at home when she went to work the next day. Capping the pen, she lay down on the sofa, steepling her fingers.

Personalized coaching? Tailored to her? Could it really be that simple? The rational part of her brain said that she should be able to handle this masturbation crap like everyone else: alone in a dark room. She looked around her. She was alone in a dark room, yet had been powerless to break down whatever mental barrier was standing in the way of her having an orgasm. She was obviously doing something wrong. But what?

Heidi would know. She'd done it before—it was the only way.

Goose bumps formed on her skin, so she drew the quilt over her shoulders. A beam of light from an adjacent apartment illuminated her face.

Dr. Costa popped to mind. Him and her chair in the spotlight. She'd jumped through so many hoops to achieve something so simple. So, human. What a mess it all was. She should have avoided fooling around with Kyle: it was too complicated. Confusing. Emotional. She wasn't ready. Their exception for her had been misplaced, as was their desire to peek in her bedroom. If anything, her romp with Kyle proved she wasn't ready.

Whatever happened felt fantastic, but was fast. Very fast. And very scary. It took her breath away, blew her mind, and incited panic, all at once. It was intense, but there were no crashing waves. No waves at all. No building and release. It happened in an instant. Her body responded to Kyle, but not fully. There was an important piece still missing.

But what is it?

She tapped her fingers.

Rebecca was a toddler driving a semi and had no business operating it unsupervised. An expert was needed to put it all together. Show her the ropes. What to do, what not to do. Answer questions. Sex was not a solitary activity. How was she supposed to learn how to do this on her own? The simple answer was she couldn't. It was impossible. She was lost without a map, compass, Sherpa, or GPS. Heidi would show her the way.

If all went well, tomorrow would mark the beginning of the end. The end of her brokenness, her isolation. Then, anything would be possible.

Chapter 30

Plumes of hot dog steam wafted over from the corner vendor's cart, triggering a tummy roll. Rebecca turned away, plugging her ear to muffle the traffic noise. Heidi Quinn's number rang and rang.

Voice mail triggered, so she hung up.

"This is not happening."

Rebecca approached the food cart.

"One hot dog, please."

Without looking up, the bearded man palmed a bun prewrapped in a paper napkin. Using tongs, he opened the stainless lid of the hot dog compartment, fished out a Sabrett, and popped it in a bun.

"Mustard, onions, sauerkraut, relish?" he asked.

"Nothing."

"Nothing?"

"Yes, bald."

He shook his head and handed it over. She paid two dollars and walked away.

Even street vendors were judging her.

Her first bite popped the crisp casing. Salty, garlicky goodness followed, putting her tummy grumbles to rest. She headed for the concrete planter in front of her office building and sat down, chewing while she redialed Heidi Quinn.

Whitney saw her and approached, but Rebecca waved her off.

Ring.

Ring.

"Heidi Quinn's office. This is Brad. Can I help you?"

"Oh, I do hope so!"

Brad laughed. "You don't know the half of it, sweetheart. What can we do for you?"

"I was hoping for an appointment with Ms. Quinn?"

"I'm sorry, but she has a lot of irons in the fire right now and is not taking any appointments."

"None?"

"Not a one."

"But, I was just on the site last night?"

"I'm a little behind updating the website. Thanks for reminding me, but we do have a wide selection of her videos."

"I've tried the videos. They didn't help."

"Sorry to hear that."

"Is there no chance of me seeing her?"

"Unfortunately, no. Heid's taking a break."

"A break? Well, that's great. When is she coming back?"

"That's the thing. She isn't. She's moving on to some new challenges and has a book in the works—"

"Brad, you don't understand. I'm desperate!" Rebecca yelled a little too loudly. Two amused businessmen walking by chuckled at her expense. She stuck her tongue out at their backs.

"Look, love. I hear you. I've worked for Heidi for years and know why women come here. But Heidi has made the difficult decision to follow another path."

"I'm in a really difficult situation here, is there any way that Heidi could make one final exception? One orgasm for the road?"

"As tempting as that sounds," Brad teased.

"Come on."

"Do you think I want to be here on the phone breaking hearts? Of course not. But she's my boss. What Heidi says goes, and Heidi is no longer taking private appointments."

"Maybe if I could talk to her?"

"That's out of the question."

Rebecca exhaled, "Is there nothing I can do?"

"I recommend trying again with the videos."

Back at her desk, Heidi Quinn stared out from Rebecca's computer screen. She had no events listed. No address. There was nowhere to show up and beg for mercy. Only Brad's insufferable "no."

Rebecca searched for past addresses and schools. Heidi Quinn graduated from Columbia University and got her PhD at Case Western, but beyond that, there were only articles. Article after article touting her miraculous track record helping the helpless. Women who had no other place to turn before they found her. Now where are those women supposed to go? Where was Rebecca supposed to go?

"Who's that?" Darcy asked.

Rebecca spun in her chair, blocking the screen with her torso.

"It's nothing."

"Be sure it is." Darcy stared down her nose. "Have you finished the print negotiations for Hollis Hotels?"

"Just about. I'm waiting to hear back from the last three magazines."

"What's the hold up?"

"Well, the preliminary estimates put us in a good position to afford a full-year campaign, but *Home Digest* is a big ticket 'must have,' so a lot will depend on their rate. Candlelight Publishing, after all."

Darcy winced.

"Exactly."

Candlelight Publishing was a bear to negotiate with, making everyone pay published rates. They only discounted based on the number of ads you bought, unlike other magazines who were open to haggling.

"I've asked to bundle other titles when estimating the frequency, add pages from *Fashionista*, *HomeBuzz*, and *Pantry* to get us a better rate. They said no, but I connected the client with the Candlelight events team, and the client is willing to offer them discounted room rates for their out-of-town company visitors to help stretch the budget a bit further. It's a long shot, but was worth a try."

She raised an eyebrow. "Bartering. That could save thousands."

"Potentially, yes." Rebecca smiled.

Darcy lifted her chin. "Very creative thinking."

"Thanks."

"Keep me in the loop."

"Of course."

Darcy wandered off toward her office, eyeglass arm clicking against her teeth.

Swiveling back, Heidi Quinn beamed from the screen. Confident, rebellious, defiant.

Then it clicked. Time for more creative thinking.

Chapter 31

Exiting the train at Broadway and West Seventy-Second Street, Rebecca scanned the masses around her. The Upper West Side masses. Tailored Brooks Brothers' suits and a stream of uber-casual twenty-somethings sporting head-to-toe ensembles with eye-popping price tags.

How can Barbara stand living up here?

She ran across the wide avenue to make the light, passing the Gray's Papaya on the corner. Totally out of place among streets lined with outdoor cafes and sparkling shop windows displaying overpriced everything. From clothes, eyeglasses, and shoes, to children's toys and pet gear, everything an affluent person could want. Rebecca paused outside a pet supply store. Stuffed dogs surfed, surrounded by the latest in sand toys for dogs.

Unbelievable.

She resumed walking. Even the air was fresher up here. Or maybe it was the proximity to Central Park. Greenery flooded the horizon as Rebecca turned the corner of West Seventy-Fourth Street and Columbus, heading toward Central Park West. Barbara's block.

It was a street lost in time: ruddy three-floor stone buildings lined both sides of the street, formidable stone stairs jutting out at regular intervals. Narrow strips of pavement lay between the bottom step and the 3x3 foot patches of earth hugging the curb. Each patch contained a frail maple tree, staked on both sides, and doing its darnedest to thrive amidst the concrete. Rebecca could picture the tree trembling as it shot out of the ground wondering, "How in the hell did I get here?" Even the pink impatiens ringing each trunk knew the trees had an uphill struggle; their own fate wasn't much better.

Pansies, begonias, or geraniums overflowed window boxes and planters. Black metal gates surrounded the stairs and front patios for some buildings, presumably to deter vagrants and provide a measure of added security. Other residents were creative with their small pieces of property. A few furnishing spaces with decorative floor tiles and potted plants, while others added planting beds, trees, and fountains. The opposite end of décor sported trash cans. Luckily, Barbara's landlord was on the floral end of the spectrum.

Barbara had not yet arrived, so Rebecca took a seat on her stone steps to wait and soak up the calm. Across the street, an older man in an undershirt and worn navy slacks belted around his protruding middle hosed down the pavement. He did his best to spray every speck of foreign matter off the sidewalk and down the nearby sewer grate. A few birds splashed and preened in the fountain next door.

"Aiden!"

A toddler scampered by, followed by a young mother navigating an overloaded stroller, doing her best to keep up.

Muffled avenue traffic was pierced by blue jay caws echoing off the buildings.

"...that is so not true..." a young woman said, eyes on the ground, hand in her boyfriend's back pocket. His hand slinked around her lanky frame and hung from her belt loop. Their steps were completely out of sync; one rising as the other fell. They were a total cloud of chaos and disharmony.

"Doesn't that look uncomfortable?" Barbara said, sneaking up on Rebecca while her attention was diverted.

"That's probably the root of their problem. Neither is secure enough to admit they should probably hold hands," Rebecca said, gathering her stuff and following Barbara up the steps.

"Have you been waiting long?" Barbara asked as she unlocked the exterior door and led the way inside the building.

"Not really. It was a welcome escape. Do you ever sit out there?"

"Are you kidding me? I'm sure the neighbors would love it if the loud Black girl hung out on the front steps with a big bottle of Colt 45."

"I didn't say anything about Colt 45. You could take a nice glass of Cabernet if you preferred," Rebecca said, noticing Barbara's skyscraper heels. "I still marvel you can walk around the city and up three flights of stairs with those stilettos."

"Nah, believe it or not, it hurts my feet more when I wear flats. I might blow out both knees by the time I'm sixty, but I'll look fabulous until then!" Barbara turned and momentarily struck a fierce pose on the stairs, snapping her fingers.

Rebecca laughed. "Oh yeah!"

"Mm-hmm," Barbara said with a sassy head flick while climbing ahead at a breakneck pace.

When Barbara reached the landing, she unlocked her apartment door, walked in, and left it open for her guest, now lagging behind. The apartment door was directly opposite the top of the stairs, and once she reached the landing, Rebecca could see inside Barbara's apartment and down the long central hallway to the bedroom. Rebecca entered and closed the door, dropping her handbag on the floor near the entryway table. Meanwhile, Barbara changed out of her work clothes and into shorts and a tank top. Rebecca couldn't remember the last time that she saw her out of a suit. Barbara walked around the apartment, dropping earrings, bracelets, and necklaces in random locations. Some habits never die.

"Where's Joe tonight?" Rebecca asked.

"He has a client dinner. Why don't you come hang in the kitchen while I chop veggies? I'll wait to put the meat on until Leslie gets here. It only takes a few minutes in the broiler." She walked over to her kitchen window and looked out.

"I wish I had a terrace right here," she said, motioning with parallel hands. "I could have a real grill. I mean, look at that view!"

Rebecca entered the small galley kitchen and squeezed by her friend to the window. Barbara had a point. There were green lawns of manicured grass where the brownstones from the next block abutted the back patios of the ones on Barbara's block. The contrasting greenery looked like a living patchwork quilt.

"One day," Barbara said while chopping onions, "I'll have a yard, and we can grill. Nothing fancy. Just a big patio with a pool, and we can sit in lounge chairs and chat, or float on those inflatable recliners with cup holders while sunning ourselves."

"You'll get there."

"Maybe so, but I'll not forget the little people I knew along the way. We can work out a visitation schedule so you won't have to mingle with all my new rich friends. I wouldn't want to subject you to that misery."

"How kind of you," Rebecca answered, rolling her eyes. Barbara dreamed big, but she had the confidence and work ethic to back it up.

Before long, Leslie arrived, and they left Barbara alone to finish her cooking. She was preparing chicken with a gorgeous salad and some sautéed potatoes she cooked with onion and rosemary.

"I miss that smell," Rebecca yelled from the living room. "Joe's a lucky guy."

"He is. And I remind him every chance I get!" Barbara laughed.

"How's it going with you two?" Leslie asked.

"Good, really good. A little different than I expected, but good."

"Different how?" Leslie asked.

Barbara walked to the kitchen doorway.

"I'm getting Joe 360 now. The full man. There's 'professional Joe,' 'my Joe' when we're alone, 'neighborhood Joe' when he's with buddies from childhood, and 'family Joe' when we're with his siblings and parents," she answered, making air quotes for each.

"That's a lot of Joes," Rebecca said.

"Yes. It is," Barbara answered, face expressionless, mind elsewhere.

"You okay?" Leslie asked.

"Yes." Barbara smiled.

Leslie and Rebecca exchanged a curious look.

"It's nothing, you guys. We're fine. I'm fine." She returned to the stove.

"The counselor dost protest too much," Leslie whispered.

"Yup," Rebecca said.

"This is delicious," Rebecca said after sampling each dish in turn. "You're such an overachiever. Salad dressing? You *made* salad dressing?"

"It's easier than you think."

"Why don't you cook for us all the time?" Leslie asked. "I would totally buy the ingredients. In fact, I think that I have bought these same ingredients, but they didn't come out so good as this," she said, motioning to her plate with her fork.

"I'd like that, but who has time to plan, shop, and prepare a meal? I'm lucky if I'm home by eight o'clock. Right, Becca?"

"Yeah, totally."

"Joe's schedule is completely random and he has client dinners several times a week. And I hate cooking alone. I used to cook with my mom all the time. She started as a lousy cook but taught herself over time out of necessity."

"You couldn't tell she wasn't a lifelong cook. Her food was super good," Rebecca added.

"Yeah, it was," Barbara said with a glance at her mother's photo.

Barbara had been close with her mother, Joyce, so her death

during their junior year in college hit hard. She nevertheless plowed through her studies, getting straight As. A lack of focus would have been totally understandable, but Barbara refused to let her heartbreak tank her GPA. Her mother wouldn't have wanted that, she said. Rebecca did her best to support her friend, but youthful empathy only goes so far. The loss of such a vibrant soul was impossible to replace.

"I was convinced she hated me," Rebecca said.

"Why?"

"Those looks. She was always watching me. Must have thought I was an idiot."

"Only at the beginning."

"What!?"

"Kidding, just kidding. She loved you. And more importantly, she respected you."

"She teased me like crazy!"

"Because you were worth teasing."

"…my flat ass, my big hair…"

"She knew you could take it."

"…my Jewishness…"

"Don't forget your bad culinary skills," Leslie added.

"Oh yeah, that too."

"It's how she showed affection. Why do you think I became a lawyer? After running the Joyce Washington gauntlet, law school was a piece of cake. Trust me, she was a big fan of yours."

"Speaking of Becca's fans, what's going on with you and Kyle? Is that what you wanted to talk to us about?"

"Not exactly. Everything is going well, though it's been hard keeping him out of my bed. I've been struggling since leaving the study and am now trying a new way to get help."

"How?" Leslie asked.

"A sex specialist I found online."

"Like a porn site?"

"No. A lady who helps women and couples have better sex. I got one of her videos."

"If you got the video, why do you need the appointment?" Leslie asked, suffering a burning stare from Barbara.

"What?"

"Well, obviously, it didn't work," Barbara said.

Rebecca interrupted, "You know how long I've been trying to figure this thing out on my own. Years. Nothing has worked. Doctors, homework, books, videos, zero. This woman is the answer. I know she is."

"Becca, we know you've tried a lot. But is this the answer?" Barbara asked.

"I just think that if I have a one-on-one private session like I saw on the video, it will finally help. I mean, how could it not? She literally walks her clients through the masturbation process step-by-step."

"Really? Do you have to be naked?" Leslie asked, wide eyed.

"It looks like it, yes."

"Orgasm or no orgasm, I don't think I could fiddle around naked in front of a total stranger," Barbara said, hugging herself.

"It's not my first choice, I'll admit. But I'm desperate."

"How does it work?" Barbara asked.

"In the videos, she had a studio, and they did everything on a carpeted floor with lots of pillows," Rebecca replied.

"Becca, do you suppose it's safe? Going to a stranger's house and being naked?" Leslie asked.

"Well, I think she's a licensed sex therapist, though I don't know what state board issues licenses for sex therapy. She has some letters after her name, and she's referred to as 'doctor,' so I don't think she's some kind of pervert. Her secretary was a guy who sounded nice."

"The bad guys always do sound nice until they take advantage of some unsuspecting victim," Leslie added. "All those girls I've been investigating. They all were fine, until they weren't."

"Will you quit that?" Barbara snapped. "Becca is a grown woman, and if she thinks that she's legit, we should drop it. Anyway, when do you go for your session?"

"That's the thing. She's not taking appointments anymore. She used to, but she's taking a hiatus. I know if I could just talk to her, tell her about my situation, maybe she'd change her mind."

"So, call her," Barbara said.

"I did. Her assistant won't let me through. 'Out of the question' is how he put it."

"What now?"

"Les, I figured that maybe you could do some of your super-sleuthing and figure out where her office is. The address is not listed on her website."

"Sure, I have some databases I can check. I'll get my laptop."

Leslie booted up, and the three crowded around.

"If public business directories don't yield anything, we can look at last known addresses associated with her business incorporation.

I have some other methods as well, but best I not discuss those. That's how I found the address for a black-market mortuary which was illegally ditching bodies."

"Are you for real?" Barbara asked.

"Yes, didn't you read the article I sent?"

Guilt crept over Barbara's face.

"Seriously? It was so well written."

"I usually read everything, but that topic creeped me out."

"Fine. This time."

Rebecca watched Leslie's fingers fly across the keyboard, opening nests of browser windows at a dizzying pace. These were not user-friendly databases Leslie was searching.

"Looks like she was once married, has two adult kids. She lived at an address in Long Island, but it doesn't look to be current…"

"Can you imagine if your mom knew her?" Barbara chuckled.

"Just ducky."

"Got it," Leslie said. "Four eighteen Broome Street. She's in SoHo."

"No way," Rebecca said.

"Way."

"I can't believe you found her!"

"Yeah, I have my ways. My editor gives me all the impossible leads, and I rarely disappoint," Leslie said with a grin.

"What's that you're looking at?" Barbara asked, looking closer at the document on screen. "Heidi Quinn's publishing contract? How'd you get that?"

"Don't ask," Leslie said, exiting the browser and slapping the laptop lid closed.

"Remind me not to get on your wrong side."

"Four eighteen Broome Street," Rebecca said. "Guess I know where I'm going tomorrow."

Chapter 32

The heels of Rebecca's cowboy boots reverberated with authority on the cobblestone streets of SoHo, slick with a mix of morning dampness and motor oil. A few near falls left Rebecca wishing she'd worn her new motorcycle boots instead. Their reinforced metal toes and thick rubber soles radiated "don't mess with me." That kick of confidence would have been useful right about now.

She had yet to devise a good reason for Heidi Quinn making an exception for her. Running through other famous damsels in distress, she'd come up with several options, including Princess Leah:

"Help me, Heidi Quinn. You're my only hope…"

The *Notting Hill:* "I'm just a girl, standing in front of an expert, asking her to help me have an orgasm."

Or her favorite: "Heidi, if you help me, I will come," from *Field of Dreams.*

Rebecca laughed aloud, thinking of it, and a stylish man to her right, freshly tanned with tortoiseshell glasses, shot her a look and kept walking.

"Someone's grouchy," Rebecca replied.

Passing 410 Broome Street, Rebecca's pulse quickened. She became aware of the light perspiration coating her body from the half-hour walk. She snuck a whiff of her armpits. Passable. She tugged her top to straighten the wrinkles and smoothed down her hair.

"You look marvelous, sweetheart," a familiar voice said.

It was Brad. For sure. He was in his mid-twenties, with slicked-back hair, wearing a short-sleeved plaid shirt with a bow tie, clean jeans with cuffs, and designer shoes.

I am so underdressed for SoHo.

He passed her with a long stride, then stopped ahead at a doorway to rummage in his messenger bag, seemingly for keys.

Rebecca hurried to catch him. "Thanks for the compliment, Brad."

He looked up, confused. "I'm sorry, have we met?"

"Over the phone. My name is Rebecca Sloane. I called the other day for an appointment."

Brad's eyes widened, darting about for a rescue.

"Seriously? You think I'm going to hurt you?"

Brad stiffened, lips pursed, chin up. "You never know."

"C'mon, do I look threatening?"

He paused to think, forefinger across his lip. "No, but you're giving off a wild untamed vibe that could do anything."

"Untamed?"

"Frizzy. You really should do something about that. Not a good look."

"It's humid out!"

"Well, that's no excuse to strut about the city like a Muppet."

"Who's attacking who now?"

"Honey, that's not attacking. It's the God's truth. You need help."

"Exactly. That's why I'm here. Can I just have a quick conversation with Heidi? I'm sure—"

"What's your name again?"

"Rebecca."

"Rebecca, as I told you over the phone, Heidi is not taking appointments."

"A minute. I only need a minute of her time."

"How'd you find us, anyway?"

"That's not important."

"The hell it isn't! We've taken every care to protect Heidi's privacy. This is a totally unacceptable invasion."

"I'm desperate. You have no idea."

"Of course I do. Who do you think I work for?"

"Then why can't you let Heidi decide if she wants to see me?"

"Because that's my job. To decide. And I say no. Now I'm going in. If you don't leave, I'll call the police."

"Is she upstairs?"

"No."

"You're lying."

Brad flushed, shook his head "no" and turned to unlock the door.

Rebecca pouted, but he ignored her. She let the glass door close, then pressed her face up against it, cupping her hands around her face to see inside. It was a vacant lobby, only an elevator bank and walls. Brad made a shooing motion with his hands then disappeared into the elevator.

Rebecca paced back to crane her neck up, then jogged across the street for a better view.

With the lighting, it was hard to see into two of the four floors, but there was only one floor without business writing on the windows; the second floor. All the windows were shut. She looked at her watch: 9:05 a.m.

Keeping her eyes trained on the second-floor windows, she called work. No way she was going in today. Not when she was this close.

Looking at the recent calls in her cell, she scrolled down and pressed the number for Heidi's office.

It rang twice before an out of breath voice answered, "Heidi Quinn's office. This is Brad. Can I help you?"

"Brad, please. I'm just outside…"

He hung up.

"Arrggh," Rebecca grunted. Then she looked up and yelled, "Brad! Brad, I only need a minute. Please!"

No response came.

"Brad. A quick conversation, then I'll leave," Rebecca yelled.

"Will you shut up!" someone else yelled.

"No, I will not shut up. Not anymore. I'm never shutting up ever again!"

"I'm going to call the cops!" the voice answered.

"Go ahead!" Rebecca answered before resuming her plea. "Brad, I—"

The window threw open, and Brad stuck his head out.

God, I'm so close…

292

"If you don't stop this, I will call the police immediately. This is no joke. You are threatening us, and I will not tolerate it!"

"This is cruel, you know, why can't I just talk..."

A second window threw open, two down from Brad. Peach wall. An auburn head popped out, both arms braced on the windowsill.

Rebecca's eyes trained on her prize for what felt like forever before the head popped back in and the window shut. Brad pivoted to talk to someone, then shut his window without another word.

Rebecca audibly gasped, then pressed her lips closed. And waited.

Nothing.

Rebecca grabbed the top of her head with both hands. "This can't be happening."

She paced back and forth before looking up again, but there was no movement. Yelling again would surely draw the police from any number of neighbors. Her head started to spin, so she reached back for the building behind her. Finding it, she braced against the cool stone.

Street sounds formerly blocked by her chaotic mind seeped into her consciousness. A car drove by. Then another. A man passed bopping to his earbuds. An old woman approached, lugging groceries. Life was resuming. No one cared that hers was over.

A two-spouted wall hydrant projected from the building wall a foot away. Rebecca took a seat.

"This can't be it. It can't end this way," she whispered.

For the first time in forever, no tears came.

After a few hours, she checked her watch; it was 11:38 a.m. Her butt probably had a hydrant company imprint by now. Any hope of ambushing Heidi Quinn was gone. She closed her eyes.

Where to go? Not home. Not work. The river? Maybe if she flung herself in the Hudson River, that'd be the best thing for everyone.

"I need coffee. Walk with me."

Rebecca's eyes popped open. Heidi Quinn stood in front of her wearing black leggings, a black tank, and a multicolored silk coverlet draped around her form.

"Oh my God!" Rebecca said.

"Not God. I like to think of myself as a conduit through which God enters the soul." She took two steps and stopped. "Coming?"

Rebecca hopped up and followed her, walking beside but slightly behind.

"You created quite a spectacle."

"Sorry. That's not how I am, normally."

Heidi looked over, surveying Rebecca. "Brad is a tough cookie, but that's why I love him. This is a tricky business I'm in. I have enemies."

"Enemies? Really?"

"Yes. The topic of sex makes people crazy, not always in a good way," she said with a sideways smile.

Rebecca swallowed hard. After all her hubbub trying to see Heidi Quinn, all she could think of was suppressing her gurgling stomach as they walked along the sidewalk.

Her breast pocket buzzed; a text from Kyle. She silenced it as she scampered to keep up.

"So, this is my proposal. I'm traveling to Africa next week for an indeterminate amount of time. My conservation work has been on the back burner for years, and I'm diving into it with all my heart. I've worked hard and deserve that," she said.

"I understand, bu—"

"I will be upstairs packing on Thursday evening and should have a few hours to see you. Come by at 7:00 p.m. and we'll see what we can do together. Bring a clear mind and $1,200. If you don't come, I'll know you changed your mind. If I see you there, I have a feeling you won't be disappointed."

Heidi opened the door of her café but held up a hand. Rebecca was not to follow.

"Are we agreed?"

"Yes. Absolutely. Seven o'clock Thursday."

"Good." Heidi entered the café and was gone.

Rebecca strode away, heading for an ATM machine to confirm what she already knew. The door she had fought so hard to open might remain shut.

Chapter 33

"Hi, Mom," Rebecca said to her stunned mother as she opened the door.

"Dios mio! What are you doing here!" Olivia Sloane said, slapping her arms around Rebecca for a lung-crushing squeeze.

"Marty, Marty, you'll never guess who's here!"

"Mom, I can't breathe…"

"Tell them I don't want any!" her father yelled from the other room, television blaring.

"Don't want any… Do you see what I have to put up with? He never pays attention."

Her mom vice-gripped Rebecca's hand, then dragged her through the doorway and down the hall.

"The door…"

"It's Port Washington. Who's coming?"

Rebecca flopped behind her mother, suppressing a smile, eyes planted up in her lids.

"Marty. Marty, look who's here!"

"Hi, Dad."

"You should have called! I would've gotten you at the train," her dad said, adjusting his glasses.

"It's okay. The walk did me good."

Rebecca bent down and planted a kiss on top of his head.

"Hold on, hold on. I need more than that," he said, shifting a messy pile of *Daily News* and *Newsday* tabloids off his lap onto the floor.

"Still keeping the papers in business?"

"Someone's got to," he said, pushing out of his lounge chair. "C'mon, c'mon." He waved her over for another hug.

"Ooof!" Rebecca grunted as her mother pile drove into her back to squeeze from behind.

"Who's loved?"

"I am."

"How much?"

"Oodles," Rebecca said, as she had since childhood. Believing it was something else entirely.

They both let go and stood beaming.

"I'll have to schlep out more often."

"Yes, you do. Come, let's go to the kitchen. I'll get you a snack."

Her dad smiled and returned to his chair and papers. Rebecca followed her mom into the small white and green kitchen, looking back at her dad before sitting down at their sturdy wooden table.

"What's Dad doing home?"

"Hmmmm?" her mother said, back turned to her as she rummaged in the fridge.

"Dad? Why is he home during the day?"

"Cheese okay?"

"Sure. Fine."

Her mother got a slab of cheddar and Havarti out, some Ritz crackers, and gave Rebecca a plate and knife before sitting across from her with two cans of lime seltzer.

"He's decided to cut back on his hours. Enjoy life a little."

"Did he get laid off?"

"Of course not! He's just cutting back a little."

"Permanently?" Rebecca asked through a mouthful of cracker dust.

"No. Just until—"

"Aha!"

"Oh, it's nothing." Her mother waved. "We didn't tell you because we didn't want you to worry."

"Worry about what?"

"His blood pressure is up. Doctor said to de-stress for a few weeks and go back for a checkup. Work has been very understanding. And he's actually enjoying himself."

"Okay, well, that doesn't sound too bad."

"It's not. Really. It's put a cramp in our sex life, but otherwise—"

"Stop! TMI!" Rebecca said, signaling time-out with her hands.

"Okay, okay! I just thought with all the sexy conversations you've been having lately, you wouldn't mind."

"What, NOW you want to have sexy conversations with me? You've always avoided them like the plague. Not to point fingers, but I could have used a little more help. Say, during puberty?"

Her mother shrugged. "It's not something I've ever discussed with anyone. My mother never discussed it with me. Can you imagine your grandma, who practically crawled on her knees to church every day, talking sex with me?

"Hardly."

"Daddy and I don't even discuss it. We just… do it. It came naturally."

"So what changed, Mom? Why are you bringing it up?" Rebecca said, crossing her arms.

"I've been going to a women's group, and that's all they talk about. Suppose it rubbed off."

"Too bad it didn't rub off sooner."

"Have you ever tried Kegels? I hear they work."

"Wow, those ladies dive deep. Trust me, Kegels aren't the answer to everything."

Rebecca had done Kegels until the toilet seat made her butt red, and only abandoned them after learning it would do nothing to induce an orgasm. The contraction exercises only increased the tone and blood flow to the pelvic floor—they didn't help her clear the hurdle. But if she ever had an orgasm, it'd be stronger than it would've been otherwise.

Rebecca gulped her seltzer dry. "Who are you, and what have you done with my mother?"

"Stop being silly."

"I'm serious. The conversation we're having, right now, this could have saved me a lot of heartache."

"I'm sorry, muñeca."

Rebecca sat, bouncing her leg. Weird. The usual indifferent hellos and how are yous had been replaced by a genuine conversation. It had been decades since her mom had shown this much interest in her life, not to mention her sex life.

"Are you doing them right? Stopping the flow as you pee…"

"Mom, yes. I've been doing them right."

"Pues…" her mother dismissed in Spanish, nibbling on a cracker.

"Kegels weren't enough, but I've decided to hire someone to help me."

"Hire someone?" She leaned in. "Like a prostitute?"

"No, not a prostitute. She's an expert. A doctor. I think she's a PhD rather than an MD. She helps women with this sort of thing."

"Really? Isn't' that something? How did you find her?"

"Online. I'm seeing her on Thursday, that is, if you can help me."

"Out of the question. I won't come with you."

"No, you don't have to. It's not that."

"What, then?"

"Are you sure Daddy didn't get laid off?"

"Of course not. He's home for rest."

"Then, I need to borrow some money."

"Oh."

"I can cover some of it myself, but I'm desperate. This could be my last chance."

"How much?"

"It's a lot."

"How much?"

"Nine hundred dollars."

"Nine hundred dollars?"

"She's moving to Africa on Monday; I don't have enough to cover the cost. I wouldn't ask if it wasn't important."

"Africa? This sounds crazy. Are you sure it's not a scam?"

"Positive. I was at her office this morning, and I talked to her and her assistant. I can show you her website if you want."

"Your dad and I usually make financial decisions together."

"Please don't. Don't mention it. Not this. I'll pay you back a little bit each month. You'll have it back by December. I never ask for anything. I'm asking you to come through for me now."

Her mom stood up and walked to the doorway of the kitchen, peering at her husband. Bursts of sports programming pierced the silence. She paced, mumbling to herself in Spanish, hands on the small of her back. It was a good sign. She returned to the table and took a sip of seltzer.

"Well?"

"I'll give you the money."

Rebecca exhaled and leaned back in her chair. "Thank you."

"If you deposit the check today when I drive you to the train, it should clear well before she has a chance to make the withdrawal. I'll give it, but on one condition: you must eat. You're too flaca."

"Skinny? You're joking."

Her mom cut a small stack of cheese slices and slid it across the table.

"Eat."

Rebecca took a slice and chewed slowly. Her phone vibrated; it was Kyle. She silenced it and slipped it into her jacket pocket.

"What else?" her mom asked.

"Huh?"

"What else. You're making your thinking face."

Rebecca sat up, laying her palms flat on the table.

301

"Since you raised the issue before, it doesn't sound like you and dad ever had any trouble in the bedroom department, have you?"

Her mom leaned back, wary.

"Oh, come on. You were bragging two minutes ago!"

She reached for her can of seltzer, taking a series of small sips while avoiding eye contact. Her wall was going up.

"The doctor may ask questions about family history. I thought it might be good to know."

"I'm sorry about not talking about this with you when you were younger. I always considered this private. Something that couples discussed, not that we did. I never had any trouble and thought you'd be fine too. I didn't mean to cause you so much pain."

Her mom offered Rebecca her hands; they were warm and soft. Familiar. She stroked the back of Rebecca's hands with her thumbs.

"I'm sorry. I'm sorry I failed you."

A lump formed in Rebecca's throat, she swallowed hard, but no words came.

Her mom's eyes dewed while she waited for a reply.

"Thank you. Having you say that, it means a lot. More than you know."

"I am sorry for all you've been through. This doctor, I pray she can help you. Do what I couldn't."

"Mom, don't say that…"

"And don't think about paying it back."

"I can't let—"

"Take it. It's our gift to you, my gift to you."

"What will Dad say?"

"I'll figure something out. Don't worry."

She stood up. Popping a slice of Havarti in her mouth, she gave the top of Rebecca's head a kiss mid-chew.

"Thanks."

"You'll be great on Thursday. You'll see."

"Why so sure?"

"You're my daughter. You're wired for it."

Chapter 34

Four days of takeout stains crusted the coffee table. Rebecca sprayed the glass cleaner, scraping the stubborn bits with her fingernail then finishing it off with a paper towel. She was probably killing the wood, but it was the best cleaning she could do on short notice.

She'd been slow to return Kyle's texts, so he insisted on coming over in person. A door slammed across the hall. Kicking her cleaning supplies under the couch, she dashed to meet him at the door.

"Beat ya!" she yelled.

"So, you did." He smiled.

Rebecca popped on tiptoes for a smooch.

He came in and flipped off his shoes, "What a week! Crazy! You must have been busy, too, huh?"

"Long and draining, yes. But I have news."

"What news?"

Rebecca followed Kyle to the kitchen doorway leaning on the threshold, as he surveyed the open fridge.

"Ahh, my beer from last week. Perfect."

He opened the correct drawer for the opener and tossed the cap in the trashcan in the cabinet under the sink. He grabbed a napkin from the windowsill holder, navigating the kitchen like it was his own.

"I tracked down Heidi Quinn. I'm going to see her tomorrow."

"What? Tomorrow? That's amazing. How'd you manage that?" He picked Rebecca up and spun her around.

She filled him in about Leslie's hacking skills and her stubborn assault on Brad's fortress.

"Are you nervous?" he said, going to the kitchen for a second beer.

"Excited is more like it. I know what to expect from the video. I'm ready. I'm actually ready."

"You're meant for great things, my love. Tomorrow is only the beginning." Kyle sat next to Rebecca, wrapping her in his arms. She snuggled in. His heart was thumping, powerful, loud, steady. It was his heart, but she drew strength from it as well.

Having him support her so unconditionally warmed places in her soul she didn't know existed. Combined with her mother's newfound maternal instincts and the devotion of her friends, Rebecca radiated a peace and contentment truly foreign to her. She could get used to this.

"The timing is perfect," Kyle said. "Yeah, I love that she could see me right away."

"Actually, I'm talking about something else. Now don't be mad at me."

"Mad about what?"

He shifted so he could see her face.

305

"Up for an adventure?"

"Tonight?"

"This weekend. A long ride out to Pennsylvania. You game?"

"Yeah, definitely!"

"I have it all planned. Pack light, and we'll make a weekend of it."

Rebecca stiffened. "A weekend?"

"A trip. Overnight. It'll be great. I know we're taking it slow, and we absolutely will. I've wanted some alone time with you, where it can be us together. No distractions. No Bessie barging in. What do you think?"

An overnight trip with Kyle? No interruptions? It's any woman's dream, so why was she terrified?

"I have it all planned out for us. I have the route picked; I made reservations. It'll be fantastic weather. You'll love it."

"We do always have fun on our rides.

"Damn straight, and you have those new biker boots. Gotta break them in, right?'

"Yes. It'll be fun, it'll be fun. We'll be away… just the two of us…" *What could happen, right?"*

"Exactly! I'm so glad you're into it. I wasn't sure if it was too much, but especially with you seeing Heidi tomorrow, we'll need a getaway. We can have some fun and unwind."

Unwind? Wound up is more like it. My crotch will be rammed into his butt for two solid days, and that's only when we're on the bike.

He snuggled close, his fingers tantalizing her shoulders.

Rebecca played with a strand of hair, wrapping and unwrapping the curl around her finger.

"Seen the remote?"

"On the sofa arm."

"Ahh." He palmed it and flipped on the television, leaning back with his feet on the coffee table.

Kyle craned his neck to see her face.

"You okay?"

"Yeah, just tired. What time do you want to leave Saturday?"

"Early. Let's plan for seven, so we can beat the traffic. We'll get breakfast in New Jersey. I know an awesome diner, then we'll make our way around and end up… Well, I want it to be a surprise."

"Kyle?"

"Yeah," his eyes were glued to screen as he flipped channels.

"Were the reservations hard to get?"

"Not too bad. I pulled a few strings. I think you'll really love the place."

"It's very sweet. For you to plan it all," Rebecca said, looking up at him.

"Anything for you." He kissed her forehead.

"Really?"

"I hope that doesn't make you uncomfortable."

"No. No. Not at all."

It's the thought of hitchhiking home from goodness knows where when you toss me to the curb after bad sex that makes me uncomfortable.

"I'll be right back," Rebecca said, heading to the bathroom.

Mind awhirl, she sat on the closed toilet lid. Maybe she was getting worked up over nothing. Tomorrow, she'd see Heidi. Heidi would put an end to this ridiculous orgasm nightmare. By Saturday, who knows? She could be a card-carrying member of the sex kitten society. She'd blow Kyle's mind and hers as well. Maybe.

Rebecca grasped the metal faucet for the cold water and turned. The icy shock jolted her senses as the water splashed her wrists. Goose bumps rose. Her thoughts jumbled as coldness crashed the party.

That's how I have to be with Heidi, she thought. No Kyle, no work, no parents or friends. Only Rebecca and her body. The body that had ached for this moment her entire adult life. To experience the rapture others took for granted would be a gift beyond measure. She deserved this moment. She'd have to put the weekend trip aside and worry about it later.

And if all went well with Heidi, her bedroom worrying could very well be over.

Chapter 35

Kyle steadied the motorcycle with his legs so Rebecca could climb off. She flipped up her visor.

A powerful energy coursed through her. A calm anticipation that'd been there all day. Even Darcy steered clear of her usual snide remarks at work. She knew something was up. The "what" would likely blow her mind.

"Ready?" he asked.

"I am. I am so ready. Thanks for driving me."

"Sure thing. See you later?"

"Definitely." She reached in for a kiss and but their helmets collided.

They both laughed.

"You got this."

"I know."

He revved and was gone in an instant. Rebecca tugged her jacket to straighten it, her head abnormally heavy.

The helmet. I'm wearing the helmet.

She tugged it off and tossed her hair. *Hmm. Badass biker Rebecca.*

Not a bad way to enter. She pressed Heidi's buzzer, swaying from side to side as she waited for a reply.

"Yes?"

"It's Rebecca. Rebecca Sloane. For my seven o'clock?"

After a beat, the buzzer sounded. Rebecca jammed the door open and took the elevator to the second floor.

The elevator opened directly into Heidi's loft. Every piece of furniture, from the sofa to the chairs and dining table, were draped in white cloths. Cardboard moving boxes were stacked everywhere. This trip to Africa was more like a move to Africa. The only remaining evidence the loft housed an orgasm den was the black and white erotic photography plastered across every wall.

Barefoot and wearing a black unitard, Heidi approached, flinging her leopard print wrap over her shoulder. A messy red ponytail streaked with gray bounced from the top of her head.

"Ah yes. The stubborn one from the other day. I didn't think you would come."

"Wouldn't miss it for the world."

"You rode here on a motorcycle?"

"Yes. My… boyfriend has one."

Heidi chuckled. "This is going to be interesting."

She turned away and walked across the room. "Take off your shoes. You'll be here a while. Or not. We'll soon see."

Rebecca slipped off her boots and shuffled to catch up. Room after room resembled haunted houses from every cliche movie she'd ever seen. Heidi stopped in one she'd seen before.

Luscious carpet underfoot, pillows, and two small sofas greeted her. The unadorned peach walls from the video were dotted with the same black and white erotica-style photographs as every other room. The coffee table was covered with a wide assortment of lubricants, dildos, vibrators, and other devices Rebecca could not readily identify. Among them, however, was a Magic Wand.

She hadn't noticed from outside, but the windows here were covered with wooden blinds and drawn closed. Rebecca removed her jacket and set the helmet next to the unmentionables on the table.

Heidi motioned for her to sit down on the sofa; she chose the floor for herself, leaning an elegant elbow on the coffee table.

"Why are you here today?" she asked.

Rebecca held her breath. Would this be the last time she'd have to tell this story? The shameful story that shadowed her life like a rain cloud?

"I…" she began, but her mouth was impossibly dry.

"Hold on."

Heidi walked across the room to what looked like a sideboard, opening a hidden refrigerator within. She grabbed a bottle of water.

"Take your time."

Frigid water cleared her throat and her mind.

I can do this.

"I'm twenty-eight years old, and despite every conceivable attempt, I've not been able to have an orgasm. I've been in clinical studies, rented porn videos—followed your videos, read erotic fantasy books, masturbated after warm baths, sensuous oils, had sex with men. Nothing. There's a block. Something I'm missing."

"Do your partners know? Have they tried to help you along; pleasure you?"

311

"I've tried to hide it from everyone I've had sex with, but every long-term partner finds out in the end. My last boyfriend went storming out because of it."

"What about Mr. Motorcycle?"

"He knows; we've been dating a couple of months."

"And how did he take the news?"

"He was great. The first guy who has been. He drove me here today."

"Good. Glad to hear it. Regardless of our work together today, you deserve to be with someone who treats you with kindness and respect. Toss the rest."

"I'll do my best."

"Believe it. Own it. You must demand what you need from anyone in your life and your bed. You will not have a fulfilling sex life unless you know what you need to feel pleasure, and ask for it."

"But what if I don't know what it is?"

"We'll begin that journey today, but your journey to orgasm will take you farther than you can imagine. It will change throughout your life and from orgasm to orgasm. To have an orgasm, you must achieve sexual pleasure for yourself. This is the time to focus on you and only you. What you're feeling, don't worry about anything else, anyone else, and most importantly, what they think about what arouses you."

"Okay; makes sense."

"You've seen my video. The one with three clients?"

"Yes."

"Our process today will be very much like what you saw on the video. I would like you to first bathe and then put on the robe hanging for you in the bathroom. Keep your hair dry, please. I'll be waiting here for you when you're done, and we'll begin."

The bathroom had a tiled shower stall with a glass door, a toilet, sink, and wrought-iron shelf stacked high with fluffy towels. *Guess they weren't going to Africa.*

The pulsating showerhead massaged the world away. Rebecca lathered thick suds with the scented body wash, careful to avoid wetting her hair. After toweling off, the satin kimono slipped down her arms, replacing the rumpled clothes she left behind in a pile on the floor.

While she showered, Heidi arranged pillows in a large pile and covered them with a black satin sheet. She motioned Rebecca to sit down.

"Have you ever looked at your vagina in a mirror?" Heidi asked.

"Yes, I have."

"Good, sit down here and let your knees each drop sideways, keeping the soles of your feet together. My goal today is to guide you as you pleasure yourself. I may occasionally help move your arms and legs into proper position but will otherwise not touch you. We will journey together, but you will do the work yourself."

The pillows were soft but firm, and Heidi added another to support Rebecca's back. She sat without using her body muscles to keep upright. She then positioned the mirror so they could both see it. As she pointed to parts of Rebecca's anatomy, she touched the reflection on the mirror with a pointer.

Pretty sneaky. Dr. Costa's team could learn a few things.

"These are your labia majora and minora, your vagina, and your clitoris is the pink pearl right here. She is poking out of her hood right now, begging for attention. I want you to take your hand and gently touch each and penetrate your vagina gently with your finger. Tell me, what feels sensitive?"

"Penetrating my vagina felt good. The labia didn't feel particularly sensitive, but the clitoris almost hurt. Is that normal?"

"My yes," Heidi answered. "Women are conditioned to think that the vagina is the be-all and end-all of sex, but the clitoris is the engine that makes everything go. Yours is protruding, meaning that you are ready to release some sexual tension. Riding a motorcycle is perpetual foreplay."

"That's why I get so horny on the bike?"

"It's an iron vibrator."

"That's hilarious. Wait until Kyle finds out."

"Back to your clitoris. She is very delicate and must be handled carefully. If you rub her too aggressively, she will get irritated, and that will diminish the sexual pleasure you derive from the stimulation. I counsel clients to stimulate the whole body then focus on the labia. Moving the labia helps to move the hood over the clitoris and gives stimulation without overdoing it and causing irritation."

The ease with which she spoke made Rebecca forget she was poking around her privates with a total stranger.

"Now that you know where everything is, I'd like you to shift back onto to these pillows, put your weight on them completely, and relax everything else. We'll start some foreplay. Do you use foreplay during sex?" Heidi asked.

"More with Kyle. Before him, it was usually kissing and petting before we'd get into bed. You know, with clothes on. Once we were in bed, it went fairly quickly."

"And what's different with Kyle?"

"He dives into me like a pool; touching me, kissing me all over, my breasts. He enjoys giving me oral and stays down there forever. I feel guilty. All the attention is on me."

"Don't. Kyle is a lover. He is loving you. Embrace it as it's giving him sexual pleasure to please you."

Rebecca exhaled. "Okay."

"It sounds like foreplay is new to you. Foreplay, especially for women, is an important part of sex. It's fuel. Foreplay helps to get your mind focused on your body's sensations and anchor yourself in the moment. Your mind must be clear of concerns and free to fantasize so you can maximize the sexual pleasure you derive from sex and your orgasmic release."

Heidi handed Rebecca the Magic Wand. "Take this and move it around your body, arms, legs, stomach, and in and around your clitoris, but not on it. We're water lapping at the edges right now."

Rebecca did as she said. "I feel a little silly."

"Why? Where are you in your head?" Heidi asked.

"I'm lying on the floor in your studio with a vibrator."

"No. That's the problem. What makes you aroused? What do you fantasize about?"

"I don't fantasize much. For some reason, thinking of me having sex with some hunky guy doesn't do it for me."

"Fine, then. Let's find something that does."

"Sometimes, when I think of naked women, it makes me aroused. I'm not gay, but the female form is very beautiful."

"Okay, is there a female body type you like, someone that turns you on?"

"When I close my eyes, I picture someone from a porno I watched."

"Perfect. It's a fantasy. Ask her do whatever you want. You can make her give you oral sex if you want. You can triple the size of her boobs if that's what you like. You can give her boobs and a dick. It's totally up to you."

"Oh, boobs and a penis would be lovely."

"Okay then, here's some oil." Heidi dribbled oil on Rebecca's breasts, exposed through the open front robe.

"Pretend that you are massaging oil on the best knockers you've ever seen. In the meantime, use the vibrator to stimulate around your vagina, like we discussed."

Rebecca followed her instructions and felt tension building in her body. The scented oils smelled wonderful, and she lost herself in the moment.

"Okay, I want you to bend your knees and hold the Magic Wand between them and grind up to meet it, increasing the pressure and stimulation on your clitoris. You're fucking your sex slave, and she is covered in oil and ready to come."

Rebecca envisioned her partner. She was blonde with full lips and round breasts, shiny from the oil. She touched them while squeezing her own. Her mouth dropped open.

She ground into the vibrations; she could see them. Red and hot. Waves. Tingles. Pulsing. They intensified. Stronger, stronger, building, spreading—then dissipating. As quickly as they came, they were gone. Her mate vanished, replaced by her never-ending reality. Alone. Sitting on the floor. Even here in the peach room, she failed.

"That always happens; it starts building and then goes away. It's maddening." Rebecca covered her face with her hands.

"What do you mean?"

"I mean, I'm on the road to somewhere and then hit a wall."

"Rebecca, that was it. That was an orgasm."

Heidi's words hit like a truck.

Rebecca pulsed her head side to side in dissent. "No. No. That's not possible."

"Young lady, are you telling me what is and isn't an orgasm?"

"No. Yes. I mean, I guess I don't understand how you know. Are you sure?"

"You tensed up and arched your back, and then flushed. You had an orgasm."

"That was an orgasm?"

"Have you felt like that before?"

"Yes, lots of times. But where are the crashing waves?" Rebecca sat up and folded her knees together. "I was expecting something much stronger. Much more powerful. How could that have been an orgasm? It was nothing. So unsatisfying."

"Rebecca, you had an orgasm and probably have them quite easily. What we have to work on now is increasing the intensity of the orgasm, so you feel more sexual pleasure."

"I'm sorry, but are you quite sure I had one? This is so hard to believe."

"Yes, Rebecca. I've been doing this for, well, longer than you've probably been alive. You had an orgasm," Heidi said with a broad smile.

"Well, I guess when you don't know where you're going, you don't know when you're there," Rebecca said. "I feel so stupid."

"Don't feel stupid. Hollywood has done a grave disservice to women's sexual education, and porn is even worse. Men are clueless. Thrusting and pumping, thinking that's what WE need to orgasm. Anyway, let's work on your breathing. You held your breath the whole time. Did you realize that?"

"Is breathing important?"

"Breathing is essential; it helps to improve the intensity and sexual pleasure of orgasms. As you have already learned, not all orgasms are created equal. You had a first one, a little one, that was less intense. Let's get you back into position, and I'll show you the mirror.

"See, from the looks of your clitoris, you have more tension to release," Heidi said, sneaking a peek at her clitoris, which was still poking out of its hood.

"This time, it will take longer to build, but will be worth the effort. Do you want another one?"

"Yes, please!"

Rebecca used the Magic Wand to start, then Heidi transferred Rebecca to a silicone dildo. It filled her up and felt incredible. Rebecca was ramming it in and simultaneously grinding up to meet it. Heidi encouraged Rebecca to squeeze her nipples and breasts and breathe loudly.

"Who are you fucking now?" she asked.

"I'm fucking a serving wench whose tits were in my face, so I've bent her over a table now in front of everyone."

"Good! You're a girl with a dick. I love it!"

Rebecca continued the motion with bent knees for a few moments longer.

Heidi yelled at her to breathe.

Then it began.

Warmth traveled from her groin up her spine, radiating around her face.

Tingles pulsed down her limbs in synchronous waves.

Face.

Neck.

Ears.

Everything.

Down to her fingertips.

Taken.

Transported.

Throughout, she heard a voice far away yelling, "Breathe! Rebecca, breathe."

A mirage of consciousness took hold. For how long, she couldn't say.

Then the contraction holding her body taut yielded, collapsing her onto the pillows in a heap. Sleepy and unfocused.

Rebecca lay heaving, her leaden limbs immobile.

"This is not possible. How is this possible?" she expelled in a breathy whisper.

"They come in all shapes and sizes. The more stimulation and patience, the bigger the release."

"I'll say."

"For an inorgasmic woman, you are certainly good at it!"

"I am. I am totally good at it," she panted.

"Want another?" Heidi asked.

Rebecca spent the next two hours making up outlandish fantasies and having six orgasms. Rebecca's mom was right: she was wired for sex. She just needed to learn how to turn the power on.

"Did you say something?" Rebecca asked.

"Haven't we come far! Now you aren't even listening!"

"I can't. I'm trying."

"Sit up a little so we can finish here."

Rebecca pushed up as much as she could on her elbows, unable to support much of her weight, or close her robe. Heidi flipped the kimono edges together for her.

"You've made a wonderful breakthrough today. I'd like you to practice on your own, without the Magic Wand, and slowly integrate your partner. What's his name?"

"Kyle."

"Now, you need to integrate Kyle into your sexual world, and as you are ready, integrate him into your newfound fantasy life. You said that he has performed oral sex on you?"

"Yes, but in truth, I don't much like kissing him afterward. I can smell me on his face."

"Yes, that's why it's so important to shower first. It is perfectly within your right to ask someone else to shower before coming to bed for sex. He can ask you, and you can ask him. If you think you may not be as fresh as you would like to kiss, take a shower on your own without him asking. Also, scented oils are great for this sort of thing. It helps with foreplay and can also improve the smell and occasionally the taste of our partners. Experiment with these types of aids. They make a big difference and add an element of fun to sex and help build sexual intimacy."

She lay unmoving as Heidi began to tidy up.

"Do you sell those dildos?" Rebecca asked.

"No, but I'll have my assistant email you the model we used."

"I feel like someone has removed all the bones from my body."

"You did a lot of work today; a lifetime of work. But it's only the beginning. Remember what we've done here together. And..."

"Yes?" Rebecca looked over to Heidi, who was standing across the room.

"Never doubt yourself again."

Rebecca stumbled to the bathroom and splashed water on her face. Droplets dripping off her chin and down the bare chest of a stranger in the mirror. Eyelids limp in a sexy way. Nose, super cute. Lips, full. Jawline tight and well angled. Hair, mussed in a "who gives a fuck" way. Had she been there all along? The skin fit the body, but this person wore it better. Fuller. Prouder.

Rebecca returned to the sofa. Heidi was waiting, sporting a sassy, closed mouth smile wisdom brings. The women of Africa were getting a priceless gift.

"Heidi, I don't know how to thank you. That insecure, quivering-at-her-shadow woman who walked in here is gone. I can FEEL it. I KNOW it. How can I repay you?"

"Well, $1,200 would be a fine start."

The glass door from the lobby swiveled closed behind her. Rebecca stood absorbing the night, entering the world reborn.

People strolled along, browsing the storefronts lit up for evening window shoppers. Diners darted in and out of restaurants, clustering around menus, bubbling, deciding.

She wondered: could they tell? Could passersby sense her transformation? If not, they soon would. She would never again waffle, lacking confidence. She was formidable, a mistress of her own destiny.

A man in a blue blazer and slacks approached. She held his gaze until he looked away.

Rebecca raised her chin in triumph. New Rebecca was going to be fun. She had places to go and people to dominate.

Rebecca raised her arm to hail a cab. She didn't raise and lower it. Wave, wiggle, look around her to be sure she wasn't undercutting another pedestrian.

She stood. Solid. Arm raised, and a cab stopped.

How could it not?

She climbed in, helmet on lap, and gave her destination.

No explanations about why she was carrying a helmet.

No excuses.

She would never make excuses again. Not to anyone. Not to her parents, not to Kyle. Not even Darcy.

New Rebecca was nobody's doormat.

Heidi saw her potential.

Kyle saw her potential.

Harry saw her potential and had data to prove it.

After her journey to O, she finally believed it herself.

Chapter 36

The whirlwind of the previous twenty-four hours was indescribable. After pounding on Kyle's door to tell him the news, Rebecca collapsed into bed for the sleep of the dead. When she woke for work, the alarm had already been blaring for a half hour.

On her walking commute, she strolled across intersections long after "don't walk" blinked its warning. No more scurrying across. Cool as a cucumber, columns of traffic ignored their green light waiting for her to pass—without a single honk.

Had life always been this ripe for the picking?

Her cell rang, and Barbara's face flashed on the screen.

"Hey there!" Rebecca said.

"How's our liberated woman today?"

"Fabulous."

"Becca, you've always been fabulous. It's fantastic you see it now."

"Yes. And I want the whole world to know."

"Even at work?"

"Even at work. Today, I made up reasons to brave Darcy's fishbowl stink just to see her avert her eyes first. By 11:00 a.m.,

Darcy entered fake phone call mode the moment I approached. It was awesome!"

"Careful now. You must only use your powers for good and not evil."

"Oh, I know. I'm just having a little fun."

"Got plans tonight?"

"Yes. I'm going on a date."

"With Kyle?"

"With myself!"

"Yourself?"

"Totally. I want to experience me a little. I deserve it."

"Well, okay. Now we're talking."

Kyle sounded puzzled when Rebecca told him she was taking the night off, but he understood. They did have the full weekend ahead, leaving bright and early the next day. And armed with Heidi's masterclass, who knew what was in store when they hit the sheets. With nothing to hold them back—and nothing to hold *her* back.

"You there?"

"Yeah. But I've got to go. I don't want to be late for myself!"

By the time Rebecca bathed and dressed, the night shift was out. Twenty-somethings throwing off the shackles of the workday as they popped in and out of cabs to their favorite haunts. Sidewalks teemed with revelers. Rebecca pushed her way through talkers surprised their pavement cliques had a party crasher, only to reform the moment she passed.

Her feet carried her away. Down First Avenue and deeper into the East Village. Her old stomping grounds. Bars and restaurants she first frequented with her parents, then with friends as a teen, and then with Ethan. Eyes clear, she surveyed the turf anew. Not as part of another cluster, but on her own. Stopping and starting where she wanted with no one else to please. How many times had she eaten Polish food when she wanted Japanese? Sat through folk music when she longed for pounding rock? No more. Her neck stretched up, testing new heights.

The light turned red, but with no traffic, the mass of humanity kept flowing. Rebecca moved among it, but at her own pace, stopping to scan restaurant and bar menus. All would be open late into the night. Manhattan. At any time, on any day, at a moment's notice you could eat or do almost anything. The options were as limitless as her newfound potential.

"You're an asshole!"

"No, you're an asshole!" Two guys joked, pushing each other; one stumbled into Rebecca's path. He bent over laughing, hands on knees. His friend kicked him in the ass, dropping him facefirst into a pile of garbage.

"Holy shit! You okay?" the offender asked, tending to his mate. Rebecca circled around them and their breathless amusement.

Where am I, anyway?

She looked up at the neon marquee of The Rose Tavern. Of all places, her feet took her there. To their place. Rebecca hadn't set foot in the bar since Ethan walked out. Too many memories. Too many nights. Fun nights. Warm summer nights like this one. Nights that ended with Ethan blissfully sleeping and her blinking at the bedroom ceiling.

She missed the fun. The music. The warm wood paneling.

Why did I let him claim it for his own?

She pulled the twisted iron door ring and went in.

Base music pounded a greeting, thumping her chest cavity as it drew her in. Energy. Life. *Delicious.*

A wall of humanity blocked her way.

Rebecca wove between sweaty men and their hoppy drinks. The crowd surged, sandwiching Rebecca face to face with a redheaded guy with crumbs in his beard.

"Hey," Rebecca said.

"Hey, there!"

Rebecca moved on.

"What's the rush?" he yelled after. "I love you!"

She shook her head and flashed him a wide smile. The absurdity earned him that much.

Rebecca sidled up to the carved mahogany bar in time to claim a sliver of space by the brass handrail. Taking hold, she maneuvered herself in.

Just like riding a bike.

"It's been a while!" the bartender said.

"Scott! Oh my God, it's nuts in here!"

"The owner wanted to liven-up the 10:00 p.m. to 12:00 a.m. time slot, so made the beers buy two, get one free."

"Looks like it's working. Give me a white wine, please. Whatever's cheap."

"You got it."

Roving spotlights passed across a crowd so thick it was impossible to see where the bar ended and the dance floor began, writing bodies being the only marker. She'd spent many a blissful hour writhing among them, not knowing or caring who she was dancing with. Ethan was more a drinker than a dancer. Looking back, her exhaustion hadn't helped her perform up to "his majesty's" standards. Hell, maybe she had, and he was too drunk to notice. And on second thought, he obviously hadn't rocked her world. She had as much claim to gripe as anyone. Why hadn't she?

Scott put the drink in front of her.

"How much?"

"On the house."

"Thanks!"

"No problem. If you're looking for Ethan, he's down at the end of the bar."

"Ethan?"

"Yeah. He's right—"

"Doesn't matter. We're not together anymore."

"His loss." Scott smiled.

"I think so too."

Eager patrons jostled from behind.

"Any seats open?"

"Sure, give me your hand."

"What?"

"Give me your hand."

Scott took Rebecca's outstretched hand and guided her toward the opposite end of the bar, which wrapped around a corner like an L. He dropped a stool over the bar into an unoccupied space. She slid onto its round leather seat.

"Done this before, have you?"

"A few times."

"Thanks."

"No sweat. I'll be back in a bit."

Rebecca got her bearings. As luck would have it, she had a perfect view of Ethan, who was standing next to a chesty blonde in a halter top.

Ethan was handsome. Trouble was, he knew it. His arm was around the back of the blonde's chair. Classic territorial move. Puffing up to be sure as many people as possible noticed. The fingers of his other hand drummed on the bar while his eyes searched the room for admirers. Periodically, he'd lock eyes with someone he knew and offer one of his patented chin flips. If you were REALLY worthy, you'd get both a chin flip and a point. Only the top-shelf folks got "the point" and the "I'll call you" gesture.

What a tool.

He had been her tool, though. But her friends' reactions after they split made it clear he had always been a tool. Now free of him, only the ugliness remained. The ugliness within. Like that famous book, *The Picture of Dorian Gray,* where the guy's outward beauty hid his rotten soul. For Rebecca, his true self was laid bare. She couldn't unsee it.

Memories gained new context. Mean comments about her hair. Never holding the door. Snide remarks about her middle-class upbringing and her mom's ethnicity. Like asking if her mom spoke English. Then, knowing her finances, still expecting her to pay for them both a little too often. That despite the fortune he was raking in as a pharma sales rep.

Yet, Rebecca had dutifully walked two steps behind. Sometimes literally.

Kyle never did any of those things. He was genuine, loving, and kind, and so vastly superior to Ethan in every possible way. Kyle cared for her. He knew her secret and loved her anyway. Now, after Heidi, after her liberation, anything was possible.

Her pants pulsed just thinking of her breakthrough. Pure erotica. No judgment. Nothing taboo or off limits. It just was. And that was okay. Rebecca never needed permission to be free. It was within her all along.

Rebecca pursed her lips to empty her wine glass. She set the stem down on the lacquered bar and lifted the cocktail napkin. The cocktail napkin with its crest: a shield bursting with coiled vines of roses. Thirteen roses. She'd counted them many, many times. Losing herself in the napkin while Ethan chatted too enthusiastically with people he never bothered introducing her to. Rebecca wished to be anywhere but with him. Now she had her wish. Yet, here she was, staring at him from across a bar. A window into a life she hadn't wanted when she lived it the first time. Not if she were honest with herself.

Would Kyle be different? The everyday Kyle? Deep in her bones, she knew he would. They were as different as two men could possibly be. Kyle had been everything she wished Ethan was, and then some. Looking at him now, she was foolish to expect anything more than the small man he was. This was his apex. He'd never be anything more. Kyle, on the other hand, was a phoenix. He'd soar as high as his wings could take him. She would fly alongside him, a phoenix in her own right. Not riding his back, but his equal. In all things; in bed.

Rebecca waved her arm to get Scott's attention.

"More wine?"

"No, I'm heading out," Rebecca reached across the bar and plastered a kiss on his cheek. "Thanks for being one of the good ones."

Scott smiled, shaking his head. "You know, every woman in this place will be copying your lead. You've opened the kissing floodgates."

Rebecca stood up. "You're welcome."

Chapter 37

Rising before an early alarm was criminal. Rebecca tossed for forty minutes before heaving her body out of bed for a shower. The trip to The Rose Tavern set her mind right, but the thought of a weekend alone with Kyle still sent butterflies careening around her insides.

She checked her watch. *Not yet.* Rebecca straightened up the living room then paced aimlessly. She ran down her overnight packing list, meager as it was given the motorcycle's limited storage space.

Out the window, life was stirring in the street below. A few joggers and early shoppers moving about. Her eyes landed on Kyle's parking spot. The spot, not the bike.

Where was he?

Her heart skipped a beat.

Had he gone out last night as she had?

Rebecca strode across the hall and rang the bell.

No response, not even Bessie shuffling.

Hmmm.

Did Bessie come down with something—or pretend to—and

drag him off?

She depressed the black button again, and the chime echoed inside the apartment.

Had it done that before? Maybe she hadn't pressed hard enough.

Faint sliding sounds grew louder as Bessie's slippered feet approached.

"It's me," she yelled through the closed door. "Kyle was supposed to pick me up. Did he go out?"

"I think he was getting gas." Rebecca could hear the brass plate of the peephole slide closed. Muted sounds of her retreating steps signaled the conversation over.

Instead of a bright and cheerful Kyle storming her gates and whisking her off to parts unknown, she got a Bessie dismissal. Presumably, her knight would soon arrive, so she spun around and headed back to her apartment.

Blank spots on the bookshelves and empty picture hooks jumped out. The wounds of Barbara's departure. With the summer flurry, she'd delayed finding a roommate. This time, it'd be someone to share the rent, but not her life. The thought of living with a stranger made her itch. Hopefully, a friend of a friend would show up. A normal friend. Someone neater than herself.

Kyle's double doorbell ring sounded.

True to form, he waltzed in with his million-dollar smile—and a bag of bagels.

"We're gassed up and ready to go. I grabbed some bagels for the road. I didn't get you whitefish salad, because I intend for us to do a lot of kissing today and I don't much care for the stuff myself."

Wrapped in his arms, Kyle planted a kiss, gently parting his lips and probing with his tongue in that dangerous way that sent Rebecca's blood stirring. He always did this when they had to be somewhere. At least today the somewhere was with him alone.

"We'll have plenty of time for that, but let's get going. You'll be proud of me; look how well I packed," she said hoisting a half-full plastic grocery bag.

"Nice! You're a born biker gal," he said. "Let's go."

His motorcycle was out front, saddlebags draped over the frame and under the seat. Kyle unbuckled one of them for Rebecca to fill. She then stood back to watch as he buckled the strap and checked the tire pressure with a measuring gauge.

"Going somewhere?"

Rebecca pressed her eyes closed. Why? Why after all this time? Did he have to show up at the precise moment she was about to ride off into the sunrise with the man of her dreams? She turned around.

Ethan wobbled, unsteady. Shit-faced, crumpled, and wearing the same clothes as the night before at The Rose Tavern.

Maybe if I ignore him, he'll go away?

She turned back to Kyle.

"Don't be like that, sweetness. You were a lot friendlier last night."

Kyle looked up from his crouched position. "What's going on?"

"Ignore him."

"Who is he?"

"The putz," Rebecca said.

Kyle looked over his shoulder then stood up. "Looks like a

333

putz."

"You weren't so frosty last night," Ethan said, approaching.

"Whoa, now, buddy. Back off," Kyle said, blocking Ethan with his body.

"Go way, Ethan. You're drunk."

"Drunk with love. I wanted to pay you back for those drinks."

"You're the cheapest man alive. Who are you kidding?"

"What's he talking about?" Kyle asked.

"No clue."

"What I'm talking about is that this sweet thing was very *generous* last night. Thought she'd want round two."

"Rebecca?" Kyle asked.

"Don't listen to him. He's drunk and crazy."

"I can see that, but why would he say all this?"

"I honestly don't know."

"And how did he know we'd be out here now?" Kyle asked.

"She told me," Ethan said, leaning in. "She told me to come now so she wouldn't have to tell you alone."

"Tell me what?"

"Let's just go. He's insane." Rebecca grabbed Kyle's shoulder to turn him, but his muscles flexed, immobile.

"Tell him, Rebecca. Tell him how you used him to get me back."

"What?" Kyle said.

"He's making it up. Let's go."

"Did you see him last night?" Kyle asked.

Did I see him? Oh my God.

Rebecca positioned herself directly in front of Kyle, his face, questioning. She had to end this.

"Please listen to me. I went to a bar last night. Ethan was way across the bar. On the other side. I didn't talk to him; I never once made eye contact. I drank some wine and left."

"That's it?

"That's it."

Kyle exhaled.

"Tell him about Scott. You forgot the part about kissing Scott," Ethan said, a cocky smile erupting.

Rebecca flipped around. "Why are you doing this? We're over."

"Are you?" Kyle asked, hands raking through his hair. "And who's Scott?"

"He's the bartender. I kissed him hello."

"The bartender?"

"Yes."

"Seems like there were a lot of kisses flying around last night."

"Not a lot. One. One hello kiss and one glass of wine."

"Are you sure? I mean, you went out. The day after Heidi…"

"This has nothing to do with Heidi. Kyle, nothing happened."

"I wouldn't call it nothing…" Ethan piped in.

Kyle's glare landed on Ethan; he stepped back.

"The timing is curious, wouldn't you say?"

Disastrous is more like it.

"It just happened to be to the same bar Ethan was at…" Kyle said.

"Yes."

"But he didn't see you. And you didn't speak to each other, and didn't hook up."

"No, of course not!"

"But somehow, he miraculously shows up here right at the very moment we're leaving?"

"I can't explain it, but yes."

"And you tossed Scott in for good measure?"

"It was a peck on the cheek. You're making way too much of it."

"Am I?"

"Yes."

"What would you think if you were me?"

Rebecca paused for a breath. "It's not what it looks like."

Kyle turned away, pinching the bridge of his nose. "It's always what it looks like. Trust me."

"Not this time. I'm not Vivian."

Kyle looked back, shaking his head.

Please... Rebecca's eyes searched his for a safe harbor, but a storm was brewing.

He lifted his helmet and climbed on the bike.

"Kyle, wait."

This can't be happening.

"Ethan, Ethan, tell him the truth. Kyle, please wait. Where are you going?"

"To gain some perspective."

"What perspective? What are you talking about?"

"I don't know, but... you... him?" The bike roared to life.

"Wait!" She extended her arm, but he accelerated out of reach, down the street. The bike rounded the corner and out of sight.

Rebecca waited for a roar to return. A signal that he'd changed his mind and come back to her. Pulling up to say it was all a terrible misunderstanding. He trusted her. But the only the only sounds came from cooing mourning doves.

Ethan's clap shattered the silence, "Well, that's that."

"Why?" she said. "Why did you say those things?"

He shrugged. "My lady dumped me."

"The blonde from last night?"

"Yeah, go figure. We had mad chemistry."

Rebecca's fists pumped, including the one holding her helmet's chin strap.

Her stalking approach forced Ethan to backpedal.

"Scott said you started the kissing frenzy. It was WILD. Girls were throwing themselves at him all night. I figured if you were kissing Scott, you'd much prefer a booty call from me."

"A booty call?"

"You look great, by the way," he said, sliding closer.

Nostrils flaring, eyes ablaze, "You're going to make this right."

"C'mon. He's old news. Admit it, you missed me."

He squeezed her butt. Twice.

"Ooh, I did miss this ass of yours."

Rebecca shifted her bottom out of reach. "Really?"

"Yes."

"You missed me?"

"Of course!"

"Wanna know how much I missed you?"

"How much? Tell me."

"This much," Rebecca yelled, windmilling the helmet in an arc, connecting with his groin with a violent thwack.

"Arrrgh!" Ethan yelled, doubling over his wound. "What the fuck?!"

"I don't miss you, asshole. I miss the man you just chased away." She landed another crotch blow despite his evasive maneuvers.

"Quit it, you crazy bitch."

"I'm not a crazy bitch. I'm an ice queen, *RE-MEM-BER?*" Helmet raised, Ethan recoiled.

"Stop, stop," he said, crouching into a fetal position.

A cab rolled to a squeaky stop nearby, its passenger silhouetted as she paid the fare.

Think. Where would he go? Where would she go to gain perspective?

Then it hit her.

"Get up," she commanded Ethan.

Rebecca gestured to the cabbie who nodded as his current fare exited the car.

"Why?"

"We're taking a ride."

"I'm not going anywhere with—"

"You damn well will."

"Or what?"

"Or I'll beat your dick to a bloody pulp," she said two inches from his face.

Ethan's eyes bulged into saucers.

"Bye-bye, booty call."

His Adam's apple bobbed a swallow.

"Let's go."

"Where?

"To gain some perspective."

The cab rolled to a stop outside Vivian's studio. Kyle's motorcycle gleamed in the morning sun.

"Your treat," Rebecca said, gesturing for Ethan to pay the fare.

She pushed Ethan out of the cab and up the stairs to the second floor, ringing her studio's bell.

"No more lies," she said.

Ethan crossed his arms, looking away.

His turn to squirm.

Vivian opened the door.

"Oh, good lord," she said, a messy top knot dangling over her sleep-creased face.

Not so gorgeous in the morning…

"He's inside," she said, standing aside so they could enter. "You two need to work on your communication."

One of Vivian's backdrops hung from the ceiling covering the entire wall. A jungle backdrop. Kyle paced in front of it like a caged tiger.

"We've got company," Vivian said.

Kyle's tortured expression vanished when he saw Rebecca, replaced by confusion.

"How did you…? You know each other?"

"Don't ask," Rebecca and Vivian said in unison, exchanging sideways glances.

"Ethan has something he'd like to say. Tell him the truth," Rebecca said, holding the helmet up like a bowling ball.

He sighed, rolling his eyes. "I made it up."

"What? I can't hear you, ETHAN," Rebecca yelled in his face, adrenaline raging.

"I made the whole thing up. I never spoke to her last night."

"You lied?" Kyle said.

Ethan shrugged.

Rebecca lunged closer,

"Yes, yes. I lied," Ethan said, cringing.

"Yes."

Kyle's palms wiped his face.

The jury was out. Deliberating.

He wants to believe me. I know it. Why won't he say something?

"Rebecca, I don't…"

"Look at me," Rebecca demanded. "Do you honestly think I could ever go back to a disgusting slime bag like him? After everything that's happened?"

She walked over to Kyle. Standing right in front of him, she looked up, "Don't be so afraid of your past that you let it ruin our future."

Kyle's exhale was a waterfall, washing their terrible nightmare away. He cracked a smile.

"I have trust issues."

"Ya THINK?" Vivian snorted. She shifted her attention to Ethan, giving him a disgusted up-down lookover. "You can leave now, cretin."

He hesitated, looking for an audience, "Rebecca. Sorry about…"

"Save it, Ethan," Rebecca said.

He turned to go, but stopped.

"You heard the lady! Out, out, out." Vivian shooed Ethan until he crossed her threshold, then slammed the door behind him.

Rebecca puckered for a kiss, but Kyle leaned back. "Wait, how do you two know each other?"

So close...

Rebecca's eyes pleaded with the returning Vivian.

"What I miss?"

"He's wondering how we know each other," Rebecca said.

"Oh, that."

"And?" Kyle said.

"You remember I mentioned doing nonprofit work? For a hospital? On a research study?" Vivian said with a grimace.

Kyle darted looks between them.

"Oh God, no. You've GOT to be kidding me."

"Small world?" Rebecca said, hiking her shoulders.

"This can't be happening. You heard every minute?" he said.

"Yes, but don't worry," Vivian said, sauntering over to kiss Kyle's cheek. "She was very complimentary."

"Really?" A glint of mischief returned to his eyes as he gazed down at Rebecca.

"Totally," Vivian said.

"Well, in that case," he said, diving into Rebecca for a thirsty kiss.

It was warm and wet, musky and delicious. It tasted of Kyle. Tears streamed down Rebecca's cheeks, mingling in.

Relief? Excitement? Belonging? Yes, yes, and yes.

Vivian rewrapped her robe.

"You kids turn off the lights off on your way out. I'm going back to bed," she said, heading toward her living area. "Oh, and next time: call first. This popping in crap has to stop."

Alone in the studio, they stood clinging to each other, grateful survivors from their tornado of the morning.

Rebecca whispered in his ear, "Let's go. I'm ready."

Chapter 38

Within moments they were on their way. Kyle zoomed up Third Avenue, red lights flipping green just in time for them to pass. Traffic picked up on the approach to the George Washington Bridge, the only bridge connecting Manhattan and New Jersey. Blue sky stretched overhead from the upper deck. Morning sun sparkled off the Hudson River below, sailboats dotting the surface like toys in a bathtub. Manhattan's glass skyscrapers glowed a fiery good morning as they sped away.

It was an escape that almost didn't happen. Rebecca shivered in the breeze, thinking about how close it had come to all falling apart. But they made it. They were together.

Kyle accelerated to join traffic on a large highway with eight lanes across, the force plastering Rebecca into her backrest. Her head bobbed uncontrollably in the wind. Reaching up to steady it meant she'd have to let go of the rails she held to secure her body.

Think. Be creative.

Rebecca slouched down to hide behind Kyle's body. The wind lessened, relinquishing control of her head. Only now, the landscape mirrored off Kyle's shiny helmet—in reverse.

Rebecca closed her eyes, yielding to motion, fresh air, and vibrations between her legs. Heidi was right. A motorcycle was an iron vibrator. Having her crotch so close to Kyle's rump... *how long is this trip?* They rode along for about twenty minutes before slowing to a stop at a red light. Rebecca pushed back with her legs to create breathing space between her and the object of her desire before looking around.

Houses and shopping centers lined both sides of the highway, which continued for miles as their trip resumed. Rarely a sustained patch of green. Rebecca once read that New Jersey was the most densely populated of all fifty states, and she could see why. Yet, twenty minutes after they crossed Route 287, the ratio of concrete to green reversed. Trees outnumbered buildings until the road shrunk to four lanes lined entirely by forest.

Kyle exited the highway, taking a succession of small county roads, snaking past homes, farms, and towns so small they were gone in a blink. Each intersection held purpose. Kyle never hesitated about which way to turn and never stopped to look at a map or ask directions. He had a plan; that much was obvious. Rebecca sank into her backrest and eased her death grip on the bike frame.

A farmhouse with a collapsing front porch whizzed by, its rustic authenticity screaming for a picture frame.

An old woman watered flowers with a pink extension rod.

Pinwheels shaped like swimmers whirled arms in the wind, a yard full spinning together. It was as if they had urgent business; somewhere to be.

Before long, they turned onto Route 615, a narrow two-lane

road that wound them through the Delaware Water Gap National Recreation Area. The scenery was solid green with small breaks of sun filtering through from above.

Ruts in the road tossed Rebecca off her seat, her handhold saving her from flipping off entirely. A minefield of potholes lay ahead. Perfectly unavoidable. Kyle slowed to weave through what he could, rising off the seat to lessen the worst impact. More tricks of the trade for her biker toolbox.

As slow as they were going, they caught up to a mobile home hauling a trailer with two jet skis, inflated water toys, and a ton of bicycles. Wherever they were headed, they intended to stay a while and didn't want a moment's boredom.

When clear of the shady forest, puffy clouds came into view. Ethereal tufts straight out of a children's coloring book. Rebecca searched for hidden forms. A lion's head with a mane? A truck? The letter Z?

They crossed a small bridge over the Delaware River, turning right to follow along the water on the Pennsylvania side. Gone were the bucolic farms, green lawns, and manicured hedges. Only arid ground and industrial businesses that had seen better days. Rebecca scanned for tumbleweeds.

I hope Kyle got enough gas…

They rolled to a stop at the side of the road near an old bridge. Rebecca hopped off but immediately collapsed to her knees.

"Easy girl! Are you okay?"

"Yeah. I just need to remember how to walk."

"I guess I should have stopped sooner, but we had really good traffic," he said, sliding off his helmet, blue eyes flashing in the sun.

"Where are we?"

"Lackawaxen, Pennsylvania. Home of Roebling's Delaware Aqueduct, the oldest wire suspension bridge in the United States. Roebling designed it about twenty years before he designed the Brooklyn Bridge. Cool, huh?"

"Yeah," Rebecca said, rubbing her thighs and calves. "What else do you know about it?"

"Well, it used to have cars on it, but not anymore. It was originally built to help lessen canal traffic from when the timber floating down to Philly would collide with a rope bridge that was here at the time. The aqueduct replaced the rope bridge, and presto! Problem solved."

"Come here, Professor," Rebecca said, fluffing her de-helmeted hair.

He sat down on the ground, and Rebecca straddled him, kissing while lightly grinding her groin into his. They both began to get worked up, in full view of whoever happened to be in the middle of nowhere with them.

"We could probably get arrested for indecent exposure if we go much further," he joked, getting up and fumbling around in a saddlebag, "Want a bagel?"

"Sure. If I can't make out, I might as well eat."

"I didn't say you can't; I just said not here on the road in full view of…"

"In full view of who?"

"Just in full view." He took a big bite of his bagel and chewed noisily with his mouth open for dramatic effect.

"Lovely," Rebecca answered and took a bite of her own bagel.

The fairy dust took immediate effect. This must be what taking drugs feels like: yeasty, salty goodness sparking a tingle of pleasure radiating from her mouth. A crisp crust and dense, doughy center, just as she liked it. These were the best bagels in the universe, even plain as hers was. She ate about half and took a swig of the water Kyle offered, warm from sitting in the leather satchel.

Stretched and fed, they resumed the trip by taking Route 590 all the way to a town called Hawley. It was just outside a more populated lakefront vacation area of Wilsonville, on the shores of Lake Wallenpaupack. It was late afternoon by the time they rolled in, having stopped a few more times for food and window shopping along the way. Living without a schedule was all part of the biker adventure.

They turned down a winding back street near what looked to be an old mill. Signs pointed to the Factory Inn by the Falls; an expansive building perched at the edge of a gorge teeming with water. They pulled to a stop, and Rebecca hopped off easily this time. Practice makes perfect.

"Wow! How'd you ever find this place?" Rebecca said, removing her helmet.

"Would I take my girl on a ride without a great place to stay?" Kyle twinkled as he secured the bike and popped off the saddlebags.

"Say that again," Rebecca said.

"What?"

"That I'm your girl."

Kyle set down the bags, took her hand, and walked to the railing overlooking a pounding waterfall.

347

"You're the only woman I think about, and I don't intend to share. Not with putz or anyone else."

The thought of how close the putz came to wrecking everything chilled her. But Kyle's sweet kiss brought her back.

"No sharing?"

"None."

Rebecca paused for a moment. "I must keep the pool boy, Philip. He gets the chlorine just right, and I couldn't bear to dismiss him."

"Okay, you can keep Philip, if I can keep," he paused to think. "Oh, I'll keep Frenchy the cook. Does that sound fair?"

"Yes. Deal. I can barely cook anyway." Rebecca flung her arms around his neck, and they kissed, their stirring giving the raging water some competition. Kyle's arms were hard, his ass was perfect, and he was all hers.

Kyle rested his head against hers as they silently watched the river cascade downstream. The world melted away. There was only Kyle and the sound of churning water.

The glass patio door burst open, and two little boys sprinted ahead to the railing, scrambling up the rungs for a better view. Their mother screamed bloody murder, tearing over to rip them down, after which the dad scolded the mother for overreacting.

Kyle and Rebecca took their cue and walked hand-in-hand back to the bike. Kyle hiked the saddlebags over his shoulder, and they went inside.

Deep blue Victorian furnishings, lush woods, and lace trimming greeted them at the hotel reception. A full battalion of wooden tables on carved legs paired with upholstered furniture scattered around the common area in intimate sitting areas.

Rebecca overheard another patron say the hotel's upper floors were dedicated to permanent apartments. Their room, however, was on the first floor, and they followed a long hallway carpeted in burgundy to the appropriate wing. The white walls had waist-high mahogany wainscoting with a glossy finish that reflected the amber sconces dotting the walls above at regular intervals. Rebecca got a strong sense of déjà vu before realizing that the hotel resembled every horror movie hotel she'd ever seen. If all went well, though, her fate would be far better.

Kyle opened the door and made a beeline to the bathroom while Rebecca performed a room inspection. The black leather binder with hotel information and area attractions sat on the writing desk near the window. The nightstand drawers were empty save for the Gideons Bible and a telephone book no one had used since the 1980s. A mauve ice bucket lined with a clear plastic bag sat on a tray alongside two upside-down glasses on scalloped paper doilies. Like the hall, the carpet was wine-colored, surrounded by more mahogany wainscoting and gold pinstriped wallpaper. Delicate lamps were strategically placed, so each illuminated area overlapped the next. It was the cozy décor Rebecca most enjoyed when staying at an inn.

The bathroom door was ajar, water splashing within. Rebecca joined him in a haven of white: white walls, white tiled floor, white sink and toilet, and a white clawfoot tub with super-high sides.

"Look at that bathtub! It's divine! Are we rushing off somewhere, or do I have time for a bath?" Rebecca asked with a tinge of urgency in her voice.

Kyle cracked a smile as he left the bathroom. "Take all the time you want. We have nowhere to be and all night to get there."

"Awesome. I won't be too long, I promise," she said, closing the door behind him. As Rebecca undressed, she heard the television switch on to some unrecognizable show. It was probably something on History Channel. She would peg him for a History guy in a minute, especially given his architecture lesson earlier in the day.

Four white, fluffy bath towels on the chrome shelf begged for attention. She wrapped one around her head, then started filling the tub. She balled-up another towel for a headrest and left another one nearby to dry off.

Soaking in a deep bathtub was a rarity. Most tubs were made with only a perfunctory thought given to baths, given the shower-dominant society. With low sides for easy entry, most tubs barely covered the naughty bits. Cold boobs would not be a problem today. Rebecca turned off the water before it reached the overflow drain and lowered herself into the tub.

The water was almost too hot, setting her nerve endings ablaze. Rebecca reached for the cold faucet but sat back instead. It was a tactical mistake; the water would get tepid too soon. She rested her toweled head against the makeshift pillow and bent her knees slightly to submerge up to her chin. Her entire body lay bare before her through the clear water, but she pushed negative thoughts away. After their long motorcycle ride, she deserved every moment of this bath. She closed her eyes. The fatigue of holding herself upright yielded to the heat.

Warmth. Everywhere. Up her arms, down her legs, supporting

her back. Tension-free, her arms floated up, breaking the water's surface as if summoned. Every movement sent gurgles of water echoing down the overflow drain.

Where did the water go next? On an adventure of its own into the wet beyond? A dark drain popped to mind, a place from children's books and movies. Dropping. Twisting. Turning. Flowing. Perhaps it would join the waterfall and then the ocean.

Faint sounds from the television penetrated from the other side, then quieted.

"Is there room for two?" Kyle said.

"Mmmm… yeah," she said, fluttering heavy lids open to view her Adonis. Muscular thighs gave way to washboard abs, pecs to die for, and longing eyes.

Kyle's tender lips connected with hers.

She pulsed approval. As did he.

Water careened over the tub edge as he slid in behind her. Their private waterfall. Her hair fell loose as he pulled her towel away, dropping it to the floor. She reclined onto him beneath the rising steam misting the room. The fog made the scene less than real. A fantasy she'd awake from in her own bed. But his nibbles on her neck were quite real.

"You're beautiful," he whispered in her ear.

She reached back, cupping his jawline as their mouths churned as one.

Kyle worked lavender-scented soap into a thick lather, then slid his hands over her slick breasts, kneading each mound.

"These were worth the wait," he said, exploring their silky roundness, caressing, squeezing, owning.

351

A shudder sent her arching reflexively into his hands, nipples ripe for attention. He pinched them, unleashing a longing at her core; sensations heightened knowing Kyle was the ringmaster drawing them out.

"I want you. I want you inside me..." she moaned.

"Not yet..." he said, slipping his fingers inside her while massaging around her pink pearl with his thumb.

Pulsing slowly, then accelerating, Rebecca ground up to meet his hands. She reached up and caressed her own breasts, her tongue sliding across her lips, drawing his.

Thoughts evaporated. Intense reds... pinks... purples shape-shifted in time with the pulsing within her. Building intensified, her longing unbearable.

"Kyle..." she gasped, his hands thrusted faster and faster. His scent filled her as he nibbled her neck.

Rebecca panted, her fingers tangling in his hair. Tension. Sensation. Her heart pounded, spreading beyond her chest, each beat radiating, lifting her, higher, farther.

"Ky—!" Rapture washed over her, flushing her face, her limbs, every cell pulsating with velvet energy that propelled her deeper and deeper into a suspended moment of intoxicating ecstasy. She soared, awash in vibration, then collapsed into Kyle's waiting arms.

He kissed her forehead as she lay breathless.

They lay together on the brink of sleep until she shivered. Goose bumps rose on her skin.

"Rebecca..."

"Hmm?"

"The water's cold, love. Let's get out."

Kyle pulled the drain stopper out with his toes, sending water bubbling down the drain.

They climbed out and dried off, leaving the towels on the floor to dry their mini-flood. Kyle draped her chilled body in a fluffy, white bathrobe while he toweled off.

"Easy now," he said as Rebecca swayed on spaghetti legs.

"I never knew I could feel this way... with someone."

"Now you know. And it's only the beginning..."

Kyle nibbled her neck as they transferred to the bedroom. His heat radiated from behind through the robe. The room pulsed, joining their bordello haze. The burgundy, rich woods, laces, and fabrics suddenly oozed sex. Welcoming her home. Freeing her to live. Breathe. Savor. Would the walls keep her secrets? Did she even care?

She inched backward onto the bed, her robe sprawled open like wings. Kyle drank her in before crawling on top. *The tiger has returned.*

He kissed her mouth, then chest, then flicked each peak with his tongue before kissing her belly, sending her writhing. He spread her legs with his shoulders to lick her, drawing her back to life.

Rebecca reached down, tangling her hands in his thick hair. Sensing him with her fingers, feeling the contours of his head and ears as he worked his magic. Tension simmered away, yet available. She pulled his head up and devoured his mouth; the muscles of his back and arms flexed as she dug in to pull him closer. Desperate to join.

"I need you."

"How much? How much do you need me?" he said, pinching

353

her nipple and sending shudders everywhere.

"Please." Her pearl pulsed for attention.

Kyle kissed her tummy, then reached for a condom on the night table. He tore it open with his teeth, then slid it down with hand-over-hand motions.

Just watching him touch himself…

Rebecca arched in anticipation, but his powerful thrust down to the hilt broke a dam within her.

"Oh my God."

"Oh, Rebecca…"

Kyle thrusted with longing of his own. He filled her bottomless depths, then pushed still farther. Harder, faster.

Deeper. More. Do what you want. I'm yours.

Rebecca rolled them over so she could straddle him. She gyrated her pleasure over him as he pushed up to meet her.

"Rebecca, you feel so good. I can't hold on…"

"Don't. Don't hold on. Let go…"

Hands on the headboard, Rebecca rocked into him, moving until she heard his groan, then intensifying. Completing him as he completed her. Thirsty for his transcendence. She moved his hands to her breasts, arching into her fullness, rubbing herself into his grip.

"Oh, Rebecca."

Wave after wave throbbed from within her as Kyle surrendered. Months of anticipation releasing with a final shudder and thrust. His hard muscles relaxing under her into a puddle of his own.

Rebecca straightened her legs and slid down until her head lay on his chest, pulling the covers about them. Wrapped in each other's arms, legs tangled, their breathing slowed into the steady rhythm of sleep.

When Rebecca's eyes opened, dawn's blueness tinted the room. *Where am I?*

She turned her head.

Naked in bed with Kyle. Where she belonged. Where she would stay. She ached for him, though they lay entwined.

Flashes of their night stirred within her, the first time she'd made love. The first time she surrendered to the moment, not worrying if she would have an orgasm or even if her partner would. But they, of course, had. A palpable force passed between them. A force completely unlike anything she experienced with Heidi. As good as that was, it was like comparing a twelve-course feast to saltine crackers. One sustained, the other sufficed.

Kyle's eyelashes fluttered; his strong profile relaxed. She traced his nose with her finger. It twitched.

He breathed deeply, his arm drawing tight around her, scooping her close.

"What time is it?"

"Early, I think."

She snuggled into the crook of his arm, warm from his unquenchable internal furnace. She fit. In that exact spot. Comfortable. Not fake comfortable like when you pretend to be resting, but are really in pain. Real comfort; like a lost puzzle piece finally came home.

Kyle's fingers bounced her ringlets, tangling and untangling in their mass.

She sought his mouth, still there, still wanting.

His arm scooped her on top of him.

"Ahh, liked that, did you?"

"I loved that," he said. "But I love you more."

A bolt shot through her.

He loves me.

Their lips met for a lover's kiss. A kiss borne of an intimacy few experienced. She hadn't herself known love until Kyle. Not really. Knowing it changed everything. She was never going back. Never returning to the empty vessel wracked by inadequacy.

"You… love… me," Rebecca said, smacking him with kisses.

It wasn't a question. There was no doubt. Kyle loved her. She would never question his love again.

His hand grazed her cheek, and she purred into it like a cat on a scratching post.

"I love you too," she said directly into his bright eyes. "Never doubt it."

She flipped his weight on top of her.

"Now, love me again."

Chapter 39

"So, my old room is now a closet?" Barbara said, sliding a brown moving box onto a growing stack. "I'm not sure how I feel about that."

"Not a closet; a studio of sorts," Rebecca said, leaning a bundle of tripods against the wall.

"He repacked all this?"

"Nah, he never fully unpacked at Bessie's. The rest he had in storage."

"You should charge an equipment fee!"

"That's awful!"

"Plotting against me already?" Kyle said, entering with a dolly stacked with lighting equipment, steadied by Joe on the far end.

"Never," Rebecca said, planting a deep kiss on Kyle's lips with a loud smack.

"We should though. I'm still not convinced you don't have body parts floating in jars around here," Barbara said, picking at a folded box flap.

"I'm not that exciting. You do know I photograph food, right?"

"So you say," she said, raising an eyebrow.

"It's paint. I promise. Paint and other crazy tools of the trade."

Kyle opened a case of lenses, sorted through, and popped one on a camera slung around his neck.

He stole a candid shot of Rebecca talking to Barbara.

"Hey, Rebecca, best keep one eye open with this guy," Joe said.

"No worries. I'd know if he were a killer by now."

"Sure, but you might find yourself on camera when you least expect it."

Rebecca looked up, in time for a shutter click. Her face bloomed into a smile.

"He knows I have a good lawyer if he tries anything funny!"

The foursome traipsed back to Bessie's apartment, where Kyle's former roommate sat in a wingback chair sipping tea out of a cup and saucer.

Each marched past their elder into the bedroom, took a box, equipment bag, chair, or garbage bag of clothes, then retraced steps.

Bessie looked up as Rebecca crossed the room.

She smiled.

Rebecca smiled back and continued walking her box across the hall. Barbara trailed behind.

"So, Bessie is really fine with Kyle moving out?"

"Surprisingly, yes. She said she wouldn't mind having her apartment back to herself. Said he was too messy anyway."

"I can't imagine WHY she'd say that?"

"Besides, she said she now has another place to go in her slippers."

"True enough."

"And Kyle is right nearby if she needs anything. You know, Bessie even gave me a key."

"A key? To her apartment?"

"Yes."

"That's big."

"It is. It is big."

"I'd high-five you if I had a free hand."

Rebecca dropped her box on a stack.

"Hey, I've been meaning to thank you for helping me. I don't know what I would have done this summer without you. Emotionally, financially…"

"You're family. You know that."

Rebecca tossed her arms around her friend for a squeeze.

"Always. You're my SSAB!"

"SSAB? Like the car?" Kyle asked as he leaned a headboard against a stack of boxes.

"Sisters separated at birth. S-S-A-B," they chimed in unison.

"Can you tell us apart?" Barbara said, cheek to cheek with Rebecca, both looking up with exaggerated blinks.

"Identical. How could I not have noticed?"

Joe smirked. "I'm going to like having this guy around."

Rebecca met Kyle's smiling eyes.

"Me too."

Acknowledgements

Love, Only Better was a labor of love, a torment, and a mission all bundled into one. I couldn't have reached my dream of becoming a published author without tremendous support from a host of corners, beginning with Ye Olden Fam.

To Markus, my husband and partner in all things, thanks for braving this journey with me and for empowering me to share this story with the world. You endured my distracted silence and writer musings with grace. I love you forever.

To my children, Max and Veronika, whose unwavering support and encouragement means more than they could possibly know. You're awesome in every way. By the way, dinner's ready.

To my parents, Martin Rosenblatt and Olga Tobin, for raising me to believe I could do anything.

To my editor, Amanda Horan of Let's Get Booked, who worked with heart, patience, and savvy to guide my manuscript to its rightful place. You truly made me a better writer, and I will be forever grateful. And your cover wasn't too shabby either.

To my illustrator Catherine Clarke of Catherine Clarke Design, for saving the day when people got us down.

To my proofreader, Diana Cox, of Novel Proofreading, for giving Love, Only Better a fine coat of finish.

To my sister, Roxanne Medina, and my dear friend, Maureen Jones, for loving me enough to tell me when things weren't working.

To Laura Henry, my partner in all things literary. Thanks for your ear, your shoulder, and for being such a fierce advocate for readers everywhere.

To my friends and beta readers: Karen Brandstein, Ginny Galletta, Gail Gecawicz, Lisa Nivison, and Laura Williams for your thoughtful attention to detail, plot holes, and my delicate psyche.

To Barbara Thau, my cousin, Ophren, and fellow writer who always understood the business behind the words and encouraged me to strive.

To Kate Imhoff, Sara Junghans, and Annemarie Stout for lending your insights and letting me prattle on about book publishing without tossing me through a window.

To Amy D'Alessio, my SSAB, for your support, interest, and beta insights. As with everything, you make me better.

To Leslie Browne, fierce friend, mother, lawyer, and inspirer of great things. Especially characters.

To Joanna Penn, though we've never met, for launching and invigorating my indie author journey with your insight and optimism.

For the members of the Women's Fiction Writers Association and the Writing Gal's Critique Group for your enthusiastic support, critiques, and feedback. You kept me going when I was alone in a room staring at a blinking cursor.

Thank you all for helping me make this lifelong dream come true.
And this is only the beginning.

Leave a Review!

Take a moment to share your thoughts and leave a rating. Your feedback means more than you know. Thank you for reading Love, Only Better!

http://paulettestout.com/review

Coming Soon:

Love, In the Pages

Join Rebecca and Kyle on the next step of their journey!

Meanwhile, get your free Love, Only Better prequel:

Love, Only Better: All About Kyle

Get your free copy now:

https://paulettestout.com/free